BUTTERFLY

Also by Simon Rae

Keras

MEDUSA'S BUTTERFLY

SIMON RAE

Corgi Yearling

MEDUSA'S BUTTERFLY
A CORGI YEARLING BOOK 978 0 440 87051 7

First published in Great Britain by Corgi Yearling,
an imprint of Random House Children's Publishers UK
A Random House Group Company

This edition published 2014

1 3 5 7 9 10 8 6 4 2

The Random House Group Limited supports the Forest Stewardship
Council® (FSC®), the leading international forest-certification organisation.
Our books carrying the FSC label are printed on FSC®-certified paper. FSC is
the only forest-certification scheme supported by the leading environmental
organisations, including Greenpeace. Our paper procurement policy can be
found at www.randomhouse.co.uk/environment

MIX
Paper from
responsible sources
FSC® C016897

Set in 12/16 pt Goudy by Falcon Oast Graphic Art Ltd.

Random House Children's Publishers UK,
61–63 Uxbridge Road, London W5 5SA

www.randomhousechildrens.co.uk
www.totallyrandombooks.co.uk
www.randomhouse.co.uk

For Susan Hitch,
First Reader

CHAPTER 1

'I shan't be long, Marcus.'

Aunt Hester stepped out of her 'indoor' shoes and stamped her feet into her fur-lined boots. Then she scooped up her shopping bag with her handbag inside it, and grabbed an umbrella from the umbrella stand. After that she glowered down the hall at Marcus as he watched from the kitchen doorway.

'Why that man can't do a simple bit of shopping . . .' she said, shaking her head and frowning. Aunt Hester's frown seemed permanently carved on her forehead. It meant she could look disapproving even when she hadn't actually got anything to disapprove of. But in this case she had. The previous evening Uncle Frank had forgotten some of the things he'd been told to pick up on his way home from work.

'Shall I come and help carry the bags?' Marcus asked, less through wanting to be helpful than from

1

a feeling that he'd been cooped up in the house too long.

'You stay here,' Aunt Hester replied. 'I'm not risking that cold getting any worse and having you off school again next week. There's a shower on the way. You could catch your death.' She twisted round and squinted through the frosted glass of the front door. Then, as she reached for the doorknob, she added: 'Don't open the door – not to anyone. Do you hear me?'

Marcus heard her perfectly. Making herself heard was not one of Aunt Hester's problems. Her frown deepened as she looked about to see if she could find anything to be cross about before she left. 'Tuck your shirt in,' was the best she could come up with. Then she turned on her heel and let herself out of the front door, slamming it behind her.

Marcus saw her shadow in the frosted glass for a moment and waited for the creak and slam of the garden gate. Only when he heard the metallic squeal of its hinges and the clunk of its latch did he allow himself to savour the peace that fell whenever his aunt left the house.

Aunt Hester was a small woman, but she made a lot of noise. She was always clattering pans in the kitchen, bumping the hoover along the skirting board and banging ornaments back down after she dusted them. And that was when she wasn't shouting at Uncle Frank. It wasn't a big house, but when she thought of the next thing to tell Uncle Frank to do – or to tell him off for not doing – Aunt Hester always seemed to be at the other end of it.

'Have you brought the coal in?' she'd shout from the landing, a minute after she'd been in the sitting room, getting Marcus to lift his feet up while she ran the hoover along the front of the sofa.

'The bulb in the downstairs hall's gone!' – this when Uncle Frank had just gone up the stairs on some other errand.

'I thought you were going to take the rubbish to the recycling depot?'

There was a lot of stuff to take to the recycling depot, now that Uncle Frank had been given the job of putting in French windows and building a patio out from the dining room – though when Aunt Hester ever thought she was going to sit there on a summer's afternoon, Marcus couldn't imagine. As far as he could see, she only wanted the patio because Mrs Hodgson three doors down had one. But it meant she now had even more things to nag Uncle

Frank about. Not that she was ever short of ammunition.

'I spend my entire time tidying up after the two of you. I really don't know why I bother. I should just pack a bag and go and stay with Megan in Rhyl and leave you to get on with it. Then we'd see.'

This threat to decamp to her sister's on the North Wales coast was always delivered as though it were her trump card. But it never happened. Marcus suspected that Aunt Megan would prove more of a match for her sister than Uncle Frank, and that Aunt Hester's habit of nagging him was too ingrained for her to give it up. So on and on it went, day in, day out. It was the backdrop to Marcus's life, and although it pained him, he was used to it.

'All I ask is a little support, a helping hand here and there. But it's too much to ask, I suppose. You'd both rather be down at the canal with your wretched fishing rods.'

She was right about that.

It was quiet along the canal. Apart from the odd gruff greeting from other anglers, no one said anything to you at all. You just sat watching your float, letting your mind drift away, free from its moorings. Marcus sometimes looked into his uncle's face and wondered what he was thinking. Perhaps he wasn't thinking at all – just enjoying not being within earshot of Aunt Hester.

How boring, people at school said, *sitting on the canal bank all Saturday afternoon*. But it wasn't. It might yield its rewards and satisfactions more slowly than other activities, but once you got into it, fishing was very absorbing. And after long hours when nothing seemed to happen, you would get a bite, see your float jerked beneath the surface and know that in the swirl of the water, you had a fish on your line.

It was possible, Marcus thought, that Uncle Frank was only truly happy when he was playing a fish; letting it tire itself out before gradually coaxing it in to the bank, lifting it out of the water on the end of the line and releasing it from the hook into the keep-net. You didn't get big fish in the canal – you'd have had to go to a carp lake for the monsters shown off proudly in the pages of *Angling Monthly* – but even a little roach could give you a run for your money. It was exciting, but also a little frightening. The intensity of the fish's struggle as it thrashed around in panic was something you shared with it before you dropped it into the net. Of course, you knew it would be released at the end of the session, but the

5

fish didn't. To the fish it was a life-or-death battle.

Letting the fish free was another of the things that riled Aunt Hester.

'You waste all that time – and you don't even put any food on the table.'

But Uncle Frank only smiled, and winked at Marcus. Fishing was their thing, the thing that bonded them – something Marcus might have done with his father, were he around.

Marcus wandered into the kitchen and picked up the latest copy of *Angling Monthly*. It was the only luxury Uncle Frank was allowed, over and above his actual fishing tackle – another bone of contention with Aunt Hester. ('How can a simple fishing rod cost over a *hundred* pounds?') Flicking through the pages, Marcus saw advertisements for rods that were much more expensive than Uncle Frank's. But he was mainly interested in the photos of champion anglers, posing with their enormous catches draped over their arms: *Ed Swillins with his 240lb catch* read the caption underneath one of a smiling man thrusting a huge fish towards the camera.

'Why don't you go in for a competition?' Marcus had asked Uncle Frank once. He'd given a short little laugh and raised his eyebrows at the question.

They both knew the answer: Aunt Hester. But Marcus was sure his uncle could catch really big fish. He could compete with Ed Swillins any day.

He imagined sitting on the bank of the carp lake next to Uncle Frank, saying nothing, hardly moving, but willing a monster to take the bait. And then the triumph of the weigh-in, and the presentation of the trophy, with lots of cameras clacking away, and there Uncle Frank would be, modestly holding up his giant catch in the next issue of the magazine. It was a lovely dream. But that's all it was, a dream.

Marcus smiled sadly, and was just wondering about making himself some orange squash when the doorbell rang. *Perhaps Aunt Hester has forgotten her key*, he thought. No; if that had happened, she'd be banging on the door and calling crossly through the letter box. Although she'd told him not to answer the door, he thought he'd better go and see who it was.

A silhouette was visible through the frosted glass. Marcus heard something being dropped on the doorstep, before the shadowy figure disappeared. Marcus could only assume the something was a parcel. He hesitated. Surely bringing in a parcel would be all right? It had started to drizzle again: he could hear the rain and it was getting harder. Aunt Hester would be furious with him if he left the parcel out on the step getting soaked. He'd be in the wrong whatever he did.

A gust of wind blew the rain against the door's glass panels. Marcus opened the door decisively, and looked down at the nondescript cardboard box at his feet. He was about to pick it up when he noticed that the delivery man had failed to shut the garden gate, which was another thing that made Aunt Hester furious. Marcus ran down the path in the heavy rain to close it. He dashed back, scooping up the parcel on his way into the house.

It was a very ordinary box: brown, square, sealed with tape. About the right size to contain a football – though he knew it wouldn't be a football: he never got anything in the post. He wondered if it was a bit of fishing tackle Uncle Frank had ordered, or a tool for his building work. Most likely it would be for Aunt Hester – a new cooking pot or something. It was certainly too heavy to be a fresh consignment of wool for her embroidery.

Marcus was weighing up the uninteresting possibilities when he found his eye drawn to the label. And there, to his astonishment, he saw his own name: M. *Waldrist, Esq.* It was slightly unsettling – as was something about the writing. Though blurred by the rain, there was a distinctive character to it, something which looked vaguely familiar, though he couldn't think where he'd seen it before. As he studied it, something very odd happened.

Something inside the box began to move.

Marcus was so startled he nearly dropped it, and ended up doing a clumsy juggling act to prevent it falling on the hall carpet. What on earth was inside?

Perhaps he'd been mistaken?

But there it was again – a slight tremor, as if whatever it was inside the box was settling itself after being shaken about. At the same time he heard a noise, though that seemed to be more in his head than coming from the box. It was an unnerving sound – like a wind from afar; a sound that conjured up lonely, rocky places, where no green things grew. And caught on that wind was another noise, one that sounded eerily like speech coming to him across a huge distance. Like the light of a long-dead star, Marcus thought. He felt a chill run through his entire body and started to shake. Whatever was in the box was having an extraordinary effect on him.

He shoved the front door shut with his foot and

stood – holding the box as though it contained an explosive device – desperately wondering what to do next.

There was more movement, and now a noise that definitely came from inside the box. He couldn't spend all day standing with it in the hall, but somehow Marcus didn't want it in the kitchen. That was the homeliest room in the house. This thing didn't belong there, whatever it was. He would put it in the dining room, he decided. Marcus loathed the dining room, the scene of so many stiff Sunday lunches during which he stared blankly at himself in the large mirror that ran along the wall opposite the door, trying not to notice how slowly the hands on the mantelpiece clock were moving. Beside the clock stood a framed photograph of his parents; a reminder of the difference between the life he had now and the life he would have had if they hadn't both died when he was young. The photo never failed to depress him, and he looked away from it as he put down the box on the dining-room table. Everything in the room had been pushed to one side to allow for Uncle Frank's work, and the table covered with a dust sheet.

Marcus stood back and contemplated the box.

He wondered again what was inside – and who could have sent it to him. There was only one way to find out, and so he walked over to Uncle Frank's work bench and fetched a Stanley knife. Just before he slit the tape, Marcus paused. You weren't allowed to send animals through the post, were you? But whatever was in the box was definitely alive. Aunt Hester hated animals, and had vetoed every request for a pet. Pets were dirty, demanding and expensive, she said. Aunt Hester also pointed out that she 'already had two high-maintenance creatures to look after in the house as it was'. Why would she want to make life even worse, with cat hairs on the sofa, or scratch marks on the skirting boards, let alone mess on the kitchen floor? *Mess.* Possibly the thing Aunt Hester hated most in the world.

Marcus looked up and froze. Damp footprints led back from where he stood – no doubt they went along the hall to the front door too. Perhaps he just wanted an excuse to put off opening the box, but Marcus set down the Stanley knife on the table. It could wait. Mess on the carpet could not. If she came back before he'd cleared it up, Aunt Hester would do her imitation of a nuclear power station approaching meltdown. Preventing that became his number-one priority.

Marcus darted into the hall, desperately thinking ahead – cloths from the kitchen? The mop from the utility room at the end of the hall? But it was too late. There was her unmistakable silhouette at the front door, the familiar impatient scrabbling of her key at the lock. And then the door swung open.

As he knew she would, Aunt Hester saw the footprints straight away, and her eyes swept down the hall to fix him in their glare. 'What on earth . . . ?' she started, swinging the door shut and then kicking off her boots to avoid adding her own wet footprints to his.

Here we go, Marcus thought. And he was not wrong. 'Didn't I tell you not to go out, not to open the door? I leave you alone for twenty minutes' – here she slammed her dripping umbrella into the stand by the door and dumped her shopping bag to free her arms for waving and pointing – 'and what do I find? You've disobeyed me. And made a mess of my house. Footprints all the way down my hall!' She took a pace forward, following the trail. She stopped by the dining-room door: 'Just what do you think you're up to?'

Marcus remained rooted to the spot.

'There was a parcel,' he managed to croak. 'They left the front gate open—'

'So you decided to walk down and shut it and then come back and stamp dirt all over my hall carpet did you? Very thoughtful.'

Aunt Hester was working herself up into the worst mood possible.

'So where is it, this precious parcel?' she demanded.

'I put it in the dining room.'

'Well don't just stand there,' barked his aunt, seeing the box, and obviously intending to go into the dining room to open it. 'You may have a cold but that shouldn't make you stupid. Go and get a bucket and mop. Now!'

Marcus had been going to warn her there might be something alive in the box, but Aunt Hester looked at him so fiercely that he shut his mouth and turned towards the utility room.

He was manoeuvring the bucket and mop from behind the ironing board when he heard Aunt Hester's scream. He nearly dropped the mop. She must have opened the parcel and found – what? He braced himself for further explosions, but there was nothing. Not a sound. Silence.

Marcus put the mop down and made his way back down the hall towards the dining room. The door was ajar still, but no sounds came from within. Not only was Aunt Hester not raging at him – he couldn't even hear her breathing.

'Aunt Hester?' Marcus said, very quietly.

There was no reply.

He pushed the door. It moved a few centimetres then stopped, bumping up against something solid. There had been nothing there only a couple of minutes ago.

'Aunt Hester?' he tried again, this time with a note of panic.

She'd had a heart attack. She was lying on the floor, dead. That was what was stopping the door from opening. He was about to squeeze through the narrow gap to check, when he *did* hear something.

At first he didn't recognize the noise. It sounded a bit like the hiss of the gas fire in the front room. But the fire made a regular, comforting sound. This wasn't comforting at all. It was chilling, dangerous, menacing. Some instinct Marcus couldn't explain made him drop to his knees. Very cautiously he reached a hand round the dining-room door.

His fingers made contact with something, something hard. Very hard.

It was like a base or plinth for – his hand groped – some sort of column. As far as he could make out, the column rose smoothly until it came to a bump, and then only just above the bump there was what felt like an upside-down ledge.

Marcus started trembling. He moved his arm further round the door. His fumbling hand found another column, a few centimetres apart from the first. He let his hand rest on it for a moment. The hissing in the background seemed to intensify.

Marcus withdrew his arm and held it to his chest, welcoming it back to safety.

His teeth began to chatter and his chest squeezed uncontrollably, as though he'd just completed a cross-country run and then been thrown into an icy-cold swimming pool.

He had often felt fear, real fear – when the Gang had taken a dislike to him in Year Seven, for example. And, of course, he still had the occasional nightmare about the car accident which had cost his mother her life. But he had never experienced terror like this.

* * *

Marcus sat on the hall carpet, his back to the doorjamb, incapable of moving.

For a moment he tried to persuade himself that this was all just his cold; a hallucination conjured up by the medicine Aunt Hester had been forcing him to take. In a few minutes she would come back from the shop, tell him off for sitting on the floor and send him upstairs to bed.

But he looked up the hall and saw the fur-lined boots, the bulging shopping bag dumped by the front door and the umbrella still dripping in the stand. Aunt Hester had already come in, had already lost her temper with him, and had flung herself in a fury into the dining room where . . .

If only he'd called out to warn her. But warn her of what? And would she have listened? Of course not. She never did, especially when she was cross.

But what had happened to her? Marcus looked at the gap left by the door. All he had to do was to push his head in and he'd find out. But something stopped him. The silence from inside the dining room was deeply sinister. There was no heavy breathing or groaning as might have been expected had Aunt Hester had a stroke or a heart attack. The silence spoke only of death.

Something was working its way to the forefront of Marcus's mind; something he remembered from school a long time ago. Something that made the ends of his fingers tingle, and his breathing slow until he almost forgot to breathe at all. But even as the memory came into focus, he tried to reject it. It just wasn't possible. Here he was in the twenty-first century. The thing that had forced its way into his mind couldn't exist in a world of light bulbs and power tools and central heating . . .

He pushed the thought aside. Marcus decided: he had to look round the door. The thought of doing it made him feel sick. But he would have to face the terrible thing waiting for him inside the dining room sooner or later; he couldn't just sit there until Uncle Frank came home.

Reluctantly he got back onto his knees, craned his neck round the door and peered in.

The first thing he saw was his own face in the wall mirror. He looked like a cartoon depicting someone frightened out of their wits. He was just about to swivel his head round when he froze. The silence was suddenly broken by that hissing noise again – obviously triggered by his appearance.

It was a horrible noise – a spiteful, hateful noise.

And it brought back the thought which he had dismissed only a few moments before.

Gradually, painfully, Marcus let his eyeballs swivel to the left, to see what else the wall mirror could show him.

It was as he had suspected but refused to believe. And far more horrifying than he could possibly have imagined.

Aunt Hester had made a thorough job of opening the box. She had picked up the Stanley knife and slashed the brown tape before pulling the sides of the box open.

And that had been the last thing she would ever do.

Marcus stared helplessly into the mirror. Spilling out of the box he could see a sort of writhing mass, like seaweed in the tide. Only the colours were wrong, and it wasn't seaweed.

It was a nest of snakes.

He wasn't sure how many there were – too many to count at a glance, anyway. They weren't looking at him – at least, they weren't looking at him in the mirror. They were looking at the real him in the doorway; they were straining and spitting, their little forked tongues slithering in and out in anticipation. As they moved towards him, the hissing increased in volume. But, terrifying though the snakes were, they weren't the worst of it. It was what they were rooted to that transfixed him.

What he saw, resting in the ruins of the cardboard box, was a human head – the head of a woman. And the snakes formed her hair. The face had faint traces of something beautiful, but now it was a blotched and ghostly green, palely luminescent, as though exhumed from a grave.

Although the face was dead, there was life in it. The lips were as colourless as worms, curving horribly in what might have been a smile, but looked more like a sneer. And the eyes – the eyes were a terror. When they caught his gaze in the mirror, Marcus felt their intense pull, their magnetic attraction. They were like whirlpools mesmerizing him, luring him into their shadowy depths. For, although the leaden pupils were terrifyingly dark, there was an understanding in them, a penetrating recognition of the gnawing at the centre of Marcus's life: the loss of both his parents. The loss that had condemned him to his dull, unsatisfactory life in a dull, unsatisfactory town. The eyes understood his sadness. And all he had to do was turn his head and meet that gaze full on, rather than in the mirror, and his troubles would be over.

Confirmation of that was right there, standing behind the door: with her arms raised in shock and disbelief, there was Aunt Hester, unmoving, blasted into stone – a perfect statue of herself.

Marcus jerked his head back. He put his hands to his mouth, willing himself not to gag. His distant memory of the lesson in primary school had been right. On the other side of the dining-room door was the most lethal of all the monsters in Greek mythology. Medusa.

CHAPTER 2

They had done a project on Greek myths in Year 6. They had read the stories, painted pictures and put on short plays about the heroes who had fought against overwhelming odds to achieve impossible deeds. And the one which Marcus recalled most vividly was the story of Medusa and the appalling fate that the gods meted out to her.

Somehow – inexplicably, impossibly, but undeniably – the product of that terrible curse was now resting on the dining-room table of 21 Brunel Street. How had that happened? Who had sent it? Where had it come from? These were all important questions, but the overriding one was: what was he going to do about it? Of course, he could pick up the phone and dial 999. But how would the conversation go from there? *Which service do you want?* The one that deals with people whose aunts are turned into stone by nightmares from ancient mythology, please . . . ?

Marcus shook his head. He had to deal with this by himself. He just had to work out how.

Marcus sat back on the hall carpet, thinking. After a while, his eye caught the bags Aunt Hester had dropped by the front door. They'd need moving. He might as well start with the easy stuff.

He put the shopping bag in the kitchen, and decided to take her handbag up to his room. There, feeling like a thief, he opened it. Inside were the usual items – a purse, lipstick, a packet of tissues – and the thing he was looking for: Aunt Hester's phone. It had taken Uncle Frank a lot of persuading to get Aunt Hester to agree to having one – partly, Marcus suspected, because she thought Marcus would then also want one, and she certainly wasn't having that. Anyway, she allowed Uncle Frank to get her the phone, though she never used it. Just to be on the safe side, Marcus turned it off before stuffing it back in the bag, which he then shoved under his bed. Now to the main problem: what to do with Medusa's head, sitting in its box in the dining room? He went downstairs again, along the hall and through the utility room into the garden.

Uncle Frank's building works were shrouded in

tarpaulin, but Marcus removed the couple of breeze blocks acting as weights, and quickly exposed the hole in the dining-room wall. He could see the back of the box on the table. The noise he'd made had alerted the snakes, which were now turned in his direction, looking like a window box of angry yellow tulips. And behind them loomed Aunt Hester, posed in the split second of her death. Because surely that's what she was now. Dead.

Flinching from that awful warning, and weak with horror, Marcus tried to concentrate on how he was going to cover the box and its terrifying contents. A dust sheet might do, but then he imagined the snakes' fangs sticking through like thorns. No; he needed something thicker – a duvet? That was more like it.

He went back into the house to get one. As he approached the dining-room door, Marcus found he was tiptoeing. He also found a sudden, irrational desire to put his head round the door and take another look. That distant wind began to blow in his head again. It was insistent, like the banging of a door. And there was a rhythm to it: *thump – thump –* like the two syllables of a word. He strained to make it out. *Thump – thump*. Was the word his name?

Mar – cus . . . Mar – cus? He gripped the bottom of the banisters fiercely and forced himself to run up the stairs to the spare room.

Marcus seized the duvet from his bed and ran out through the house with it. He stood outside the door for a moment. He had to get everything right – or be turned into stone, like Aunt Hester. With a deep breath, he pushed back through the hole in the dining-room wall.

He glanced again at Aunt Hester. She looked, he couldn't help thinking, a bit like Mr Bishop conducting orchestra practice on a Saturday morning, with arms flung up and an intense expression on her face.

The snakes were restless, darting to and fro like the flames of a hungry fire.

Marcus let half the duvet drape down. The snakes stopped their writhing as though trying to fathom his intentions.

He advanced slowly. He was frightened, but he was also focused, concentrating the way he did when reeling in a fish – though obviously the stakes here were far, far higher.

Another step, and the snakes started swaying and hissing again.

Another step. They were watching his every move.

They stretched their jaws wide, baring their needle-like fangs, and flicking out their forked tongues.

He paused. It was not too late to turn back, to run away and call for help. But then he glanced again at Aunt Hester. How would he explain that? How would he admit that he'd let her open the box? Of course, he couldn't have known it contained the Gorgon's head – how could he? The guilt, he told himself, was only because of what had happened. No one could accuse him of wanting it to happen. Could they?

As he approached the table, he let the rest of the duvet unravel. With every step, the hissing grew louder and the heads strained in fury. Now he was within a metre of the table. One more step, that's all it would take. But his closeness stirred up an even greater frenzy of snake rage which stopped him in his tracks. So much hatred, so much pent-up malice, was intimidating. *They can't hurt you,* Marcus told himself. *Not if you get the duvet over them.* He lifted it above his head. *Throw it – throw it NOW!*

In a blind panic he jerked the duvet over the box. A trailing corner snagged on the table, but the snakes were covered.

Marcus let out a sigh of relief, then he looked again at Aunt Hester.

What was he expecting? Approval? No chance of that. There would be no response from the familiar figure frozen motionless before him.

Giving the table a wide berth, and ignoring the frantic undulations of the duvet, Marcus went up to his aunt. As he did so, he stepped on something hard. It was Uncle Frank's Stanley knife which she had obviously dropped in the last nanosecond of her earthly existence. Marcus picked it up and placed it on the duvet.

Then he turned to his aunt once more, and put his face close to hers. It was incredible – a face he'd known all his life, petrified into the most accurate sculpture. How could it happen? What unearthly power could do that? He stared into the eyes he had never dared to meet when she was alive. Her eyeballs bulged but were quite lifeless, impenetrable, the lids above them incapable of ever blinking again. Her nostrils flared, as they so often did in life, but now they were distended in terror, not anger. The mouth remained open, blasted into a surprised 'O'; her last cry frozen into silence between stone lips. And the frown line that crossed her forehead was as deep in death as it had been in life. Marcus reached up his hand and ran his fingernail along it. It was extraordinary: every molecule in her once-living body, every thread of her coat and the cardigan beneath it, every pleat of her no-nonsense skirt, her woollen stockings and her slip-on 'indoor' shoes; every last atom of the entity known as Aunt Hester was now converted to stone.

It's my fault, he thought. He knew he could have tried to warn her, whether it would have made any difference or not. At least he would have tried. But instead he'd backed off down the hall to get the mop. And now she was dead, transformed into a stocky stalagmite in the deathly cave of the dining room. He knew he was going to feel guilty about it for a very long time.

The words 'I'm sorry' formed in his mind. But he never uttered them, because just then the phone started ringing.

An intrusion from the outside world was the last thing Marcus wanted or expected, and it caught him off guard. But the phone was nothing compared to the ring at the door, followed by a few urgent thumps on the glass pane.

He stood there, caught between his urge to answer the phone – which was the other side of the dining-room table – and the need to find out who it was at the front door and send them away as fast as possible.

Assuming it was Uncle Frank on the phone, he would ring back later, though he'd have to think of a good reason why Aunt Hester hadn't picked up. In the meantime, he couldn't leave whoever it was waiting on the doorstep. He squeezed out of the dining room, shutting the door firmly behind him.

The silhouette in the door pane was quite short, and he'd guessed it was Hannah before she'd called through the letterbox:

'Mrs Armstrong – is Marcus in?'

How had it got so late? Marcus wondered. It was the end of the school day.

There was another thump at the door.

'Please, Mrs Armstrong.'

There was a note of panic in her voice, and Marcus rushed down the hall to let her in.

'Oh, Marcus, thank goodness,' Hannah said, pushing past him and leaning hard against the door. 'You saved my life.'

Marcus felt the same. It was so good to see her.

He could see the relief on her face. There was probably relief on his too.

'Didn't you want to answer that?' Hannah said.

Marcus shook his head. 'My aunt doesn't like me answering the phone.'

They stood awkwardly in the hall. The phone stopped ringing.

'Where is she?'

Not out doing the shopping, Marcus thought, remembering the shopping bag left prominently on the work surface in the kitchen.

'Oh, she just popped out to see a neighbour. Church flowers or something.'

He could see Hannah's interest fade.

'Are you all right?'

Hannah nodded. 'I am now.'

'What happened?'

'They were waiting for me at the park gate, but I saw them in time.'

Marcus knew who 'they' were, and nodded sympathetically. The Gang tended to leave him alone these days – he'd grown a lot since Year Seven – but they still ruined life for a lot of people at school. They were led by a vicious boy called Arran. Arran wasn't much to look at, but you didn't want to cross him. His eyes burned with a psychotic fury if he was crossed, and if he didn't deal with you himself, he'd hand over the job to his side-kick, Digger. Digger was huge, a great lumbering oaf with a boxer's hands. Together they led a reign of terror, which the Head and the teaching staff seemed unable to halt. And it wasn't just Arran and Digger. There was a group of girls who took particular delight in persecuting anyone different, anyone vulnerable. And with her unhappy home life, Hannah was one of their favourite targets.

'Do you want to tell me about it?'

Suddenly Hannah turned her head away as her face began to crumple.

'You don't have to.' He put out a hand to touch her shoulder.

She kept her face turned from him, and then with a sob, said: 'It's Dad. He's hit Mum. Again.'

Marcus hated conflict. Aunt Hester's constant shouting at Uncle Frank was bad enough, but actual violence . . . It made him feel sick.

'And that cow Sasha Henderson. She saw the police car outside the house last night.'

Marcus glanced at her sympathetically.

'Then she told Chelsea Holbrook.'

Enough said. Once Chelsea Holbrook got to know something, you could guarantee it would be round the school by lunch time.

'Melissa got wind of it and it just sort of built up over the day. You know – whispering – little conversations I was meant to overhear. "My mam says he'll go to prison" – "He'll murder them in their beds, my Mam says" – "She'll have to go into care".'

Hannah produced a handkerchief and wiped her eyes.

'I hate them all,' Marcus said, more loudly than he'd intended.

Hannah gave him a sharp glance. Then she scrunched her handkerchief up in her fingers.

'You can understand it, I suppose,' she said. 'School's so boring. They all like a bit of juicy gossip. It's just like the papers, really. They don't mind how badly people are hurt provided they get a good story.'

Marcus dropped his hand from her shoulder and clenched his fist.

'But it's not a good story, is it? Not your dad lashing out at your mum.'

Something in his expression made Hannah take a step back.

'I know it's upsetting,' Hannah said. 'But there's nothing you can do. Honestly. It's just good to have one person I can trust.'

Marcus felt his face getting hot, but at the same

31

time a steely cold resolve seemed to be forming within him. He heard the banging in his head again, a powerful, vengeful banging. An image flashed across his inner vision – a frightening image – familiar figures in a ring, the Gang surrounding Hannah. But although their hands were pointing and their mouths were open to jeer and shout abuse, they made no move. No move at all.

'Marcus – what is it? You look awful.'

Marcus had to pull his mind back from the image in his head. He realized he was standing right outside the dining-room door. That wasn't where he wanted to be. And it certainly wasn't where he wanted Hannah to be. He put his hand on her shoulder and gently steered her into the kitchen.

'I'm all right. Just the end of my cold. Let's go into the kitchen.'

'I should go. They'll have given up waiting for me by now.'

'No,' Marcus insisted. 'Come and have a drink.'

Hannah sat at the kitchen table and he got two glasses of squash for them.

'So, you're still feeling bad?' Hannah asked.

'I'm nearly over it. I'm just so tired of being cooped up at home.'

Hannah nodded sympathetically.

'Are you coming to orchestra tomorrow?'

Marcus shook his head. 'I shouldn't think so. I don't think I could play a note.' He put his hand up to his mouth and coughed. He did still feel a bit wheezy. 'I'm sure Mr Bishop won't mind. As long as he's got you.'

Hannah and Marcus were the only two clarinettists in the town's youth orchestra. Hannah was the one who could really play.

'Nonsense. Anyway, last week he was talking about a piece he wants us to do in the spring concert – and it's got two clarinet parts.'

'Well, you take the hardest. I'll catch up when I get back.'

'I'll tell him you'll be back next week, shall I?'

'Sure,' said Marcus, though that would depend not on his cold clearing up but on him surviving the next half hour or so.

Sensing his preoccupation, Hannah pulled her schoolbag over her shoulder.

'I'd better go. Your aunt'll be back in a minute.'

Marcus remembered how uncomfortable Aunt Hester had made Hannah feel the last time she'd called round, peering suspiciously at her and asking questions about her parents.

'No she won't. I mean, not straight away,' Marcus said. 'I haven't seen anyone all week. Stay a bit longer.'

Neither of them had any other friends, close friends. Marcus was the weirdo who preferred fishing to football, and Hannah . . . well, with problems at home, she preferred to keep herself to herself. She didn't talk to Marcus about it much, any more than he talked about the pain of losing his parents, but he often thought that the shadows in both their lives strengthened the bond between them.

Of course, being friends exposed them to a barrage of sneers and innuendos at school, which inevitably reached its peak around Valentine's Day. But their friendship meant so much to both of them, it was worth all the aggravation. Ignoring provocation was the best policy, and the Gang usually got bored and found easier prey.

They sat and talked about school for a while – Hannah had run her best time in the cross country and looked certain to get a county trial.

'That's brilliant,' Marcus said. He meant it, but a glance at the kitchen clock reminded him of all the things he had to do before Uncle Frank came home.

Hannah also checked the time. She finished her drink and stood up.

'I'd better be off,' she said.

Marcus stood up too and put his hand on her arm.

'Are you going to be all right? How's your mum?'

'She's OK. Bit of a bruise.'

Marcus frowned.

'Where's your dad?'

'At home. The police wanted to take him in, but Mum said he could stay. He's devastated. Can't stop saying how sorry he is, how he's going to give up drinking.'

She looked at Marcus and gave him a watery smile. Her face was drawn. She looked exhausted. Marcus squeezed her arm gently.

Then the phone rang again.

'I'll go,' Hannah said.

Marcus nodded, moving to answer the phone by the door.

'I'll let myself out.'

'OK,' Marcus said, plucking the phone from its cradle on the wall.

It was Uncle Frank.

'Marky! Are you all right? I tried phoning half an hour ago.'

Marcus waved goodbye to Hannah, who gave him a brave smile and slipped out into the hall.

'I'm fine, Uncle Frank. I was in bed. Couldn't get downstairs in time.'

'Is your aunt not there? I just wanted to see if she had anything to add to the shopping list.'

'It's all right, she's done the shopping,' Marcus said.

'Oh, that's good. She was a bit peeved with me for forgetting those bits last night. Where is she? I tried her mobile when no one answered the landline.'

Marcus didn't answer. He couldn't tell Uncle Frank the truth. It would sound so unbelievable, as though he'd gone mad. And even when his uncle realized it *was* true, there'd still be the terrible responsibility for having let it happen.

'Marky?'

'She's gone,' Marcus said.

'Gone? What do you mean, "gone"? Gone where?'

'Wales. To stay with Aunt Megan.'

What if Uncle Frank got straight into his car and drove home?

'Gone to Wales? How do you mean, "Gone to Wales"? She didn't say anything to me about going to Wales.'

'But she's always saying she's going to go and stay with Aunt Megan,' Marcus reminded him.

'But she never does.'

There was a pause while Uncle Frank tried to take in what Marcus had told him.

'But when – when did she go? She shouldn't have left you on your own. Why didn't she ring me?'

'I think it was a spur-of-the-moment thing.' Marcus paused, panic rising, making his voice sound untrustworthy. 'I think,' he went on, striving for a measured delivery, 'I think she was a bit cross. Like you said. About the shopping. She went out to get it and when she came back she was fuming. Said something about letting you see what it's like running a household on your own. I don't know. She wasn't really talking to me. Anyway, when she came in from the shop, she just went upstairs and packed her suitcase.'

There was silence at Uncle Frank's end now. Marcus heard him mutter something like 'Drat the woman' to himself. Then he said: 'I never thought she'd do it; not in a hundred years. She should have rung me. At least we could have talked about it. And if she really wanted to go, I'd have come round and driven her to the station.'

'She got a taxi.'

'I can't believe it,' Uncle Frank said, and Marcus imagined him shaking his head, a deep frown forming on his forehead. 'How long will she be away?'

'She didn't say.'

Marcus was relieved. Uncle Frank's question suggested he was buying into the story. Marcus just had to make sure he didn't make any serious mistakes. He had already realized that he would have to pack Aunt Hester's suitcase to make her visit to Rhyl believable. He looked again at the kitchen clock. There was barely going to be time, and that was assuming Uncle Frank didn't come home early.

'What did she say, exactly?' Uncle Frank was asking.

'Nothing much. Just that she was going to Rhyl for a few days – and that she didn't want you to phone.'

'And then she just left you on your own?'

'I'm fine, Uncle Frank. Honest.'

'Well, it's not right. I'd come round now—'

'You don't need to. Really. I'm OK.'

'Are you sure? It's just that I've got a few more clients to deal with.'

'It's not a problem, Uncle Frank. I'm feeling a lot better. I've had a good rest.'

'Well, if you're sure. And you say she did the shopping before she went?'

'Yes.'

'Do you know what she'd planned for our tea?'

'No. But I'm sure we can find something in the freezer. How about fish fingers?'

'Good idea.' Frank sounded distracted. 'Look, I'll get home as soon as I can.'

'OK,' Marcus said. 'I'll see you later.'

'Good lad,' Uncle Frank said. 'Look after yourself.'

Uncle Frank hung up. Marcus's hand was trembling so much he had difficulty putting the phone back in its cradle.

Still, that was Uncle Frank taken care of. For the time being.

Now all he had to do was dispose of Aunt Hester and find a safe hiding place for the . . . *thing* that had turned her to stone. In less than two hours.

Going back into the dining room was an ordeal. The break he'd had with Hannah, and then talking to Uncle Frank on the phone, had allowed him to reacclimatize to the normal world. But as soon as the dining-room door banged against Aunt Hester's stone heel, Marcus was back in the nightmare of venomous serpents and stares that turned people into statues.

It was still hard to believe, and he had to touch Aunt Hester's solid, unyielding arm to make sure. But if he'd been in any doubt, he only had to look at the seething duvet on the table. He could feel his hair lifting as he stood staring at the undulating material. The snakes were obviously angry at being draped in the dark, and, Marcus saw with horror, they were working together to move the duvet so it would eventually slip off.

He burst into action, rushing for something heavy from Uncle Frank's building site. He found a breeze block, which he took inside and banged down on the table to moor one end of the duvet. The snakes took a moment to react, but they soon started pulling the duvet in the opposite direction.

Marcus fetched another breeze block. Fangs still tore through the material and wrenched it about, but when it became clear to the snakes that they could not shift the two blocks, all movement stopped.

Marcus felt exhausted. Perhaps he should wait for Uncle Frank, after all? Tell him what was really going on? But again, he tried to imagine the conversation, which would now be further complicated by the lie about Aunt Hester going off to Wales. That would make it seem as though Marcus had been more involved in her terrible fate than he had been. He looked into her stone features again. She looked grotesque, like a gargoyle. He couldn't let Uncle Frank see that, have it as the last memory of his wife. It was a nightmare, but it was Marcus's nightmare.

CHAPTER 3

Marcus kept staring at Aunt Hester's harsh features, as though, if he looked at them for long enough, they would eventually soften back into her familiar flesh. But in his heart, he knew that wouldn't happen. There was nothing so final as stone.

He had to get on. But when he turned he had such a fright that he stepped back into the hard bosom of his aunt. Sticking out of the duvet was a snake's head. It looked like a single flower in a vase – except that it was moving from side to side. It caught Marcus's eye and lunged towards him, hissing violently.

It was a terrifying sight, but Marcus was now wound up like a piano wire. Almost before he realized what he was doing, he stepped forward, seized the Stanley knife, and slashed.

The hissing stopped. Marcus blinked.

There in front of him was the snake's neck – if a

snake could be said to have a neck – the head cleanly severed.

Something was beginning to ooze out of it, but before Marcus could see it properly, the now-headless snake slithered back down through the hole in the duvet.

A moment later, the whole duvet started to seethe like a cauldron of boiling water.

Marcus looked to see where the snake's head had ended up. There it was by the skirting board, its jaws apart, its eyes still staring angrily.

One to me, Marcus thought, grimly, his heart racing and the blood in his ears beating like a drum. There was a long way to go, and he felt a spasm of dread at the thought of everything he had to do.

The first job was to move Aunt Hester.

Fortunately she was a small woman, but even so Marcus had no idea whether he would be able to shift her on his own. He was quite big for his age. This had its inconvenient side – like being put in the scrum and shouted at a lot in rugby. But there were occasions when it was useful, and this looked like being one of them.

The only way he could possibly move her was on the builder's trolley Uncle Frank had bought for the patio job. He wheeled it into the dining room, skirted the table and positioned it behind Aunt Hester. With one hand on Aunt Hester's neck, he pushed her forward so that her heels rose fractionally. He then shoved the trolley with his shoe so that the plate at the bottom slipped under her feet. When he was confident she was properly on, he clasped his aunt round the middle and braced himself. He eased her to the tipping point, and then just that little bit more . . .

He lurched back against the door. For a terrible moment Marcus thought he wouldn't be able to bear the weight. But when he'd got a better grip on the handles and was sure Aunt Hester was properly balanced, he found he was – just – able to support her. And then he began, very uncertainly, to push her towards the hole in the dining-room wall.

He nearly lost her when the trolley wheels wobbled over the extension lead Uncle Frank had left trailing from the plug out to the patio. He paused to wipe a bead curtain of sweat from his forehead.

It was this scare that made Marcus turn and take Aunt Hester through the dining-room wall backwards. Uncle Frank had built a crude ramp, and he bumped her down onto the patio towards her final resting place. There really was only one option.

The garden ran down towards the railway cutting. Uncle Frank had a shed at the bottom, right up against the rickety fence beyond which a wasteland of brambles and bushes dropped steeply towards the track. Marcus was forbidden to explore beyond the garden fence – but of course he had. It was the perfect place for Aunt Hester. He was thankful she had insisted on letting the hedges grow so tall. The towering dark walls jealously rationed the amount of sunlight getting through to the lawn, but they also provided an impenetrable curtain, preserving the garden's privacy – especially from the curtain-twitching retired librarian, Mrs Prewle, who lived next door.

When Marcus got to the end of the garden, he surveyed the overgrown wilderness beyond the broken-down fence. Aunt Hester would lie hidden by elderflower bushes and willow herb, protected by brambles.

He wouldn't have to push her far in to be out of sight. First he had to get the trolley through the gate, which sagged from a single hinge and had weeds and a tendril of bramble growing between its rotten woodwork. Marcus looked at his palms, which were already covered in blisters

He yanked Aunt Hester through, but it was tough going beyond the fence. Every bit of vegetation seemed intent on clogging up the trolley wheels. A fly buzzed around his face, as though the sweat running down his cheeks were nectar. He couldn't brush it away – he had to keep his grip on the trolley whatever happened.

Then the slope suddenly became alarming, and at the same time he got his foot caught in a bramble and very nearly fell. The last thing he wanted was to be crushed under the statue of Aunt Hester. Marcus looked desperately over his shoulder and saw a towering clump of brambles a few metres further down. Testing every step, he started to ease the trolley towards it, struggling all the time to keep Aunt Hester balanced. He wheeled the trolley round, so it was facing down the slope. Then, with a sudden surge of energy, he propelled the trolley and its load as far into the bramble bush as he could.

Aunt Hester rose vertically, and then toppled forward. It reminded him of the statues of dictators being tumbled from their plinths that he'd seen on one of the history channels. Only instead of cheering

46

crowds there was just the sound of a dead weight tearing through the vegetation.

His aunt came to rest, face down, her arms stretched out above her head. Marcus stood looking at her. What did he feel? Relief at having got her out of the house; but also a kind of shocked sadness. And behind that, he could feel the brimming tide of guilt, lapping at his conscience.

Perhaps he should say a prayer?

He was just wondering what form it might take when, from along the railway track, came the mournful two-note bray of a freight train. These tore through the cutting two or three times a day, their dozens of trucks clanking along at high speed. The noise was overwhelming, filling your head like a torrent. Marcus watched the tops of the trucks as they hurtled along the track below him, all thoughts of appropriate last words for Aunt Hester lost in the ringing of his ears. Then the train disappeared as quickly as it had arrived. With a last glance at the stone pleats of Aunt Hester's skirt, Marcus took hold of the trolley and started lugging it back up the garden.

Marcus felt a strange hollowness in the pit of his stomach as he returned to the house alone. There

47

was no point pretending he had liked Aunt Hester. But he knew she had looked after him as best she could by her own harsh standards, and for that she surely deserved better than to be tipped into a bed of brambles and left to the mercy of the elements. He'd only ever been to one funeral and he had been so young he couldn't remember much more than the long black cars, the tall black-clad people and the sense of being an object of sympathy and horror at the same time. Of course, Aunt Hester couldn't have a funeral – how would you get a statue into a coffin? As he had just discovered, the weight meant manoeuvring it was not something you could do with any decorum.

He parked the trolley back among the patio paving slabs. He didn't want to go back into the dining room, but he forced himself to duck beneath the draped tarpaulins. The room seemed quiet, almost peaceful. There was no angry hissing, and no seething movement beneath the duvet.

Now the question was how to shift the thing. In the Medusa story, Marcus remembered, the hero who had cut off the head took it away in a bag. But how would you get it into the bag in the first place? You couldn't plunge your hands into that violent mass of snakes – you'd need serious protection.

Marcus glanced around the room in search of inspiration, his eyes resting on the fireplace. They seldom had a fire because Aunt Hester was constantly worrying about how much they spent on fuel. When they did, he enjoyed watching Uncle Frank setting the twists of newspaper among the kindling and then loading on the lumps of coal. There were tongs, but quite often Uncle Frank didn't bother with them. Instead, he pulled on one of the leather gauntlets that were tucked away behind the coal bucket and dropped the coals on by hand.

Marcus went over and dug them out.

He found one and plunged his right hand inside. It was too big for him, of course, but it was made of good thick leather, and although it was stiff, he could still move the fingers. It was a start.

He turned back towards the dining-room table.

Then he screamed.

Coiling out of the tear in the duvet was a snake. But it wasn't like the one he'd beheaded earlier. It was a lot worse.

Sometimes a nightmare gets so bad you have to wake yourself up to escape it – but Marcus knew there was no waking up from this one. He stood trembling, looking at the latest twist in a story that was already completely out of control.

This new snake was a towering king cobra, with a huge spread hood, zigzagged with black markings – like the danger warnings on electricity pylons. It swayed menacingly, mesmerically, its beady black eyes fixed on Marcus's, and the long forked tongue slipping in and out of its mouth, as though anticipating the moment it could sink its fangs into his flesh.

Marcus looked round for the Stanley knife. But then a terrible thought crashed into his mind. What if the cobra had replaced the snake he'd decapitated? Wasn't there something in the myth about that? The more you cut their heads off, the more they grew new ones. Or was that another story? It didn't matter. This wasn't a myth. This was what was happening now. In his house. To him.

He glanced down at the coal bucket, but couldn't imagine himself dropping it over the cobra – let alone all the others. He wasn't sure it was even big enough to hold the head. Maybe there was something in the attic that would do. He took a step forward. The cobra lunged towards him. The great hood flared and swivelled as Marcus eased past the table and dashed towards the dining-room door. It was a relief to be running up the stairs and along the landing to the attic. Marcus pulled open the door and climbed the uncarpeted stairs.

The attic was the home of things no longer wanted but which were kept anyway: piles of Uncle Frank's old angling magazines, pictures wrapped in newspaper, a pedal bin they'd once had in the kitchen, and box after box of glassware and crockery. He dimly remembered a row between Uncle Frank and Aunt Hester about how much of his parents' stuff they could be expected to keep for when he grew up. His father had been an archaeologist, and his work had taken him from one ancient site to another around the Mediterranean. There were still stacks of tea chests full of his parents' belongings from their last home and, in a far corner, piles of suit-cases from their travels.

Marcus hadn't done much travelling. Apart from a couple of visits to Aunt Megan in Wales, he could only remember one 'family' holiday – a long time ago now. They'd gone to Minehead on the Devon coast. It hadn't been a great success. Somehow there were even more things for Aunt Hester to get het up about away from home. Sand had been an issue, though, as Uncle Frank had patiently suggested, there was always going to be sand when you went to the seaside.

'Not all over the house,' had been Aunt Hester's response. 'I'm meant to be on holiday. With the amount of sand that boy brings into the chalet, I've got even more housework than I have at home.'

There had been one good day. The rain had let up, the wind had dropped, and Uncle Frank had hired a rod and done some fishing. The two of them had sat together behind the windbreak, while Aunt Hester had gone off to search out the cheapest post-cards to send to her sister and her handful of friends back home.

Uncle Frank had caught a brilliant fish, which for once he didn't have to throw back, and Aunt Hester had grudgingly acknowledged that it made a tasty meal, though she couldn't help asking: 'But what did you pay for the hire of the rod?'

The next day it had rained, and it kept raining till it was time to go home. After that they seemed to have given up on holidays.

'More trouble than they're worth,' Aunt Hester had said, adding, 'all you two want to do is fish – and you can do that at home.'

Marcus's parents, on the other hand, had travelled

all over the place. He pulled their suitcases out one by one and gazed at the labels – Cairo, Marseilles, Athens, Tunis, Istanbul. These were names he'd only encountered in his geography lessons. If his parents hadn't died, he would have shared their wonderful life, moving from one exotic destination to the next. He still could have seen the world – had his father, who survived the car crash which killed Marcus's mother, not gone missing soon afterwards. His disappearance had been a complete mystery. No one ever got to the bottom of it and it was assumed he had died, though his body was never found.

If only he'd taken me back to his dig with him, Marcus thought bitterly. But as Uncle Frank had told him once when he'd asked about it, his father had not intended going back for more than a month or two. 'You were too young, lad,' Uncle Frank had said: 'He was busy, and there was no one to look after you out there. Whereas your aunt and I – we were very happy to have you for a few weeks.' The 'few weeks' had turned into months, then years. And in the end Uncle Frank and Aunt Hester had formally adopted him, even though Marcus insisted on keeping his father's surname: Waldrist.

Although he missed them bitterly, Marcus could

hardly remember his parents, however hard he stared at the few surviving photos; and he certainly couldn't recall what it was like living with them. Everything was blocked out by the few black seconds of the car crash which changed his life for ever.

He pulled himself back to his present problem. Most of the suitcases were far too big. He pulled a shoulder bag off the pile, but that wasn't right, either. Nor was the leather briefcase with his father's initials on. But below that there was something that looked more promising. It was an old fashioned wicker picnic basket, which stirred a vague memory – of a meadow by a river, a blanket spread on the grass, and a succession of treats handed out by his mother. The memory evaporated. What mattered was the basket. It had a lid which secured in the middle of the front panel. In addition, the front panel itself could be released by two catches at the side. Inside was a sort of shelf with a hole in it for a bottle or a thermos flask. He looked at the space beneath. Would it be big enough for the monster waiting for him downstairs? He hoped so, but there was only one way to find out.

CHAPTER 4

As he re-entered the dining room, the cobra puffed out its hood. Marcus did his best to ignore it. He'd worked out a plan, and he had to stick rigidly to it. He took a low stool from beside the fireplace and put it beneath the table. Then he put the picnic basket on it. He stood back, sizing things up. The king cobra stretched out of the mound of the duvet like a periscope. It was certainly interested in him, even slightly anxious, Marcus thought. When he fetched Uncle Frank's spade, the creature looked positively alarmed. For the first time Marcus felt he had the upper hand. He lifted the spade threateningly. With a hiss of rage, the cobra's head disappeared rapidly back through the hole in the duvet. Marcus placed the spade against the wall, then removed the two breeze blocks.

As he bent down to place it on the floor, he heard a noise, a very soft rustling noise. He straightened up, and as he did so took a precautionary pace backwards.

It was just as well; with a coordinated effort,

55

the snakes had sunk their fangs into the duvet – they were pulling it off. It was an extraordinary sight, the duvet slithering towards the edge of the table like a great manta ray rippling on the bottom of the ocean.

Marcus did nothing to prevent it; the snakes were doing exactly what he wanted them to. But he had to control what was going on. He moved swiftly round to the other side of the table again and picked up the spade. Then, standing to one side, he brought the blade down hard on the writhing duvet. There was a moment's silence, then an almighty hissing. But the movement of the duvet stopped.

Very gently, Marcus pushed the spade under the remaining half of the duvet. With a single shovelling movement, he lifted it away from the box and flung it onto the floor.

The snakes exploded in fury. For a moment, he was terrified. But when he threatened them with the spade they cowered down – even the king cobra, though he gave Marcus a baleful stare.

But that wasn't lethal, Marcus reminded himself. It was the glare of Medusa that would kill him. Even as he thought of her, the ancient wind began to blow through his head, and again, he heard the insistent rhythms of communication. He stood, transfixed. And then the voice began.

Mar – cus . . . Mar – cus. I have travelled so far . . . so far . . . to meet you. And how do you treat me? How do you honour my presence?

The voice was foreign – but it wasn't just the geographical distance it had travelled. Somehow the voice carried the weight and ruin of great age. Marcus felt he was being addressed across centuries, millennia.

But he was being addressed by the creature who had turned his aunt to stone. How could he trust her? Everything he knew about Medusa told him he was seconds away from sharing Aunt Hester's fate. He had to resist her voice; however gentle, however persuasive, however seductive it was.

He had to act quickly. Reaching for the nearest dust sheet, he flung it over the snakes. In seconds the sharp fangs pierced through it and started to pull it off.

He steadied the spade and thrust it in, feeling the horrible give of deteriorating flesh as it slid under the severed neck.

The snakes were working more rapidly now, and the dust sheet was more than half off. Marcus lifted his gruesome load, gritting his teeth in determination. Then, with great care, though every nerve in his body was urging him to hurry, he laid it inside the basket and withdrew the spade. He was only just in time. Standing safely behind the basket, Marcus watched as the snakes pulled the dust sheet away completely so that it fell on the floor. Stooping, as though taking cover from sniper fire, he pushed up the front panel of the picnic basket and latched it at either side, before slamming down the lid. The picnic basket thrummed with outrage as the snakes realized they had been outwitted.

Marcus was barely able to stand. But he had done it. He leaned against the table, looking down at the lid of the picnic basket. A hamper of very angry vipers, growing out of the head of a monster condemned to turn every living creature she saw to stone. Well, she hadn't turned him to stone – yet.

The best place to store it would be the cellar, he'd decided. No one ever went down there, and he was sure there would be piles of junk to hide it behind. Not that he felt like picking the basket up and carrying it to a tightly confined space accessible only by a very steep, narrow set of steps. The cellar was full of things that had never been moved up to the attic:

paraffin heaters, in case the central heating broke down; an ancient hoover, in case the new one stopped working; an antique sewing machine, preserved on the same principle; and a couple of mildewed deckchairs – in case, Marcus assumed, they ever went on another summer holiday. *Not likely, now,* he reflected grimly. The only holiday he could think about was the fictional one he'd just made up about Aunt Hester.

After looking around in the dim light, he found a promising corner where a jumble of items leaned untidily together: his first bicycle which he could just remember learning to ride under Uncle Frank's watchful eye; a garden parasol with a couple of broken spokes; and an old clothes horse, which had a pair of faded curtains hanging from it – the perfect cover. It didn't take long to move everything out of the corner, shove the basket into it, and then return everything to its place. With one last look, Marcus climbed back up the wooden steps and then turned the light out. He leaned against the cellar door. The house was silent. The fomenting rage of the snakes was stilled, the terror of their murderous glare sealed away – for the time being.

Where had the head come from? Why had it

been sent? And what was he going to do with it long-term? These burning questions rang through Marcus's head demanding answers. But they could not be addressed now. Now he had to throw himself into chivvying the house back into the state it had been in that morning, when Uncle Frank had called a casual 'Goodbye' from the front door and driven off to work.

Marcus went into the dining room to return the stool to its place by the fire; he needed to take the breeze blocks and the spade back out to the patio too. There was something else, he thought, as he ducked back into the room. The Stanley knife reminded him: what about the snake's head he'd sliced off?! There it was, lying inert by the skirting board. He edged round the table to pick it up, but something made him pause. Just to be on the safe side, Marcus decided to get the protective gauntlets from the fireplace. There was no point in taking risks now. One scratch from a venom-laden fang could be fatal.

Having put one of the gauntlets on, he approached the snake's head for a second time. Marcus hadn't really thought what he was going to do with it. Perhaps wrap it up in old newspaper like a fish head and shove it deep into the pedal bin in the kitchen.

He crouched down to reach for it – and it jack-knifed. With a terrible hiss, the jaws extended and the fangs plunged upwards. Marcus leaped back, catching his rib painfully on the table.

Was there no end to it? Not only had the decapitated snake been replaced by the king cobra; but it was still alive itself! It lay there squirming and spitting venom. If he hadn't put on the gauntlet, he was sure he would be writhing on the floor beside it, dying in agony.

Something fired in his brain. This was war, and he had to win, by whatever means he could. Thinking quickly, Marcus ran upstairs to his own room. There was a pencil box on his desk. He emptied the contents onto the desk. Sliding the lid to and fro nervously, he made his way downstairs again.

Marcus put the gauntlet back on, and held the pencil box in it. The snake head eyed him as he approached, its jaws wide. He veered round so he was coming at it from behind. The snake's jaw widened and snapped, the black eyes smouldering. But there was no escape. Marcus slammed the box down, trapping the snake, and, with his other hand, pushed the lid shut.

When he lifted the box off the floor, he could feel it vibrating with fury. Marcus went into the kitchen and grabbed three or four of the thickest elastic bands he could find, quickly fitting them down the length of the pencil box before running upstairs to hide it in his room.

Having lugged the duvet back upstairs, he went outside and checked that everything was as Uncle Frank had left it on the patio, and secured the tarpaulins in their original positions. He was just congratulating himself on having done the job properly, when he heard a sound behind him. It was Mrs Prewle's cat, Decimal – a daft name for a cat, Marcus thought, but then having a cat in the first place was pretty daft. Like all cats, Decimal seemed to prefer the neighbours' garden to his own, and had clearly been making himself at home in the long grass beyond the clothes line. There was a field mouse hanging from his jaws. Marcus knelt down and tickled it under its chin. 'Decie, Decie, Decie,' he whispered. The cat began to purr. Marcus stroked it, tickling its ears and milk-white throat. The field mouse fell to the ground, ignored, and for a moment

Marcus continued his tickling. Then he stopped, dropping his hand to claim the mouse. Mission accomplished. Decimal gave him a slightly hurt look, but then decided that the mouse was a small price to pay for friendship. As Marcus stood up, prize cupped in his hand, the cat wound himself round his ankles.

'Not now, Decimal,' he whispered, bending down to give the cat's ears a last tickle. Then giving Decimal a gentle nudge with his shoe, he sent him on his way and went back into the house. He was pleased with his trophy, which he placed almost reverently in a small freezer bag before taking it up to his room. What else did he need to do?

The box! The cardboard box in which the head had been delivered.

He stared at its ruins on the dining-room table, and looked again at the label. How could anyone have known his address?

M. *Waldrist, Esq.* 'Esquire?' He peered again at the blotted writing, and at the foreign-looking frank, which had also run in the rain, obliterating any clue as to its country of origin. But a glance at the clock reminded him he didn't have time to think about the mystery sender now. The box had to go down the garden to rest in the brambles with Aunt Hester.

*　*　*

Uncle Frank was coming home any minute to get to the bottom of Aunt Hester's impulsive disappearance to Wales . . .

Marcus ran through her last moments once more. He could see her bustling down the hall, shouting at him because of the footprints on the carpet, ordering him to fetch the mop from the utility room, and, at the same time, getting up a head of steam about whatever Uncle Frank might have ordered from the mail-order angling company.

Marcus needed to imagine an alternative sequence of events so that he could make his story sound convincing to Uncle Frank. There would have been shouting – he could work out exactly what was said later – followed by a determined charge up the stairs and then some drawer-banging as Aunt Hester packed for her spur-of-the-moment trip.

Marcus would have to do the packing for her, of course. He reluctantly climbed the stairs, hesitating on the landing outside the main bedroom. But there was no avoiding it. He had to go in. It was immaculately tidy – the twin beds neatly made and not a thing out of place – from the brushes and combs on Aunt Hester's dressing table to Uncle Frank's polished shoes drawn up in a row beneath his bed.

Marcus scooped up the brushes, nail files, lipsticks and lotions and then stopped to think. What would she have taken? Clothes – probably lots of clothes. There were two small drawers at the top, opening the one on the right he stood back aghast at the neatly folded piles of underwear. *Well, go on then*, he told himself. However furious she was, she wouldn't have gone to her sister's without any knickers, would she?

Cautiously he pulled a pair out. They were surprisingly baggy, and he stretched the elastic to see just how far it would go, before telling himself to concentrate on the task in hand. How many pairs would she have taken? That would depend on how long she was going for, of course. And he was in charge of that as he was inventing the whole trip.

He plunged his hand into the drawer and came out with quite a bunch, which he threw on the bed. Then he reached in for the stack of beige tights, following them with some handkerchiefs and slips. Shouldn't there be something else? He tried the other small drawer. There they were, dozens of them. He gingerly lifted one out and held it for a second up to his chest. He felt a snigger coming, but the sound of a car outside in the road made him freeze. Uncle

Frank could arrive home at any minute. The bras joined the other things on the bed.

Marcus went rapidly through the rest of the drawers. In the bottom one he found jumpers and scarves. It was still quite cold, so why not? He pulled out two jumpers and a pair of slacks that he had hardly ever seen her wear. But she might want them if she went for walks or spent an afternoon in the garden. When the pile looked like the right amount of clothes for a few days' stay, he looked around for something to put it all in. There was a suitcase on top of the wardrobe. He fetched it down, knocked the dust off it and flung in all the things he'd selected. He opened the wardrobe and pulled out a couple of skirts and a smart jacket. What else?

Shoes!

There they were, all over the floor of the wardrobe. He grabbed three pairs. Was that enough? Another car drew up in the street outside. That had to be Uncle Frank, he thought, pulling the suitcase lid down and pummelling it into place. There wasn't time to take it down to the garden. It would have to go under his bed. He took a last despairing look round the bedroom. Bedroom! He reached under Aunt Hester's pillow and yanked out her nearly-forgotten nightie. Hanging from a hook on the door was her dressing gown. Her slippers waited patiently by the side of her bed. Scooping them up and hugging the suitcase, Marcus made his way back out onto the landing and flung himself into his own room, just as he heard Uncle Frank's key in the lock.

'I'm home, Marky. Where are you, lad?'

CHAPTER 5

Marcus stood at the top of the stairs, hoping Uncle Frank wouldn't notice the signs of his mad rush to throw his aunt's things under his bed. His uncle looked up at him from the doormat, his briefcase hanging limply from his hand. He looked about him, head cocked slightly to one side, taking in, Marcus thought, the tell-tale silence.

'Well, well,' he said, eventually. 'So she really has gone. You'd best come down and tell me all about it, lad.'

An hour and a half later, they pushed back their chairs from the kitchen table. Their plates were clean, apart from smudges of ketchup and the odd orange-yellow crumb from the fish fingers. Marcus wiped his mouth with the back of his hand.

'Well,' said Uncle Frank, 'we survived the first meal on our own.'

It was meant to be a light-hearted comment, but

Marcus could sense the weight of feeling behind it. He'd already given an account of Aunt Hester's departure while Uncle Frank was pulling cupboards open and searching for the fish fingers and peas in the freezer, but he didn't imagine for a moment that that would be end of it. He was right. As he got up to clear the table Uncle Frank touched his arm.

'Leave it. Come and sit down and tell me about it all once more. I just don't seem to be able to get my head around it.'

So Marcus went through it all again, adding the odd detail here and there – and having a nasty moment when he realized that the fictional call to the taxi firm could be checked – if Uncle Frank had a mind to – when the next phone bill came through. Not to mention the call to Aunt Megan! He hoped it wouldn't cross his uncle's mind, but it was a warning to keep the story as simple as possible.

When Marcus finished, Uncle Frank sighed and pushed his fingers through his hair.

'Well, she's been saying that's what she was going to do for as long as I can remember,' he said. 'I just never thought she would.'

'I think it might have been me that set her off,' Marcus said.

'How come? I thought she was mad at me for forgetting the shopping.'

'She was. But – I don't know. She seemed mad at me too.'

'For having a cold?'

'Just for being around – under foot. She said she didn't want me off school next week.'

'But she was the one who kept you at home. You said last night you felt well enough to go to school, and she wouldn't let you. Look, lad, don't fret yourself about it. If it's one thing, it's probably me taking so long over the French windows and the patio. I bet you that's it. Though why she couldn't just have said she was going off to let me get on with it, I don't know.'

Why didn't I think of that? Marcus wondered. But then, of course, there'd have been no reason for the ban on calling her in Rhyl. Anyway, once you'd made up a story, you had to stick to it.

Uncle Frank stared ahead, trying to get his head round the situation.

'And you're quite sure she said not to call her?'

Marcus found his uncle's eyes suddenly refocused on his own. Despite the sorrowful appeal in them, he hardened his heart: '"Tell your Uncle Frank not to call me",' he recited in a slightly singsong voice.

Uncle Frank put on a brave smile. 'No point winding her up by doing the one thing she told us not to do then, is there?' He looked tired, but at least he seemed convinced. Sending Aunt Hester off to Wales was working.

He just had no idea how long it would work for.

Although he was exhausted, Marcus couldn't sleep. There was so much pulsing through his brain. Eventually he heard Uncle Frank making his way to bed, and acknowledged his sombre 'Goodnight, Marky'. Then he must have drifted off. But it wasn't a peaceful sleep – more that state where you seem to skim along the surface of slumber, where dream and reality weave into one another.

First there was the sound of wind, a low whistling noise that made him twist uncomfortably in bed. A part of his brain protested that there had been no breeze earlier. When he carted Aunt Hester down to the railway cutting, there'd hardly been a breath of wind. Another part of his brain tried to remember why the wind sounded familiar.

Marcus screwed his head deeper into his pillow, but there was no avoiding it. The voice was back. It demanded his attention, and, whether waking or sleeping, he had to surrender to it.

Marcus . . . Mar . . . cus . . . the wind whispered, though the voice seemed to come from a long way off, and the two parts of his name seemed barely joined together. Although he hated the wind-whispering, he couldn't block it out.

Mar . . . cus . . . Mar . . . cus . . . And soon there were other sounds, other syllables, fragments of words:

I came . . . Mar . . . cus . . . I came . . . such a . . . long way . . . such a long time . . . Marcus . . . to bring you a message.

It was as indistinct as a badly-tuned radio station. Marcus was listening intently, sitting up in bed now.

He found his mouth opening. He wanted to ask questions. What was the message? And why was this monster from mythology the one to bring it to him?

But the voice began to fade, the wind-blown whispering was lapsing back to whistling. And then the wind itself was dying down, blowing itself out in faltering little wisps of noise.

Marcus was left grasping for meaning, but was pulled down into the undertow of sleep. There was no peace there. The depths were haunted by nightmares: Aunt Hester taking her fatal stride into the dining room, her scream of terror, and then the monstrous face of Medusa leering at him, her dead eyes searching for his like dark lasers. The snakes of her hair writhed around her graveyard features, dominated by the king cobra. As much as he struggled, Marcus's eyes were drawn, slowly, inevitably towards the black vortex of her deadly gaze. He felt his head being held in a vice-like grip, and was forced to face her. His eyes desperately fought to look away, but in vain. They took in the ragged edges of the severed neck, the mottled green of the chin, and then the mouth which seemed to move. The lips began to part. He heard the echo of the whispering wind. *Mar . . . cus . . .*

She was speaking to him. She knew his name.

Mar . . . cus . . . Mar . . . cus . . . I have come to you.

The lips closed but then stretched into a smile. He knew he was only a second away from catching her fatal glance.

Marcus whipped his head to one side, his whole body turning to escape.

And then he was awake, his sweat-soaked duvet

clinging clammily around him. He fought his way from under it and lay in the dark, shivering. The relief at breaking out of his nightmare was great. But with a sinking heart he realized he had just returned to the world in which Medusa was real. He may have trapped the monster in the cellar, but she was still powerful enough to infiltrate his dreams. He lay there hugging himself, too fearful to risk going back to sleep.

He must have dropped off again at some point, because he was asleep when Uncle Frank came into his room and drew back the curtains.

'Morning, Marky.'

How many weekends had started like that – with Uncle Frank's friendly face looking down on him, and the glad thought that he didn't have to go to school?

'Did you sleep all right? I thought I heard you in the night.'

'Had a bad dream,' Marcus said, yawning.

'I'm sorry. How are you feeling now?'

'Fine.'

'Do you want to go to orchestra?'

Marcus shook his head.

'I haven't practised.'

It was true. He'd had plenty of opportunity, but he hated playing within earshot of Aunt Hester, who never complimented him and whose unsmiling face suggested she thought he was wasting his time.

'Fair enough. What about an hour or two by the canal then – if you're feeling up to it?'

'Can we?'

'Don't see why not. As long as you wrap up warm. It's a lovely day. Come on, get yourself up and I'll cook some breakfast.'

'Strangest thing,' Uncle Frank said, half a sausage poised on his fork.

'What?' Marcus asked.

'She forgot to take her toothbrush. Most unlike her.'

Marcus felt a cold flush under his shirt. How could he have overlooked something as obvious as that?

'Still, if she was in a state . . .'

Uncle Frank chewed slowly, though his mind was clearly not on the sausage.

Marcus felt a spasm of shame. He hated lying to Uncle Frank. But now he'd started, he had to make the lie as effective as possible.

'I think it was the taxi.' He looked down at his baked beans. 'It came sooner than she expected, and she got flustered when the man parped his horn.'

Uncle Frank gave this some consideration and then nodded his head. Marcus prayed that he didn't ask Mrs Prewle for confirmation. She would have certainly have noticed a taxi outside and Aunt Hester getting in with a suitcase. He suddenly felt depressed. There seemed no chance of keeping this up, even for the weekend.

Uncle Frank didn't say anything but carried on eating.

'I think I'd better do a proper shop,' Uncle Frank said after they'd done the washing-up together. 'We can't just live on stuff from the freezer. Imagine what your aunt would say.'

Marcus had to work hard to imagine a world in which Aunt Hester would ever say another word.

'Do you want to come with me or stay here? You can stay here if you like,' Uncle Frank read the answer in Marcus's eyes. 'No need to drag you round the supermarket. You rest up at home, lad; and we'll get out to the canal after lunch. Let's do a list, so's I don't forget anything.' They exchanged a brief smile.

However terrible the situation was, Marcus

thought, there was no denying that spending time with Uncle Frank was a huge bonus. They pored over a piece of paper on the kitchen table, and planned out the meals for the days ahead. 'And I'll get one of those Marks and Sparks shepherd's pies your aunt likes. Just in case.'

Then Uncle Frank got up and took his car keys off the hook by the telephone.

'I'll not be long – though having said that, it can get a bit mad on a Saturday can't it?'

Marcus nodded. Uncle Frank walked down the hall and let himself out of the house. A moment later, the car coughed into life, and he drove away.

The first thing Marcus did was to go into the front room and turn on the computer. The computer had been the cause of much friction in the household, as Aunt Hester was deeply suspicious about what people 'got up to' online. They already had a set of encyclopedias (leather-bound, and taking up two shelves of the glass-fronted bookcase by the fire). But Uncle Frank had persisted, pointing out that it would put Marcus at a disadvantage not to allow him the same access to the internet as his fellow pupils. She had given in with a bad grace, banned any sort of social networking, and insisted the computer remain downstairs, never to be moved to Marcus's room.

Marcus typed 'Medusa' into the search engine. In a few seconds the screen was flooded with links. It didn't take him long to piece together the story.

Medusa was an exceptionally beautiful young woman, he read – a bit like a supermodel. Men travelled from all over to try to marry her, and the attention went to her head. She started saying she must be more beautiful than the goddesses in Olympus.

Big mistake. The goddess Minerva took it upon herself to punish Medusa and transformed her into a Gorgon – a zombie-like monster who could turn any living being to stone with just a glance. As Medusa was particularly proud of her lovely blonde hair, Minerva turned it into snakes to make her even more terrifying.

Of course, the next lot of men who came to propose to her didn't get very far, and word soon got out – Medusa became even more famous, but for all the wrong reasons. No one else came along to ask her to marry them.

Marcus remembered the outline of the story from his primary-school project; he skimmed on to the bit he was really interested in: how the hero, Perseus, cut off the Gorgon's head. This came about because the wicked king, who was keeping Perseus's mother prisoner, challenged Perseus to bring back the monster's head. The cruel king thought Perseus would die in the attempt, leaving the way clear for the king to force his captive into marriage. But Perseus didn't fail. With help from the gods – in the form of a pair of winged sandals and a brilliantly polished shield – he flew rapidly to the Gorgon, and, using the shield as a mirror so he didn't have to catch her eye directly, sliced off her head. Putting it in a special leather bag, he set off on his return journey, and after a few adventures in which he unleashed the devastating power of the Gorgon on anyone who stood in his way, he returned to the wicked king's palace. With the king and all his courtiers gathered round, Perseus pulled out the Gorgon's head, and turned them all to stone. He had saved his mother, and proved himself a hero.

Marcus had been right. Somehow, so far, he'd dealt with this mythical – but all too terribly real – monster, without being a hero, and without any help from the gods. He felt he had to give himself some credit for that. But it was all so weird – and very frightening. And Aunt Hester was now a lump of stone abandoned on the railway embankment.

Marcus felt a sudden anxiety: perhaps she could be seen from the fence. He should probably go down and check on her. He also decided to take the packed suitcase down and leave it in the bramble bed with her.

He ran upstairs to his room, and pulled it out from under the bed. He decided it would be safer to move the handbag as well, but first he took out Aunt Hester's phone, flicking it on briefly and noting there was one missed call – from Uncle Frank. Marcus weighed it in his palm, thinking hard. Perhaps, rather than just being something that could expose the terrible lie, the mobile might provide a means to keep it going . . . He placed the phone in his bottom drawer, then stuffed the handbag in the suitcase.

Marcus walked briskly down the garden, pausing at the gate to look over the wasteland beyond. There was no trace of anything out of place. On he went with the suitcase and found Aunt Hester exactly as he'd left her, face down in the brambles.

He heard the morning freight train and the inhuman clatter of its wheels as the tops of the brightly-coloured containers flashed briefly through the embankment and disappeared round the bend. Aunt Hester was indifferent to the torrent of noise of course – just as she was to the slug that was crawling up her left leg. Marcus reached down and flicked it off. Then he laid her suitcase beside her. It felt a bit like laying a wreath on Remembrance Sunday. Beside his aunt sagged the remains of the cardboard box. Marcus peered forward and inspected the label again. How could a mythical horror arrive on his doorstep via the modern means of the postal service? For some inexplicable reason it had been sent to him. Again the question Who had sent it? rattled through his head. Who, and why?

If only Marcus still had his dad. Dr Waldrist would have been fascinated by the head of the Gorgon turning up on the doorstep. There had even been moments when Marcus thought he might have had something to do with sending it. But then, how could you explain the ten-year gap since he went missing from his dig? That initial flame of hope was soon doused. If his dad were alive, he'd be coming home – not sending the equivalent of a small nuclear bomb to his son.

At which point Marcus came full circle. He'd just have to accept it was a mystery. More important than solving it was dealing with it; making sure he didn't follow Aunt Hester into the stone halls of death.

Once in the house, Marcus went up to his room. There, he fished out the pencil case from its hiding place and let it rest on the palm of his hand. He could feel the movements of the snake's head inside. A plan was beginning to form. His head was cloudy with images of fear and punishment that would never have formed in his mind before the arrival of the Gorgon's head. What was it doing to him?

Putting the pencil case to one side, Marcus went through the drawers of his work station. Somewhere he had another one – from primary school. When he found it, he emptied it out. Then he tipped the dead mouse into it and placed both boxes at the back of the bottom drawer.

Uncle Frank returned shortly afterwards. They had an early lunch and then loaded their fishing paraphernalia onto their bikes: rods, bait boxes, camp stools, keep-nets, along with a flask of tea and a generous ration of biscuits ('Got to spoil yourself sometimes,' said Uncle Frank smiling).

The sun shone, a few high clouds scudded by, and they heard birdsong as they skirted the park.

Once they had set up their little camp, they sat in companionable silence for two hours, lazily monitoring their floats as they bobbed in the dark brown water. On the surface it was just a typical day on the tow-path. The odd canal boat chugged past, sending a bit of a wash rippling to the bank. They'd wave at the people on board, and gradually the water would still to its usual muddy calm, with just their lines reaching out to their two floats.

But beneath the surface, Marcus's mind was in turmoil. For a couple of minutes he might be able to forget; but then his anxieties would crowd back in. And Marcus guessed it was the same for Uncle Frank. Although he did all the things he usually did – he even caught a couple of small roach – he seemed restless, obviously going over, again and again, the events that had led up to Aunt Hester's astonishing disappearance.

Marcus realized they were doing the same thing: going through the motions so as not to spoil it for the other one. In a way it was a relief when Uncle Frank gave the signal to pack up and head back home. Though of course, it meant returning to the house with its appalling secret in the cellar.

They had a quiet night in, watching a talent show

with their supper on their knees, something they never normally did. Uncle Frank even put the gas fire on, though Aunt Hester would only have allowed it if the night had threatened to be frosty. Marcus thought they might get through to bed time without Aunt Hester coming up in conversation. But he wasn't really surprised when Uncle Frank asked: 'How long did she say I wasn't to call?'

'She didn't.'

Uncle Frank nodded: 'I suppose she'll phone when she's good and ready.'

Marcus felt bad, but what could he do? Once you start telling a lie, you have to keep going. And it has to keep growing. A branch here, a twig there. Marcus briefly closed his eyes, picturing the lie as it stood. He would not only have to remember it in exact detail, but would have to be prepared to add to it as the need arose.

'I'd better get on with the patio tomorrow,' Uncle Frank said as they sat in the kitchen over a bedtime mug of cocoa. 'If I get it finished, I can ring her to say it's done. And then she'll come back. Perhaps I could text her? She didn't say anything about texting, did she?'

Marcus looked at Uncle Frank's pleading

expression. *Yes*, he thought, *Aunt Hester's phone could be useful.*

'No, Uncle Frank, though whether she'd pick a text up . . . you know what she's like. Anyway, I'd leave it for a day or two.'

'You're right – I wouldn't do it now – not immediately. But when I've made some progress on the patio?'

Marcus nodded and smiled encouragingly.

When they'd finished their drinks, Uncle Frank got up and went into the hall. Marcus joined him outside the dining-room door. He felt a pang of unease. Had he left everything exactly as it should be? Uncle Frank pushed open the door and switched on the light. Marcus looked in hesitantly, half expecting the nightmare box still to be on the table with its venomous contents biding their time. But everything was as it should be. He'd even remembered to wipe the Stanley knife clean.

Then he saw the right hand gauntlet on one of the dining room chairs.

There was an agonizing moment as he waited for Uncle Frank to see it and, worse, ask him whether he'd been in there.

But Uncle Frank didn't notice anything out of

place. He just stared down the room, nodded to himself and said, 'Yes, I really must press on.'

He flicked off the light and they went back into the hall.

'We'll roll our sleeves up tomorrow, lad – make a big effort. What say we skip church?'

Marcus nodded vigorously. He'd hoped – almost prayed! – that Uncle Frank would let them off this once.

They said their goodnights and Marcus went to bed. If he were going to pray for anything, it would be for a peaceful night untroubled by nightmares.

At breakfast, Uncle Frank asked how he'd slept.

'OK, thanks,' he said. This was only partially true. Medusa had let him be, but he'd felt an underlying sense of unease. Even when she wasn't manifesting herself in dreams, he could never entirely block her out of his mind, awake or asleep. Even now, the thought that they were sitting down to breakfast only a few yards away from the cellar sent a chill up and down his body.

He steeled himself to give his attention to the full-English breakfast Uncle Frank said they'd need to keep them going as they worked on the patio.

It was hard lifting the paving stones, but Marcus enjoyed physical labour. He enjoyed working with his uncle, and he felt good about the fact that they had moved things around so much there would be no possible trace of his activities on Friday afternoon.

'You handle that trolley well, lad,' Uncle Frank said at one point.

You don't know the half of it, Marcus thought to himself.

When they stopped for lunch they had made measurable progress and stood back admiring their work.

'Shall I get you a beer, Uncle Frank?'

Uncle Frank always had a beer before Sunday lunch, and Marcus always got his glass and opened the bottle for him.

'Thanks, Marky,' Uncle Frank said. 'And get yourself a Coke.'

Coke was a rare treat; Aunt Hester had a thing about fizzy drinks and E numbers, whatever they were.

They clinked glasses, two workmen celebrating the end of a decent shift.

After lunch, Uncle Frank pushed back his chair

and said: 'Now what are we going to do this afternoon?'

'I better do some homework,' Marcus answered. 'I've been away a week.'

'Course you have,' Uncle Frank nodded. 'I might take a load over to the recycling depot.'

'Do you want me to come?'

'No; I'll manage. You get yourself sorted.'

Marcus nodded. Good. There certainly was a fair bit to be done. But it wasn't what you would normally call homework.

CHAPTER 6

Marcus had a troubled night. Familiar figures approached him in his dreams, then threw up their arms in horror, their faces split with silent screams. Others crowding behind pressed in, freezing in a last spasm of terror. Straining eyeballs; heads flicked sideways in a futile attempt to avoid a stony fate . . . Marcus found himself surrounded by the hapless victims. As the circle of stone figures multiplied, an increasing weight pulled his shoulder down. His discomfort turned to pain, and his eyes dragged down. There, at the end of his arm, was the tangle of snakes writhing from the Gorgon's head.

The pain became unbearable; his elbow stiffened and his wrist turned against his will, gradually raising the Gorgon's head. Her eyes were nearly level with his so that he would soon find himself looking straight into her face. He rolled and thrashed, kicking out his legs, trying like the other victims to scream his terror. He tried his utmost to wake himself, fighting like a drowning man. But the Gorgon's power held him, like the tentacle of a vast octopus, until her head finally turned, and her eyes blazed straight into his. As he made one last frantic effort to be free, he saw the ruined face break into the ragged tear of a smile – a smile that said: *You are mine, Marcus, mine* . . .

Then he was awake, sitting up in bed, shivering in the cold dawn of Monday morning. But for all his exhaustion, Marcus felt a weird and growing sense of power. The Gorgon, he realized, had empowered him. She had given him her blessing for the action he had decided to take. He was going to take on the Gang. He was going to end the bullying that had brought Hannah running to his door on Friday. *Arran Woods has been having things his own way for far too long,* Marcus thought, still shivering from the strange aftermath of his dream. Despite his slight build, Arran had been a willing and punitive fighter from his first day in the school. Not that he did much fighting these days, because he had his huge hench-man, Digger, by his side. No one wanted to fight Digger, but Digger was always ready to fight anyone Arran told him to. They weren't proper fights, more carefully judged beatings, supervised by Arran who, by all accounts, enjoyed watching Digger in action.

Of course these 'fights' happened after classes and away from the school premises, but word got around, feeding the fear of them both, so that Arran continued to enjoy his power unchallenged. Just below him in the hierarchy was Melissa Gray, a big unpleasant girl, who was always surrounded by sycophantically laughing sidekicks.

The thought of them all ganging up on Hannah made Marcus so angry, and now he had developed his plan, he would exact revenge. The plan had required a certain amount of rehearsal the night before ('homework'), but now, as he looked at the two primed pencil boxes laid out on his work surface, he was confident it would work.

He ran downstairs for breakfast. Uncle Frank looked as though he hadn't slept well. Perhaps a day at work would do him good, Marcus thought. They didn't speak much, Uncle Frank just asking the routine questions about text books, PE kit and the contents of his lunch box, before going off to get his briefcase.

Then Marcus went upstairs to get everything ready. The two pencil cases were placed carefully at the bottom of his school bag. He could always leave them there unused, he told himself as a wave of nerves hit, immediately knowing he would despise himself if he did. He had been given the means to do something about Arran and Melissa. He would be a coward if he ducked the opportunity.

'Come on, Marky!' Uncle Frank called up the stairs. 'Got your key, lad?' he asked when Marcus joined him by the door.

Marcus nodded, and was soon blinking in the sunlight, and setting off up the road towards school.

'Had a nice holiday, then?'

'All right for some, skiving off 'cos their auntie says they've got a cold.'

Marcus ignored them. Minor members of the Gang. Small fry. He was going to strike at the top. Word would soon filter down.

His first target was Melissa Gray, Hannah's tormentor.

Second period, the one before break, was the one he'd chosen for the launch of his campaign. It was a science lesson, one of the few that he and Melissa shared. In the science block, pupils sat at high work surfaces on tall stools. ('Like a bar,' someone had said, and certainly some of the chemicals they mixed made lively cocktails.) Seating was pretty much a free-for-all, and for once Marcus made sure he sat close to Melissa and her associates. The lesson was quite bad. Mr Day was away, and he had left the history of space exploration as the topic for the supply teacher. The man covering the class was so old he looked as though he could remember it all personally, going all the way back to Yuri Gagarin and the moon landings. He got them talking about the space race and asked a few soft questions like 'What was the Cold War?'

Marcus put up his hand once or twice, just to attract Melissa's attention. But then he made it seem as though he'd switched off and that he was much more interested in his pencil case, which he peered into repeatedly.

'Are you conducting a scientific experiment in that pencil case?' the teacher asked, to a ripple of laughter. 'Because if you are, perhaps you'd like to share it with the rest of the class?'

No, just with Melissa, Marcus thought, covering the pencil case with his hand. The last thing he wanted was to have it confiscated.

At the end of the lesson, Marcus volunteered to

collect up the text books. He slipped down from his stool and was delighted when, out of the corner of his eye, he saw Melissa reach across and take the pencil case. He pretended not to notice, and when the bell went shoved his books into his bag and was amongst the first to the door.

Once outside, though, he stopped, letting everybody else push past.

Then the screams started – long, loud, and very genuine.

Marcus smiled, and quickly made himself scarce.

One down, one to go.

'I'm disappointed in you, Marcus.'

Mrs Faversham, his form tutor, was looking sternly at him.

'She shouldn't have taken it, Miss,' he said.

He had to focus really hard on Mrs Faversham's piercing eyes to prevent a broad grin spreading over his face.

He had experimented with the spring device for ages, but it was beyond his wildest dreams that the dead field mouse he'd taken from Mrs Prewle's cat could have catapulted right down Melissa's blouse.

Mrs Faversham sighed.

'No, she shouldn't,' she agreed. 'But then, she could hardly have expected it to be booby-trapped with a dead mouse, could she?'

Here Marcus had to look down at his feet and bite the inside of his lip.

'It's not in the school rules, Miss,' he said eventually.

'Perhaps not, but many things aren't in the school rules. And it's quite clearly against the spirit of the school rules, isn't it?'

'Yes, Miss,' Marcus said, thinking: *If only she knew what I've got in my second pencil case. That one is definitely against the spirit of the school rules.*

'All right, Marcus. We'll overlook it this time. But no more silly stunts like this in future, all right?'

'No, Miss,' Marcus said.

'Off you go, then. Here, you better have this back. But just use it for pencils in future, OK?'

Marcus hadn't expected to get the pencil case back, but he took it with a grateful smile.

He still had it in his hand as he walked out of Mrs Faversham's classroom.

'Got your secret weapon back, then? Thought you might have been suspended.'

Arran Wood's sharp features were uncomfortably

close to Marcus's face. For once, he was on his own. Marcus's pulse quickened. Here was his chance.

'Let's see, then.' Arran stuck out his palm.

Marcus handed it over.

Arran slid back the lid, and looked disappointed when he found it was empty.

'I've got another one,' Marcus said.

'Yeah? What's that got in it? Poison gas?'

There was a mocking look in Arran's eye, but Marcus could also see signs of curiosity.

'I'll show you.'

'Go on then.'

'Not here. I've just been given a warning.'

He nodded his head in the direction of Mrs Faversham's room.

'All right then,' Arran said, and led the way down the stairs. 'It better be good,' he said over his shoulder.

It will *be*, Marcus thought to himself; *it will be*.

There was a group of pupils at the bottom of the stairs, but it parted as Arran approached. Marcus was aware of the looks he was attracting. Usually being led somewhere by Arran meant something bad was going to happen to you.

Marcus looked forward to reversing the tables.

Arran led them down a long corridor at the end of which there was a door. A locked door.

Arran produced a key and pushed open the door.

This was Arran's 'office', which he shared by agreement with Mr Jarrold, the caretaker.

It wasn't so much a room, more a big broom cupboard. There was a rickety table and one broken-down chair. Mr Jarrold's mop and bucket stood in a corner and on a shelf were old plastic bottles of cleaning fluid.

'No Digger?' Marcus remarked conversationally.

'Relieving Year Sevens of their sweetie money, I believe,' Arran said with an unpleasant look. 'Do you think I can't handle you on my own, Marcus?'

Marcus shrugged and dropped his eyes.

'Well come on, then. Let's see. I haven't got all day.'

Marcus put his bag on the table and opened it. Arran craned to see as he shoved his exercise books to one side and reached in for the second pencil case.

'Oooo, lacky bands. Are you sure this isn't a tech project?' Arran cocked a mocking eye at the pencil case, but Marcus noticed that he had edged away a bit. Perhaps he was having second thoughts. It was too late now.

Marcus held the pencil case in his right hand, and pulled off the first elastic band, just as he'd practised the day before.

Arran's eyes were now fixed on it.

'I hope you haven't got anything stupid in there.'

Arran's voice struggled for its usual authority. Marcus gave him a bleak smile.

'You'll see,' Marcus said, removing the second elastic band.

'If you try anything funny—' Even as Arran said it, he took another step back.

'Funny?' Marcus said.

'You know what I mean. You try anything on and—'

Arran stumbled against the chair and sat down unexpectedly.

This played into Marcus's hands.

Before Arran could get up, Marcus took a stride forward. Standing over him he released the remaining elastic band, and thrust the pencil box right under Arran's nose.

'Get away from me!' Arran shouted, the panic rising in his voice. 'What is it? I'm warning you—'

Concentrating very hard, Marcus slid back the lid about a centimetre.

The noise Arran made was very different from Melissa's scream. It was a sort of welling gurgle of terror. His feet kicked for purchase on the dusty floor as he tried to push the chair back, but there was no escape. Marcus kept the partially opened box right there, right in his face. 'Stop! Take it away. Please! I'll do anything. Anything.'

Marcus inched the lid down just a little more. The snake that had been violently tossing its head from side to side in an attempt to get out sensed its moment, and opened its jaws, exposing its fangs dripping with venom.

'Poisonous, Arran. Just like you.'

Arran flinched away. He had his hands on Marcus's arm now, and his face was contorted with terror. Beads of sweat appeared along his hairline.

'Two minutes,' Marcus said softly, almost whispering it. He didn't know where this 'two minutes' came from, but he went with it: 'Dead in two minutes. But the pain, Arran. The pain. You'd never believe.'

'Marcus, please – no. I've always liked you, really. I've never done anything to you.'

'Not me, Arran. But plenty of other people.'

'I'll stop.'

'You will,' Marcus said.

'It was Digger. He kept upping it.'

'You gave the orders, Arran. And now you're going to order him to stop. All right?'

'All right, all right. Just put that thing away.'

Marcus looked down at him pityingly. The boy who had held the school in a grip of terror was now squirming in abject panic. It was good to see. And it had been strangely easy to bring about.

'It's the end, Arran. For you; for Digger; for everyone.'

'I've said. Now take that thing out of my face.'

'Just so you know I will use this again, if I have to. I could slip it into your pocket, or your bag – or your football shorts . . . You'd never know when it might strike.'

'OK, OK. Stop it – please . . . I'm begging you, Marcus!'

Marcus gave the pencil case a little shake, and the forked tongue shot out again.

'Two minutes. Two minutes of agony. Then you'd be dead.'

'I'll stop. I will. I promise. Please . . .'

'And Digger?'

'I'll tell him.'

'You better.' Marcus took a step back. He felt Arran's hands relax their grip on his arm.

'If anyone steps out of line – not just Digger – I'm holding you responsible. Understood?'

'Yes. Oh God. Just take that thing away!'

Marcus slid the pencil case shut, but he didn't put the elastic bands back on for the time being.

Arran sat slumped in the chair, his chest heaving and sweat running down his face. He couldn't meet Marcus's eye, and when he did get to his feet, he hardly seemed able to stand.

The school bell rang to mark the end of lunch. In a moment the corridor would be crowded with pupils jostling to get to their classrooms.

'Better give me the key,' Marcus said as they left the office.

Arran handed it over without a word.

Marcus had Geography next. He sat at the back and half-listened as Miss Kelvy explained how ox-bow lakes were formed. But he was more interested in the map of Europe stuck on the wall. His eye roved hungrily around the Mediterranean. He found Greece, with its myriad islands and multiple myths; where heroes pursued quests and faced up to their impossible challenges.

His last lesson was in the computer room. This was good news – it meant he could do more research on Medusa. He just hoped his log-in would work. Sometimes it didn't, and you could waste half a lesson waiting for someone to get you online. That's why he and Hannah knew each other's passwords. It saved time to have a back-up.

But today there were no problems, and he was soon scanning the pages of websites dealing with Greek myths in general and Medusa in particular. There were also a vast number of images. Some of these were quite rude. Medusa had certainly been a great beauty and many of the artists had followed that line with relish. Not wanting to get caught viewing 'inappropriate' material, Marcus switched to browsing the articles. A lot of it was dull, with scholars discussing the origins of the story and speculating on the date at which it first entered Greek mythology. Marcus skimmed through, stopping only when he came upon new elements. There were apparently three Gorgons, not just Medusa – though Medusa was the only one who was mortal, which explained why Perseus was able to cut off her head. She was also the only one to have snakes for hair. The three Gorgons lived at the entrance to the Underworld, and were so fearsome that images of them were common all over the ancient world. Mosaics, wall paintings and plaques could be found over doorways, above windows and on the walls of temples to ward off evil, or to remind mere mortals of their place in the scheme of things. Those were the sort of artefacts his father had spent his life excavating on his digs. Marcus imagined the excitement of brushing away the last layer of caked-on antique dust to discover something that hadn't been seen for two or three thousand years.

'I didn't know you were interested in Greek mythology.'

With a start, Marcus swung round. Mr Glanville was looking over his shoulder. 'Sorry, sir. I—' He had been so absorbed he had completely forgotten to keep a lookout.

'No, that's all right, Marcus. The history of the Channel Tunnel was only a suggestion. Greek myths would make an excellent project topic. At least you're actually doing some research instead of trying to play games behind my back.'

He smiled, then looked up at the clock and announced: 'All right, everybody: time to log off.' Two minutes later the bell rasped out, and Marcus was lost in the pandemonium of the end of the school day.

With his bag slung over his shoulder, he kept his head down and headed for the gate. If one or two pupils made way for him, he didn't notice. He was still lost in thought.

Medusa had been only Gorgon who was mortal: that was why Perseus was able to kill her. The story didn't say what happened to her body; maybe it rotted away, or was buried by the other two Gorgons. But clearly the head remained alive in some sense. For one thing, when Perseus used it as a weapon, the eyes were still capable of flashing their furious glare that froze men into stone. And now, centuries later, Medusa was still capable of terrible destruction. None of the accounts that he'd found made any reference to what had happened to the head. As people accepted it was just a myth, they probably didn't think about it.

He was still lost in thought when Hannah stepped

out of the bushes at their usual meeting place in the park.

'Hey, you! Why so serious? Thought you'd be grinning ear to ear!'

She certainly was grinning, and without waiting for a response, she launched into an excited account of how she'd heard Melissa's scream in the art block, along with everybody else in the school, apparently.

'It was amazing the mouse actually going down her front. How did you get it to do that?'

'Just luck, really.' Marcus spread his hands. 'I put a spring in it – like a jack-in-the-box – so it would ping out.'

'I wish I'd seen it,' Hannah giggled. 'But the screams were good – 'specially when I found out it was Mel. How did you get her to open the pencil case?'

I just sort of made it look as though it had something interesting in it – and . . .'

'You caught her, hook, line and stinker!' Hannah exclaimed. 'You clever angler, you!' She smiled broadly at him. 'Just right – a nasty shock for a nasty girl. I thought it was brilliant.'

Marcus smiled, but he still couldn't look as pleased as Hannah obviously expected him to.

'There was a rumour you'd had a run-in with Arran. Did you?'

Marcus nodded.

'Well, what happened? How did it go? Did he threaten you with Digger?' She looked concerned.

Marcus shook his head.

'Arran won't be a problem anymore.'

Hannah stared in disbelief.

'What did you do?'

'Just showed him my other pencil case.'

'Your *other* . . . what was in that one?'

'Well, that would be telling, but Arran won't want to see it again, I promise you.'

Hannah frowned.

'Marcus, what's going on? You come into school after a week off, perform a couple of practical jokes, and the two nastiest kids in the school are suddenly put in their place. How come?'

'Are you complaining?'

'No, of course I'm not. But who are you to suddenly decide to stop bullying at school?'

'Someone had to.'

'Yes, but why you, and why now? And how did you manage it? There's something you're not telling me, isn't there? Come to think of it, you were acting strange on Friday. I know I was in a state, but when you came to the door you looked as though you'd just seen a ghost. What's going on?

She looked him in the eye. He turned his head away.

'I thought you'd be pleased,' he said weakly.

Hannah gave him another look. It wasn't easy to interpret, so he changed the subject.

'Anyway, how is it – at home?'

'OK,' she said tonelessly.

'I'm sorry, Han.'

'It's all right.' She was quick to reply. 'If you don't want to tell me about the devastating contents of your pencil cases, that's up to you.'

'I'm sorry,' he said again: 'I really do want to know. Is your mum OK?'

Hannah gave him an 'all right then' look and sighed. 'Yes, she is, thanks. Dad's all "Oh Sorry, oh my God I can't believe I did it. I'll never do it again. I'll never drink another drop". But we've heard that all before.'

Marcus raised a sympathetic eyebrow.

'And the police?' he said, knowing what the answer would be.

'What can they do, with Mum clinging on to him

and saying she forgives him and won't press charges?'

'And you?'

Hannah ducked her head. Marcus saw her wipe away a tear. He put his hand out, but she didn't want to be touched.

'If there's anything I can do—' he started.

'But there isn't,' she said fiercely. 'Dad's not a school bully. He's not a kid. He's a grown man with a drink problem, so frightening him with a pencil case isn't going to work.'

There was no answer to this, so Marcus simply stared at his shoes.

He heard a sniff and felt Hannah's hand on his arm.

'I'm sorry, Marcus. That was unfair. But . . .'

And then she put her head to his chest and started sobbing.

Marcus found this unsettling – not least because it made him want to cry as well – for Aunt Hester, for the lies he'd told, for the terrible state his life was in.

'Oh God,' Hannah said when she eventually stopped crying. 'I'm sorry. Your blazer's soaked.'

He looked down and saw the damp patch.

'Doesn't matter,' he said. 'It'll soon dry. Walk you home?'

She gave him a watery smile and sniffed.

'Thanks. Oh' – she opened her bag – 'I'd better give you this.'

It was the score for their clarinet duet. He looked at it quickly, and saw to his relief that the second clarinet had only a few bars to play solo.

'Yours is easy,' she said.

A glance showed that hers was anything but.

'You'll be brilliant,' he said.

Hannah's house was an ordinary brick terrace, with greying render and peeling paint on the front door. It was further out than Marcus's, nearer the ring road and close to the canal.

Marcus had never been inside. Hannah didn't mind him walking with her to the corner – but no further. He understood that, even though he hated watching her walk into a home where her dad could kick off at any time.

Hannah's dad. Always getting drunk, always liable to hit out; always begging to be forgiven and promising to stop. From time to time Hannah talked about it – the jobs he'd lost, the friends who didn't want to see him anymore, the feeling of isolation in the house, and the terrible difficulty her mum had to make ends meet.

Marcus had only seen her father a couple of times – when he'd been clipping the hedge or doing something to the car outside the garden gate. He looked like a perfectly ordinary man: dark-haired, quite handsome in a way, though Marcus didn't like his two days' stubble and tousled hair. He was slightly below average height, but with broad shoulders. You wouldn't have picked him out as a dangerous man. But then you didn't have to be two metres tall to hit people.

As they walked in silence through the empty streets, Marcus thought how different it was – or had been – in his own home. Uncle Frank had never once raised his voice in response to Aunt Hester's constant nagging; whereas Hannah's dad was capable of lashing out over the slightest thing because he'd had too many pints in the pub. Marcus glanced at Hannah. She hadn't said anything for five minutes at least, and was now walking with grim determination, her eyes fixed on the pavement ahead. Marcus couldn't help feeling how unfair it was. He wanted to comfort her, but didn't know how.

'I'll go on by myself from here.' Hannah stopped and put a hand on his arm. 'Thanks, Marcus. See you tomorrow.'

110

They exchanged weak smiles, and then she turned away hurriedly.

Marcus stood watching her: just an ordinary girl going home from school, her bag over her shoulder. But he knew how much fear she had to swallow down just so she could walk up to her own front door, not knowing what was waiting beyond it.

He felt a sudden rush of anger. He hated Hannah's dad and the way he kept getting let off because Mrs Yarder stood by him. He should be stopped. He should be punished. The only thing Marcus could do was too awful to think about. He didn't even know why he'd thought of it. But he thought about it nonetheless. And if Hannah's dad ever hit her he would think about it a lot more.

He watched until she disappeared. There was an empty plastic drinks bottle lying on the pavement by the roots of the tree. He kicked at it fretfully and then felt guilty when he saw a woman glaring at him from her front window. To a respectable householder he was just another ill-disciplined kid from the local comprehensive. She had no idea – could have no idea – what he was going through.

Even though the day could hardly have gone better, he turned for home feeling unsatisfied. He had embarked on a long and dangerous journey that meant telling lies to the people he was closest to. He wished he had been able to tell Hannah the truth about how he'd toppled Arran; but that would have led her to ask about things he simply couldn't share with her.

As he walked, he stuck his hand in his pocket. His fingers closed around the key to Arran's 'office'. He had intended handing it in at reception. But as he ran the tip of his finger over its dull serrated edge, he thought that he would keep it for a bit. Access to Arran's cubby hole might prove useful.

Marcus cursed himself when he saw Mrs Prewle's lace curtains twitch. He should have approached the house from the other end of the street so she wouldn't have seen him go by.

She caught him just as he was opening the front door.

'Hello, Marcus. Back from school?'

What does it look like? he thought, but didn't say, offering a polite smile instead.

'I'm so glad your cold's better. I know Hester was really worried about you.'

'I'm fine, thank you.' He suppressed a sigh of impatience.

'I noticed you weren't at church yesterday.'

'No,' Marcus said.

'And I haven't seen your aunt for a day or two.' Mrs Prewle went on, giving him the penetrating stare she'd perfected at the library to make readers bringing books back late feel uncomfortable. 'Is she all right?'

'She's fine,' Marcus said. But he realized he couldn't leave it at that.

With a suppressed sigh, he started on the Gone Away to Wales story.

Mrs Prewle looked at him with beady attention.

'On Friday? Really? How astonishing. She didn't say anything about it when I saw her on Thursday.'

'It was a sudden decision,' Marcus said, cursing himself for saying anything at all.

'Did your uncle take her to the station?'

'No, she got a taxi,' Marcus said, mentally crossing his fingers.

'A taxi? I'd have given her a lift, but I was away all day Friday. I went over to Cheltenham to see an old friend. I could have done that any day, though . . . What a disappointment to have missed her. How long will she be away?'

'I'm not sure. She didn't say. She just decided she needed a break.'

'Well, I'm not surprised. Perhaps she's giving your uncle a chance to finish off that patio. It's very vexatious living on a building site.'

Marcus had the front door key in his hand.

'Well I must let you get on with your homework,' Mrs Prewle said. 'I hope you and your uncle are managing, but if you need anything, you only have to ask.'

'Thank you very much, Mrs Prewle,' Marcus said; 'but we're fine.'

'Of course you are, dear. I'm sure you'll have a lot of fun, just the two of you.'

She gave Marcus a glassy smile and started to retreat to her own front door.

Marcus thrust the key into the lock and swung open the door. It was a relief to shut it behind him and slip his school bag off his shoulder.

Not that home felt particularly homely these days. As he walked down the hall, he found his eye drawn to the cellar door. He had the feeling that he needed to open it and go down the stairs . . . That was the last thing he actually wanted to do, though, but he had to force himself to go into the kitchen and fix himself a squash instead. As he poured it into the glass, he noticed his hand was shaking and felt a clammy sweat crawling all over his chest. He tore off his school tie and undid his top button. But he still felt he was fighting for breath.

CHAPTER 7

The fact that Marcus had gone into Arran's 'office' and come out in one piece was news that travelled like wildfire round the school. It didn't take long for the shift in power to become common knowledge too. Arran wasn't himself. His confidence, his arrogant unpleasantness, had gone. Instead of striding through parting throngs of pupils, he now slunk about, avoiding eye contact, unaccompanied by Digger. No one knew what had happened, but clearly something had. Arran's fall was clear, complete and irreversible.

All attention was now focused on Marcus. Everyone was agog to know how he'd managed to depose Arran so completely, and rumours of a second pencil case ran like wildfire through tutor groups and across the playground in break. Because of his pre-occupation with his own problems, it took Marcus a while to notice he was the centre of attention. Some people looked at him with nervous awe; others –

minor gang members – avoided him. When he met Melissa in a corridor, she cowed back against the wall in exaggerated terror. But mostly people seemed pleased. The one member of the Gang who seemed untouched by the previous day's events was Digger.

'You ain't going scare me with a pencil case, Marcus,' he said with his unpleasant face thrust close. 'I ain't a girl – an' I ain't a coward. You just remember that, Mar-cuss.'

Marcus gave him a weary 'whatever' look and moved away. Digger, he knew, was pure brawn – malicious, but far less dangerous without Arran's guiding hand.

He met Hannah after school as usual.

She looked at him anxiously, enquiringly.

'What's wrong?' he asked.

'You tell me.' She looked fixedly into his eyes.

He shrugged.

'Marcus, you can't pretend you haven't noticed.'

'Noticed what?'

'Everybody in school's been watching your every move all day.'

'Why?'

'To see what you're going to do next.'

'I'm not going to do anything next.'

'They don't know that.'

'What do you want me to do about it? Stand up in assembly and make an announcement?'

Hannah gave him a slight frown.

'What?' he protested.

'You can't just overthrow Arran and Melissa and not expect people to react. They want to know the secret; they want to know what happened. How you did it, and how you're going to use the power you've obviously got. And frankly, I don't blame them.'

'You mean you want to know too?'

'Why shouldn't I? If there's nothing wrong, there's no reason not to tell me. Perhaps if I knew I could – you know – steer people in the right direction, and all the fuss would die down.'

'It'll die down anyway.' Marcus evaded her challenge. 'I'm not going to do anything, and in a day or two they'll all be gossiping about someone else.'

'Fine.' Hannah turned her head.

There was an awkward silence.

'How're things?' he said, breaking it awkwardly.

'OK.'

'Good.'

There was another pause.

Then Hannah looked at him again.

'Marcus, I don't mind if you want to keep a secret from me – well, I mind a bit, but it's up to you. I just want to know you're not doing anything . . .' she tailed off, her eyes attempting to lock onto his.

'Anything – what?' He dropped his gaze.

'I don't know – wrong, dangerous, stupid, cruel. In one day you do two amazing things, and I know for a fact you didn't take Arran and Melissa to one side to reason with them. We know what you did to Melissa, and she's obviously completely milking it; but you can hardly have terrified Arran with a dead field mouse.'

She stopped to give him the chance to respond. When he failed to, she said: 'Arran's an evil bit of work, but he's hard as nails. He wouldn't have got a boy like Digger to do his bidding without being a tough nut. Ten minutes with you in the janitor's room, and he's broken. It's not unreasonable to wonder how you did it.'

'Well, I didn't pull a gun on him, if that's what you're thinking.'

'It isn't, actually,' Hannah said. 'But whatever it was, it's obviously powerful. Power can be dangerous, Marcus.'

Again she pleaded with her eyes. 'Marcus, it's you I'm worried about. If you play with fire, you can get burned.'

'It's not fire,' he said.

Hannah gave a little snort of impatience, and gave him a last look.

'Just be careful,' she said, and then, looking at her watch, turned to go.

'And you,' Marcus said. 'You take care as well.'

But Hannah was walking away from him towards the park gate. She didn't look back.

The next day proved Marcus right. He was no longer the big story.

It didn't take him long to find out who was.

Hannah's friend Rose ran up to him as he crossed the yard to go to his tutor group. 'Friend' was perhaps an overstatement; they lived close to each other and sometimes walked to school together.

But not today.

'Han's not in school,' Rose said breathily.

'Why not?' Marcus asked, aware of faces turning in their direction.

Rose dropped her voice to a whisper. 'Chelsea Holbrook says her dad hit her.'

'How does she know?' Marcus whispered back fiercely.

'Dunno. But I'll find out.'

By break the school was buzzing with rumours.

Marcus saw Rose pushing through the crowds towards him. They slipped away on their own.

'She was going for a training run—'

'Hannah?'

'Hannah and Louise Parker, you know the captain of the girls' cross country, and one or two of the others. Anyway, she – Hannah – didn't turn up. Louise tried to ring her but just got voicemail. So they went for the run, but afterwards, Louise went round.'

'To the house?'

'She was worried. Hannah never misses training – and she was fine yesterday. You saw her. She was right as rain wasn't she? And she wouldn't just have changed her mind and not said, would she?'

'So what happened when Louise went round?'

'I'm not sure exactly. Chelsea—'

'Chelsea Holbrook?'

'That's right.'

'What's she got to do with it? She's not in the running team.'

'No, she overheard a couple of the girls who are – but she didn't get the full story.'

Marcus sighed. No wonder the news was all over the school, if Chelsea Holbrook had got hold of it. And how typical that she was peddling a botched and no doubt highly exaggerated version of it into the bargain.

'So what does Chelsea say happened?'

'Well,' Rose said, dropping her voice, 'Louise went round bold as brass and knocked on the door. No one answered for a while, but she was sure they were in, so she knocked again. In the end Hannah's mum came to the door. She looked awful, all teary and upset. Then we come to the bit Chelsea didn't hear properly, but she thinks Louise demanded to know what had happened to Hannah, and when Hannah's mum wouldn't tell her, she pushed in past her and went up to her bedroom where—' here she lowered her voice to a whisper, 'she found Han with a black eye and cut lip, where her dad had hit her.'

Even allowing for Chelsea Holbrook's likely embellishments, this made Marcus's blood boil.

'Isn't it awful?' Rose said, as much to remind him she was still there.

He clenched his jaw in anger, barely looking her. This was exactly what he'd been fearing. Her dad had clocked her one. And if it was true, what was he going to do about it? Was he going to do anything? Was he tough enough and brave enough?

The rest of the school day was a torment. The rumour mill was working overtime. He noticed people looking at him and then pretending they weren't when he looked back. He saw Melissa and her friends staring at him from a safe distance. It was as if the whole school was waiting to see how he would react.

Someone passed him a note in his last lesson. It was from Rose.

Meet at the usual place – you know where. I know more.

It was written in big, childish writing, and annoyingly signed 'you know who'.

He ripped it into tiny pieces.

But he still went to the rendezvous in the park.

'Coo-ee – Marcus?'

Rose was calling him from about ten metres away. She gave him a little wave and pointed to the secluded bench he had shared so often with Hannah.

They sat awkwardly together, Rose pulling down the hem of her very short skirt.

'Well?' Marcus asked.

'I saw Jenny Mills.'

Jenny Mills was another girl on the cross-country team.

'And what did she say?'

'Not much. She didn't really want to talk. Louise had told them not to say anything to anybody. But as she said, the story was out, and as I said, I am a big friend of Hannah's.'

She paused and gave Marcus a look as though to confirm her credentials.

'And?' Marcus prompted.

'Well, it's true. Han's dad did hit her. But it wasn't as bad as Chelsea made out. Though it was bad enough to leave bruises. Anyway, when Louise saw her she was very upset, but the thing that worried her most was it getting out, and she swore Louise to secrecy.'

'Which she didn't keep to.'

'Well, I suppose she thought she had to explain to the rest of the team why Hannah had missed training. And then of course when Chelsea overheard them talking about it.'

You might as well have had it broadcast over the school tannoy, Marcus thought grimly.

'Anyway, the really important thing is to stop any member of staff finding out. Han was terrified the police and social services would be involved – cos, you know, they might take her away from home. Or even put her dad in prison.'

Marcus had his own ideas as to what should happen to Hannah's dad, but he certainly wasn't going to share them with Rose.

Not getting a response, Rose continued, barely pausing for breath.

'Isn't it terrible? I mean last week there were all those rumours about her dad hitting her mum, which was awful. You weren't in, but they were saying dreadful things – Melissa and her lot – well she's wound her neck in a bit since then, hasn't she? That was brilliant, Marcus, and whatever it was you did to Arran – which was even more brilliant. I mean, what *did* you do?'

Marcus shrugged off the question. In her eagerness to engage his attention, Rose had moved even closer. Their legs were nearly touching. He looked pointedly at the tiny gap between them until Rose reluctantly shuffled a centimetre or so away from him.

She looked slightly flushed, but soldiered on.

'So you see, Marcus, I found out for you, didn't I?'

She gave him what was meant to be an engaging look.

'You did brilliantly, Rose. Thank you.'

Rose's face lit up.

She looked at him from under slightly lowered lids.

'Do you want to walk me home?' she asked.

'I can't, I've got things to do.'

Rose's face registered her disappointment.

'I thought you'd be pleased, Marcus,' she said, and then, realizing that had come out wrong, added: 'I mean about me finding out for you.'

'I am.' Marcus tried to sound friendlier. 'Really. Like I said, you did brilliantly.'

'So don't I deserve to be walked home – just a bit of the way?'

'Rose, I really have got stuff to do. I was off all last week, and I've got loads of homework to catch up on.'

'Well, if you'd rather do homework than walk a girl home . . .'

'Rose . . . it's not like that. I'm really, really . . .' – he reached for a word – 'grateful.' Then he added,

'And I will—'

'Walk me home?'

Her face had lit up again and her smile was bright.

'Yes,' he said.

'When?'

'Dunno. Soon.'

'Promise?'

'Promise. And, Rose?'

'Yes, Marcus.'

'Keep your ears open. Anything you hear, let me know. But don't add anything to the gossip. Can you do that?'

Rose's arm shot out and rested on his cuff.

''Course I can,' she said.

She gave him a conspiratorial wink, and then she was off. He watched her clipping down the path to the gate, swinging her school bag jauntily.

He readjusted his own bag and headed off in the opposite direction, walking as fast as he could. His head was full of questions: How hard had he hit her? With the flat of his hand, or a fist? How many times? The more the questions hammered through Marcus's brain, the faster he walked. Now he knew the truth, his anger could harden into purpose. By the time he was within a street or two of home he was practically running. Even so, he remembered to take the detour which brought him into their road from the other end, avoiding another Mrs Prewle ambush.

Once inside the house, he rushed up to his room and changed out of his school uniform. Then he went into the other bedroom and helped himself to Aunt Hester's hand mirror.

After that he came downstairs, and opened the basement door.

He decided he didn't want to practise with the picnic basket indoors. The basement was far too pokey and the dining room was too depressing. Besides, he didn't want to become dependent on the wall mirror as there was unlikely to be one when he actually came to deploy his weapon. (He liked the word 'deploy'; it gave things a reassuringly military feel.)

It was a nice afternoon – quite mild for the time of year – so his plan was to take the hamper down to the bottom of the garden. He was confident he wouldn't be disturbed there, though there was a gate which joined their garden to Mrs Prewle's, so he'd have to be quiet. If Mrs Prewle did happen to come trespassing, well, she'd just have to take the consequences. He wouldn't have to lug her far to get her to the railway embankment.

The first thing was to get the picnic basket out of its hiding place.

'Up you come', he said under his breath as he lifted it out from behind his old bike. There was an immediate stirring within – hissing, and the sound of fangs scratching against the wickerwork. He also noticed the lid rising fractionally, like a pan lid when the water starts to boil.

He'd almost forgotten how frightening the Gorgon's head was and felt tempted to put the basket back in its hiding place and forget all about it. But, no: he had a mission, and he was going to see it through.

The sunshine felt good on his face and he heard a couple of doves cooing in the branches of the tree by the shed as he walked down the garden. The snakes had obviously sensed a change in the air and became even more restless. That was something to be aware of, he noted, wondering whether they would settle down on a longer trip. He hoped so.

Generally, though, the picnic basket was a success. It hung from his shoulder by its strap at a convenient height, and wouldn't, he thought, look too conspicuous if he rested his left arm casually on top of it. Perhaps the best way of deflecting attention from it would be to pretend it wasn't a picnic hamper at all. If he went out with a rod, people would assume it contained fishing tackle. Taking it out in public was some way off. First he had to learn the best way to handle it.

And he had to concentrate – really concentrate.

He positioned the hamper at an angle to the tree, and leaned Aunt Hester's mirror against the base of the trunk. Then he moved behind the hamper and undid the latch at the front. There was instant pressure from the snakes, forcing it open. Marcus lifted it up and back completely, and sure enough, there was the cobra, unwinding itself through the hole meant for the wine bottle or tea flask.

It took the snake a moment to find Marcus, but when it did, it favoured him with a long, disdainful and hate-filled glare. Even though he was expecting it, it gave Marcus a nasty turn. So much destructive power was packed into those two black pinhead eyes. The cobra puffed out its hood, and bared its fangs.

Marcus looked around and found a stick. He then reached forward so that the stick was nearly within the cobra's range. It hissed and lunged. Marcus moved the stick from side to side, and once gave the cobra a playful tap with it. The snake recoiled and then shot its head forward in a real temper.

Marcus wasn't teasing it for fun. He was establishing the extent of the cobra's reach, and was pleased to see that it couldn't stretch outside the basket. Just. This was good news, as it meant he could undo the side fastenings without having to worry about putting the gauntlets on. He would still have to be super-cautious about the rest of the snakes that made up Medusa's hair, but none of them had anything like the cobra's reach. However, he would make sure he got his hand out of the way with lightning speed when he released the catches, just in case.

Getting the flap back up and secured again would also need thinking about. With a last look to check the position of the mirror, he reached down and opened the front flap of the picnic basket. It sprang open, and the snakes spilled out into the sunlight, glinting and gleaming with malice. But Marcus's attention, as he gazed into the mirror, was fixed on Medusa's blotched, once beautiful face. Terrifying though it was, there was something tragic about her ruined features. When she caught his gaze, she locked onto it and seemed to redouble the power of her unblinking stare. As they gazed at each other,

Marcus felt sucked into the depths of her black eyes. She was trying to claim him for herself. Even though she was a mortal terror, there was something so sorrowful in her expression that he felt a surge of sympathy for her. And with it, a desire to please her, by giving in to her. As his resistance weakened, Marcus heard a voice. Her voice.

Although her lips moved in the mirror, the voice was in his head.

Marcus, the voice said. *How lovely. How lovely to be outside. I cannot tell you how long it is since I saw the sky, felt the breeze on my face . . .*

She closed her eyes, and a dreamy smile drifted across her mottled skin.

Yes, Marcus, the voice in his head said. *It seemed like an eternity.*

How could anyone endure that? he found himself thinking. It was terrible.

Yes, Marcus, terrible. More terrible than you can possibly imagine.

Marcus felt such a strong pity for her that he was tempted to turn his head and look directly at her . . .

But then the spell was broken. He heard a scrabbling in the hedge, and for a moment of sheer panic thought it might be Mrs Prewle.

But it wasn't. Instead, Marcus saw a grey squirrel streaking across the grass – head down, tail up, making a beeline for the tree. It was in such a state of panic that it looked neither left nor right.

Mrs Prewle's cat was in hot pursuit.

Had the cat been content to concentrate on its prey, all might have been well, but Decimal made the fatal mistake of turning his head slightly mid-pounce. He gave a tiny fraction of a cry, and then there was a thump.

While the squirrel frantically clawed its way up the tree trunk, the cat remained completely motion-less. There on the grass, right in front of the hamper, was an exquisite statue of a cat in flight – jaws apart, claws extended. Decimal's days of chasing squirrels in other people's gardens were over.

Marcus was still gazing at this dramatic reminder of the Gorgon's power when he heard another noise – and another, lesser, thump. There, at the base of the tree, was another statue – of a squirrel, its tail extended, its big eyes peering with alarmed curiosity. Marcus caught sight of his own expression in the mirror. Then he moved to see Medusa's reaction. There was the faintest hint of a smile in the curl of her lip.

He felt weak with the realization that he'd come within an inch of death.

He reached for the stick and slammed the front of the hamper shut. There was a hiss of protest, but he ignored it, quickly securing the side latches.

Then he gently tapped the cobra on the head while dropping the lid. With a last venomous glance and a darting flicker of its tongue, the great snake reluctantly slunk down into the darkness. Marcus was just allowing himself a moment of recovery when he was catapulted back into panic mode.

'Decimal, Decimal, Decie, darling! Come on in for tea, dear!'

The last thing he needed was for Mrs Prewle to discover him admiring a stone effigy of her beloved pet. Seizing the hamper with one hand, he leaned down to scoop up the cat statue. It was surprisingly heavy, but he lugged it under his arm and hurried across to Uncle Frank's shed.

He emerged, having jettisoned both hamper and petrified cat on the floor, only to find Mrs Prewle standing by the gate, continuing to call for her wretched animal.

'Oh, Marcus,' she said, obviously startled. 'I didn't expect anybody to be down here. You haven't seen

Decimal, have you? The silly creature won't come in for his tea. So unlike him.'

'No, I haven't, I'm afraid.'

He was suddenly horribly aware of the mirror and the stone squirrel at the base of the tree. He had to steer Mrs Prewle away before she saw them and started asking more of her awkward questions. But it was too late.

With an excitable little yelp, Mrs Prewle strode over to the tree and bent down.

'How extraordinary! What a marvellously lifelike piece. Where on earth did that come from? And what's this mirror doing here?'

What possible reason could there be for him to have a stone squirrel and a mirror at the bottom of the garden? He caught Mrs Prewle's severe gaze.

'Art!'

It was almost a squeak.

'Art?' said Mrs Prewle suspiciously.

'Art project.'

Yes, that would do. Brilliant! You could produce absolutely anything for an art project.

'The squirrel's exquisite.' Mrs Prewle turned back to it. 'It's so lifelike – you could almost imagine—'

'—It was alive just a minute ago, yes.' Marcus

finished the sentence for her.

'But what's the mirror for?'

'Um – it's to do with . . .'

What was Mr Lambert going on about the other week?

'Art – it seems real, but really it's not. It's just made up – an illusion. Like seeing something in a mirror. Like holding up a mirror to nature' – he was sure Mr Lambert had used that expression. 'And I thought, Why not hold a mirror up to nature out-doors? Where real nature is.'

'I see,' Mrs Prewle said, doubtfully. 'Who'd have thought they'd be filling your head with such compli-cated stuff at your age?' She looked at Marcus to check that he wasn't pulling her leg. Marcus didn't want to give her time to think of another line of enquiry.

'I'm going to present a tab– tab—'

'Tableau?'

'Yes, tableau – about nature. Nature and art. The nature of art. The art of nature.'

He smiled winningly. This stuff wasn't so difficult when you got into it.

'That's why I was doing it down here, in the garden.'

Then, with a nod towards Uncle Frank's shed, he

added: 'Just thought there might be something I could use in the shed, but all I could find were some horrible big spiders.'

Mrs Prewle recoiled.

'But no sign of Decimal?'

Marcus shook his head. Then he called out, 'Decimal, Decimal!' before shrugging at the mystery of the disappearing cat.

'Naughty boy,' Mrs Prewle exclaimed. 'Well, thank you, Marcus. And good luck with your art project. Any word from your aunt? I hope she's enjoying her break in Wales.'

Marcus gave a non-committal nod. The question of hearing from Aunt Hester was going to become more pressing, he could tell. Reluctantly he admitted he would have to intervene. The woman who lay transformed into stone not twenty metres away would have to be given a voice.

Mrs Prewle turned back to her own garden, leaving Marcus to tidy up after what could be described as an alarmingly successful experiment. He hid the stone cat under some old boxes in Uncle Frank's shed, and carried the picnic basket, mirror and squirrel back to the house. He returned the basket to its hiding place in the basement, then went into his own room and sat with the squirrel. It was hard and heavy in his hands. He felt sorry for it. It seemed unfair that having escaped the life-or-death chase across the garden to reach the safety of the tree, the squirrel should have suffered the same fate as Decimal. Marcus studied the little face, its mouth agape in astonishment and fear. He stroked the now-unyielding fur of the face and neck. The claws, extended to keep a firm grip on the bark of the tree, were little needles and the bushy tail was like a frozen fern. Maybe, as there really was an art project he was meant to be working on, he would take it into school and put it in a tableau. At least it would have more dignity in death than Aunt Hester.

CHAPTER 8

Hannah wasn't in school the next morning. Marcus wasn't surprised, but her absence hardened his resolve. He passed the day in a bubble of thought, reviewing all the options for putting the next stage of his plan into operation. Lessons passed over his head, and at break he kept himself to himself, making it clear he didn't want company. Even Rose, who didn't have anything new to tell him, anyway, left him in peace. The only person who wasn't prepared to leave him alone was Digger.

A heavy hand fell on Marcus's shoulder towards the end of the lunch break, coming as an unpleasant surprise.

''Ello, Marcus,' Digger leered. ''Ow's it going?'

'Go away, Digger.' Marcus shook the hand off his shoulder.

'And why would I want to do that?'

Marcus looked into the stupid, belligerent eyes beneath the low brow sprinkled with acne.

He really hadn't got time for this.

'I told Arran—'

'You told Arran. But Arran doesn't tell me what to do. Not anymore. Not since what you did to him. What was it you did, Marcus? Cos whatever it was, it sorted him out, didn't it? Proper job.'

'You don't want to know, Digger.'

'Yes I do. Arran said something about a pencil case. What you got? I want to see it.'

Marcus said: 'No you don't, Digger.'

'I do. Cos I'm telling you this, Marcus. It ain't going to turn me into a scaredy cat. An' if it's as good as you think it is, then maybe we could work together. Otherwise I'll just have to carry on by myself.'

Digger grinned. He was like a big stupid dog, Marcus thought. The kind that hangs around, getting in the way, unless you take control. But he really didn't want to give the solo snake another outing. It was nerve-wracking: he only had to make one mistake, and Marcus could be the one feeling the venom in those fangs.

He made up his mind quickly.

'All right,' he said. 'I'll see you in the office after school.'

'Arran gave you the key?' Digger's doughy features moulded themselves into a frown. 'You *did* do a job on him, didn't you?'

'Don't come if you're scared,' Marcus said.

'Me – scared? You bring that pencil case, and let me have a look-see. Then we'll see who needs to be scared, yeah?'

The bell rang for afternoon lessons, and Digger turned and slouched away, pushing through a gaggle of Year Sevens as he went.

Marcus headed off to his science lesson.

Melissa made a few melodramatic gestures when Marcus placed his pencil case on the desk beside his exercise book, but he ignored her, and she was only too happy to stay away from him. Marcus had always enjoyed science, and it was nice having Mr Day back instead of that hopeless supply teacher. He scrawled a few instructions on the whiteboard and left them to get on with it. As usual, a number of people put up their hands and Mr Day went round patiently telling each one what he'd already told the whole class. This was convenient for Marcus, because it meant he could slip away from the bench and collect the things he wanted from the bottles on the rack on the wall.

He was back in front of his Bunsen burner by the time Mr Day got round to him, and the pencil case with the two corked test tubes was safely put away in his bag.

The colour in the flask on his workbench turned the impressive purple Mr Day had promised, and he recorded the temperature at which this had happened. The follow-up homework was pretty straightforward too, and he'd got most of it written down by the time the bell rang for the end of school. He needed a few moments to himself and slipped into an empty classroom to prime the pencil box. Then he made his way down to the caretaker's room to meet Digger.

Normally, a one-to-one with Digger would be an ordeal, but Marcus felt full of confidence. Digger was all brawn and very little brain, and Marcus knew his strategy would work. But it still had to be carried out properly.

Digger was there outside the office. As Marcus fished out the key and opened the door. Digger gave him a grudgingly admiring look.

'Jarrold know you've got the key now?'

'What do you think?' Marcus said, as he led the

way into the 'office'. He'd met the janitor when taking a quiet moment for thought the day before. 'Regime change, eh?' he'd said with a humourless grin. 'Well, just keep it tidy.'

Marcus looked around the dismal cubby-hole with its one chair and rickety table. *Keep it tidy!* Sure. But at least Digger was impressed that he had the run of the place. Clearly going through his sluggish mind was the notion of business as usual, but under new management – if Marcus could prove himself a worthy replacement for Arran.

Marcus had other ideas. He didn't want Digger to turn into a constant nuisance.

'Let's see it, then,' Digger said, his large hand extended and a foolish grin playing around his mouth.

For a moment Marcus wished he had gone to the trouble of using the snake, but consoled himself with the thought that what he was planning would be a lot more painful, if less frightening. He reached into his bag and pulled out the pencil case.

He could just hear the clink of the two test tubes, and checked that the hook he'd made out of a paper clip was in place over the end of the lid.

'Here you are,' he said.

'What is it?'

'That's for you to find out. If you're not scared.'

Digger leaned forward. He was like a greedy fish gobbling bait.

Marcus pulled back the sliding lid of the pencil case. This in turn removed the corks from the two test-tubes that he had primed in the Science lesson. Their gaseous contents mingled and reacted impressively, producing an acrid vapour that had Digger reeling back, coughing, spluttering, and rubbing his streaming eyes with his huge knuckles.

Marcus stepped forward and punched him hard in the solar plexus, and Digger dropped like the bag of cement Uncle Frank had had delivered for the patio. Marcus quickly straddled his chest. He pulled his fist back and held it just above Digger's face, poised to punch again. Dealing with Medusa had taught him the effectiveness of direct and unhesitating use of power. Digger was still fighting for breath, his mouth wide open and his eyes watering.

'Any more trouble from you, Digger – any trouble at all – and I'll . . .' He waved his fist centimetres from Digger's nose. 'Understood?'

Digger managed a desperate gurgle.

Marcus drew back his hand. Digger turned his

head to one side spluttering 'No – Yes – don't hurt me!'

Marcus got up and yanked Digger to his feet. Gripping his collar, he marched the other boy to the door and threw him out into the corridor.

Alone, he stood panting for a moment, surveying the grubby little room with its bare bulb, its wonky table and the one chair. Then he bent down to pick up the pencil case. He waved away the last odours of his makeshift stink bomb, and tipped the empty test tubes into the bin.

After that he sat in the chair, lost in thought, head thumping.

The wind started softly, almost inaudible at first; but then it gained in strength, blowing more insistently, beginning to speak of huge distances and vast measures of time.

Marcus shifted in his bed. He wanted rest – and peace. But even as he slept, he knew he would be denied both, and that his night would be tormented by more terrifying dreams.

The wind was getting louder, harsher. It began to rasp. Images of blowing dust began to form. Small stones rattled across a bone-dry landscape; a desiccated thornbush cartwheeled across his vision.

Then dark shadows loomed; tall, slow-moving. As well as the rattle of stones, he could hear the *clip-clop* of hooves. The shadows were figures on horseback. Marcus didn't know why, but he was terrified by them. Their faces swathed in cloth against the dust storm, they sat on their gaunt steeds, galloping forward, relentlessly, never changing their pace.

The wind was howling now; he could feel it lifting the duvet, beginning to probe the warm nest of his bed. He tried to press the duvet down, but all heat had vanished, leaving him shivering before the relentless advance of the riders.

He felt a cry rising in his throat.

Then suddenly the wind dropped and the faceless riders disappeared. Gradually, light began to dissipate the darkness. He was in a low-ceilinged room. A stone chamber, cold and bare like a prison cell or burial vault. He looked around him and saw strange markings on the wall, inscriptions, he guessed, but in a combination of symbols he didn't recognize and certainly couldn't understand. And then, as the light grew stronger, he saw it: a plaque of the Gorgon, Medusa.

It was a crude representation of her, but instantly

recognizable nonetheless. Her mouth stretched in a cruel grimace, her eyes open wide – intense, implacable. The snake-locks spread out on either side of her head, just like in the pictures he'd seen on the computer.

There were a few tools on the floor, open boxes, an open folder of papers.

Then his eye was drawn back to the Gorgon.

Marcus had to stifle a cry.

The carved plaque had come to life; the face still had the grey-green colours of the grave, but it was certainly not an inanimate carving. The eyes were riveted on his, and the lips, those thin cruel lips, were moving.

Oh, Marcus, if only you could have seen me . . . seen me then . . . More beautiful than the stars, but closer, Marcus, so much closer . . . Suitors from across the known world waiting on me, Medusa; princes, warriors, the pick of a generation . . . All seeking me, all worshipping me, Marcus, me . . .

She let her eyelids flutter shut. It was no good telling himself it was only a dream. Marcus was trapped in the living nightmare of the Gorgon, whether he was awake or asleep.

You could see the perfect symmetry of her face,

even though the mottled skin pulled across the fine, high cheekbones was repellent.

Marcus felt again the stirrings of pity he had experienced in the garden.

Suddenly the eyes blazed open.

Yes, Marcus . . . I am to be pitied. But what use is pity? None. The only balm is revenge, Marcus – revenge. Where harm has been done, there is blame, and where there is blame, there must be punishment.

She almost spat this out, and as she did so, all the snakes of her hair turned and hissed in unison, creating such a terrifying sight that Marcus cried out and flung himself violently to one side of the bed. But something was holding him, restraining him.

'Marcus . . . Marcus . . . It's all right, lad. You're all right.'

Marcus sat up feeling he'd just been given a huge electric shock.

Uncle Frank's face was only a few centimetres away and his big gentle hands were holding onto Marcus's wrists.

'My word, Marky, that was a nightmare and a half, my lad.'

Marcus relaxed, relief flooding through him.

He hugged Uncle Frank, felt strong hands

clumsily joining behind his back, and knew that for the moment at least he was safe.

When the hug ended, Uncle Frank gazed down at him, his face frowning with concern.

'It was only a dream. That's all it was. You're all right. I'm here. There's nothing to worry about.'

Marcus lay back exhausted. Tears filled his eyes. Uncle Frank was so good to him. He deserved better than the web of deception Marcus had fabricated.

But he couldn't stop now. *When harm has been done, there is blame, and where there is blame, there must be punishment.* The Gorgon had spoken.

Hannah didn't come into school all week. Marcus agreed to meet Rose after school on Friday, but she still had no news. They say no news is good news, but Marcus knew it wasn't. He would go to orchestra on Saturday morning, and if she didn't turn up then he would act.

This, he realized, was the moment to fulfil his promise to walk Rose home. He wanted to go out to Hannah's street anyway, so he might as well. Rose was delighted, but it was a largely silent walk, and when they parted, she said thank you in a way that showed she was disappointed. Marcus told himself he would make it up to her, but all he was really thinking about was Hannah.

He walked on a few more streets. It wasn't that he expected to see her, and he certainly wasn't going to ring the doorbell and ask if he could come in. He just wanted to be nearer to her.

When he got there it was exactly as he'd expected: there was no sign of Hannah, no sign of any activity at all. But he couldn't stop himself picturing Hannah unhappy in her bedroom, or tip-toeing round the house in fear of another blow from her dad.

When harm has been done, there is blame.

He turned away and set off for home, though he hardly noticed where he was going, there was so much careering around in his head. The new plan was a far more dramatic intervention than anything he'd done so far – a huge step up from facing down the bullies at school. But he knew it was justified. It just needed very careful preparation.

'Marcus?'

Oh, no. He'd walked past Mrs Prewle's house, giving her an opportunity to grill him.

'I still haven't found Decimal. You haven't seen

him, I suppose?'

'No, no I haven't, Mrs Prewle. I'm sorry.'

Mrs Prewle sighed.

'They do say they always come back eventually,' Marcus offered in a half-hearted attempt at sympathy.

'Decimal's never gone away like this. Not even for one night. I fear the worst, Marcus, I really do. I have a horrible suspicion he may have gone down the embankment and . . .'

The sentence petered away sadly. Marcus's senses went onto red alert. He didn't want Mrs Prewle nosing around on the waste ground below the garden fence!

'Oh, I'm sure he wouldn't go down there,' he said with conviction. 'It's terribly overgrown. He'd have kept to the gardens, I'm sure.'

'That's what I'd have thought, Marcus. But if that were the case, then where is he? What can have happened to him? I mean, there's no way he could have got out at the front – at least, not on my side.'

Marcus shook his head. 'We always keep our garden gate closed too. Mind you, if he'd really wanted to, he could have climbed out, I suppose.'

'Could he? Do you think so? Could I come and have a look?'

Marcus nodded, though he wasn't happy about it. This was all taking up valuable time, and a prowling Mrs Prewle was a complication he could do without. Still, if keeping her occupied with the front meant she was distracted from thinking about the railway embankment, it was worth the trouble.

She joined him on the pavement.

'There,' he said, pointing to the gate by the side of the house. 'A cat could get up there if it wanted to.'

'Oh dear: poor Decimal.'

'You could get some posters and put them up on lampposts and things,' said Marcus.

'I suppose so.' Mrs Prewle looked dolefully up and down the street.

'I could do them for you at school, if you liked.'

'Could you? Could you really? Do they have the facilities?'

'The art department does.'

'That would be most kind, Marcus, if you really think you could.' She gave him a fleeting smile. 'Shall I get a photograph of him for you now?'

Before he could stop her, Mrs Prewle sped off into her own house, coming back a minute or two later.

She handed Marcus a snapshot of the cat and a piece of paper.

'I've put my phone number and address on here. And the name, so people know what to call him if they see him.'

'Decimal' had always struck Marcus as an odd name for a cat, but he'd never bothered to ask about it. Mrs Prewle must have seen the question in his eyes.

'It is rather a silly name, I know. It's just a little librarian's joke – have you heard of the Dewey Decimal system?'

Marcus looked blank.

'Not to worry: it's just the system we use for cataloguing books. It's used all over the world.'

Marcus looked up at her. The joke didn't seem to be making her very happy, and he felt bad. 'I'll do it for you on Monday,' he said.

'Thank you, Marcus. That's very kind of you.'

Then, as she turned back to her own front door, Mrs Prewle asked: 'Any word from your aunt?'

Marcus shook his head. 'But you know what they say: no news is good news.'

Leaving Mrs Prewle to chew on that little pearl of bogus wisdom, Marcus let himself into the house and raced upstairs to change.

Ten minutes later he was pushing his bike out through the garden gate and, with a glance around to check that Mrs Prewle wasn't waiting to ambush him again, he started pedalling towards the canal towpath.

CHAPTER 9

I t all seemed so familiar when he returned the
following afternoon, after going to orchestra and
finding Hannah hadn't turned up. The boats were
the same, as were the anglers sitting on the towpath
gazing at their floats. The only difference now was
that, loaded into his bicycle basket, he had the
picnic hamper containing the Gorgon's head. As a
result, he felt so nervous he could hardly steer his
bike straight.

He'd spent a sleepless night going over the plan in
minute detail, yet it still seemed insanely daunting in
the clear light of day. He really couldn't believe he
was capable of even thinking such a thing, let alone
actually doing it. But seeing Hannah's empty place
beside him at orchestra had given him a spurt of
anger. And as he walked home, the now familiar
voice inside his head started up.

*Marcus . . . Marcus . . . it is right. It is your duty.
The girl needs to be avenged. You must administer*

vengeance . . . I will help you. I will give you the strength you need . . .

He walked purposefully down the familiar pavements, avoiding the other pedestrians instinctively, without seeing them. He was going to go through with it. Nothing could stop him now.

Uncle Frank had said he would push on with the patio, and had been happy for Marcus to go fishing by himself. 'A bit of fresh air'll do you good. Blow the cobwebs away.'

Getting the picnic hamper out of the house was the worst bit. Marcus had already moved it from the basement to his room where it was well smothered with blankets, but he'd felt very exposed carrying it downstairs and out of the utility room door. However, Uncle Frank had remained absorbed in the complexities of laying the patio, and so with a cheery goodbye, Marcus wheeled his bike through the garden gate and set off on his mission.

The first flush of that success had long since worn off, and he was feeling increasingly nervous with every step. There was a bend in the canal and as he came round it, he saw the bridge just next to the Jolly Bargeman, the pub where Hannah's dad liked to drink. It was an old building with exposed beams and

a beer garden which ran down to the w:
and Uncle Frank had stopped there for a
afternoon after fishing.

But shandy and a Coke were a very dif
matter from the pints and pints that Hannah's dad
put away. Marcus's grip on his bike handle tightened.
He found the place he had identified yesterday as the
best vantage point from which to see both the bridge
and the pub door.

He leaned his bike against the hedge and
unpacked his kit. The Medusa basket almost looked
the part, he thought, plonking it on the bank next
to his folding chair. But it would only take one in-
quisitive fellow angler wanting to look inside it for
things to get awkward. He draped his jersey over the
basket, and quickly assembled his rod. Marcus was
just beginning to feel a little bit excited about actually doing some fishing when a car shot over the
bridge. There was a squeal of brakes, and the vehicle
turned sharply into the car park. A group of men
climbed out and made their way noisily into the
pub. Suddenly he felt deflated. Strong and confident
men, hard men – not gentle, like Uncle Frank. How
could he tackle someone like that? Especially
Hannah's dad.

Perhaps he wouldn't come today. Maybe the shock of actually hurting Hannah had made him stick to his promise. But in the meantime, Marcus had to look the part, so he got out his bait box and primed his hook. Soon his float was bobbing gently in the water. The sun was out, and the day was pleasantly warm. It was almost like an ordinary Saturday, except that on an ordinary Saturday, Uncle Frank would be sitting there beside him, staring companionably out over the dull green waters of the canal.

'Caught anything, then?'

It was one of those stupid questions you always got. But the voice was friendly, and when Marcus looked up, a man smiled down at him. All was well until his dog, a little terrier, started sniffing around the picnic basket. He growled, dropped down to his belly, with his little stumpy tail wagging furiously.

Then he started to bark – loud, nervy yaps, as he rushed up to the wickerwork, and then just as suddenly darted away.

'Don't know what bait you're using, son, but it's certainly got Mylo excited!'

Marcus forced a smile, and glared at the dog. He

was not keen to add to his collection of animal sculptures. Fortunately the man reached down and grabbed the dog's collar and fixed a lead on it. Then he dragged the dog away, though it kept twisting round and snapping and yapping.

Marcus went back to staring at the bridge, but he wasn't happy. The man had taken a good look at his face, and would certainly remember the picnic hamper, now. Two motorcyclists roared over the bridge, their black helmets gleaming in the sunlight. They were followed by a white van, another car that turned in to the pub car park, and a horse box that wobbled cautiously over the bridge's hump. Finally, he saw what he had been waiting for.

A slouching figure approached the bridge from the town. Marcus felt a surge of adrenalin. It had to be Hannah's dad. Mr Yarder had his coat collar up, his hands thrust deep in his pockets. He had a paper under his arm and kept his head down. He looked furtive, like a man seeking a guilty pleasure. Although he tried to seem nonchalant, there was an unmistakable purpose in every stride. This was a man for whom a drink meant more than anything – or anybody. He looked so ordinary – just like any middle-aged man, making his way to the pub for a lunch-time pint. But Marcus knew better. He suddenly felt detached, as though he were fate's delivery boy.

While these thoughts were going through his mind, the man had paced across the bridge and up the few dozen yards to the pub. Marcus reckoned that when Mr Yarder came out of the pub again, he would have time – just – to get up onto the bridge from the towpath and be ready to meet him with the picnic hamper. But he would have move fast. Knowing Hannah's dad it could be quite a long wait, but that was the beauty of angling. It taught you patience – how to sit still for hour after hour without getting restless, without getting bored.

Marcus reeled in his line and inspected the bait. Most of it had washed off the hook. He reached into his bait tin again. Then he sailed his line across the water, and the float made a discreet *splosh* as it landed.

The pub was in the same arc of vision as the float, so he could cover both at the same time. All Marcus had to do for now was sit on his stool and keep alert.

Marcus was motionless, but he hadn't dozed off. Quite the opposite: he was in a state of heightened awareness, conscious of everything around him. Suddenly he stirred. A movement caught his eye, and then he felt a tug on his line as his float dipped under the surface. He had got a fish, and something told him it was an experienced one, a canny old campaigner who would give him a good run for his money. Like any angler, Marcus loved a hard-fought duel – one in which you felt you were engaging in a battle of wits as well as wills. The float suddenly bobbed to the surface, and Marcus caught a glimpse of a swirling blur of scales. *Game on!* This was what nobody at school could understand. These moments of excitement more than made up for all the hours sitting waiting.

The float bobbed up and down again. The fish was trying desperately to dislodge the hook from its jaw. Let him tire himself out, Marcus thought, paying out the line again.

For the first time since the float had ducked out of sight, he raised his eyes to the Jolly Bargeman. A couple came out of the pub door, and he heard a sudden rush of laughter and loud voices. They came towards him, crossed the bridge and then set off down the towpath towards the town. No one else exited the pub, so he turned his attention back to his line.

Although the float swung this way and that, the fish could not shake free, and eventually Marcus reeled it in and hoiked it out of the water. It was a roach, and a fair-sized one. Marcus looked at its tinfoil eye and nodded a brief acknowledgement of the fight it had put up. He disengaged the hook and slipped fish into the keep net, and then sat back on his stool enjoying a moment of triumph. But his mind soon veered back to the real reason for being on the canal bank today. He looked at his watch. Hannah's dad had been in the pub nearly two hours. The more he drank, the more dangerous he would be, Marcus thought; but then, the more he drank, the more he deserved what was coming to him.

A few more people left the pub. Every time the door opened, the noise from inside seemed louder. Marcus could even hear individual voices raised above the general roar. He stared moodily into the muddy water of the canal, hoping it would be deep enough – and muddy enough – for his purposes.

With these thoughts, he decided he'd better get ready. He reeled in his line, threw the untouched bait into the canal, and broke his rod into sections. He unhooked the keep net and let his catch go free. With a disdainful flick of its tail, the roach slipped into the murky depths. After that, there was nothing to do but sit and wait.

Another burst of laughter from across the canal. The pub door was open and Marcus could see Hannah's dad standing in the doorway, shouting something back into the bar.

Marcus was on his feet, reaching down for the basket. He threw the strap over his shoulder. It felt heavy – heavier than he'd remembered. And his feet seemed leaden. He glanced across the canal. With one final shout, Hannah's dad was on his way.

The furtive, shamefaced figure that had approached the pub two hours ago was gone. He had turned into a loud, arm-swinging man, setting out carelessly for home. Marcus had to hurry.

He forced his legs to move and set off down the towpath towards the bridge. When he reached the steps onto the bridge, he paused, and checked the catches on the basket. There was a lively buzz from inside, and he could see the upward pressure on the basket's lid. Taking a deep breath, Marcus started up the steps.

As he came onto the bridge he could see Hannah's

dad a mere thirty metres or so away. He hadn't got to the bridge yet, but was standing in the road with his hands cupped around a cigarette. Once it was lit, he put his lighter away and continued walking down the gentle gradient.

Marcus's hands were shaking. How could he do this?

Where there is harm, there is blame, and where there is blame there must be punishment.

Was the voice in his head, or was the Gorgon talking to him from the hamper? What did it matter? He had heard, and hardened himself to obey. Surely he had to protect Hannah? He looked around to check there was no one else in sight. No – no witnesses. It was just him and Hannah's dad. This was it – the best opportunity he was ever going to have. But as his fingers played on the picnic basket's latches, they felt like sticks of ice. Everything seemed to be happening in slow motion. Hannah's dad kept coming toward the bridge. Marcus felt so weak, he found himself sitting down on the low parapet. He realized this was a good option anyway, as it gave a solid platform for the hamper. He was adjusting it on his lap when he heard a shout.

The shout came from the doorway of the pub,

where a man was waving a newspaper in the air. Hannah's dad had obviously left it on the bar. Mr Yarder had reached the bridge, and turned to see who was calling him.

It all happened so quickly. Marcus only had a blurred impression of Hannah's dad swinging round, and his legs getting tangled. Suddenly Mr Yarder was falling, his arms flailing, his face a picture of shock. And then he was gone.

Marcus heard the man's cry of panic – and a terrible, blood-chilling thump, followed by a splash. The man at the pub door shouted over his shoulder and then sprinted down the lane, throwing the news-paper away into the ditch.

Marcus's instinct was to go to the other end of the bridge and look down, but as two more men emerged from the Jolly Bargeman, he had second thoughts. He gathered up the picnic hamper and made his way down the steps back to the tow-path, where he had a good view of the rescue operation. The first man from the pub threw himself to his knees on the opposite bank and grabbed hold of Hannah's dad, who was floating face-down in the water. Seconds later, the two other men arrived and helped haul the limp and dripping body out of the water.

Hannah's dad had a terrible gash on his head, and he looked more dead than alive. Marcus saw a big man with tattoos all over his forearms stabbing numbers into his mobile phone and heard him shouting into it: 'Ambulance. We need an ambulance. Jolly Bargeman – by the canal. Quick!'

Everything that could be done was being done, Marcus thought, loading his fishing gear onto his bike. Having had no part in the accident, he decided he had no part to play in its aftermath. More and more people were gathering on the other bank, talking excitedly about what should be done and asking what had happened and who had seen what.

Marcus started pushing his bike, hoping that no one called him back. Nobody did.

Marcus was exhausted. His fingers had been on the latches of the picnic hamper. He'd been seconds away from the most explosively important moment in his life. And then his victim – his intended victim – had self-destructed right in front of him. In a way he was relieved he hadn't been put to the test. Would he have opened the picnic basket if it had just been him and Hannah's dad, face to face on the bridge? He had wound himself up to a pitch of determination, and now he felt a terrible emptiness, as though all the electric charge that he'd built up had been suddenly released, draining him completely. His eyes looked vacantly ahead; his mind was numb. It was a relief, when he finally reached home, to find a note from Uncle Frank saying he'd gone shopping.

Marcus didn't know how long he had, so he raced down into the cellar to stow away the picnic basket. When he came back up, he sat in the kitchen with a drink. But his right hand was shaking so much he couldn't get the glass to his lips. He sat at the table, images running unbidden through his head: Hannah's dad approaching the bridge; falling over the low parapet; lying in his dripping clothes on the far bank of the canal. Did he feel guilt at what he'd been intending to do, or disappointment that he'd been deprived of the opportunity to see his plan through? Marcus couldn't tell. What he did know was that he felt bad – so bad that he didn't want to explore the various things he felt bad about. There were so many layers of guilt, he wouldn't have known where to start. It didn't help telling himself he'd actually done nothing. Hannah's dad had barely seen him. It certainly wasn't Marcus's fault Mr Yarder had tripped over his own feet – it had been the man shouting from the pub, making him turn. And because he'd had so much to drink. He lost his footing and over he went.

Whatever happened to him – whether he lived or died – it was no one's fault but his own. It wasn't anything to do with Marcus. And yet ... in his head the footage of what he'd intended to happen began to play. Hannah's dad was coming towards him smoking his cigarette, whistling tunelessly. He glanced at Marcus – with maybe the faintest flicker of recognition. But it was wiped out immediately by a look of horror as the front flap of the basket opened and the life froze out of him. And all Marcus would have needed to do was push the statue over the parapet into the canal, and that would have been that. He felt a cold sweat breaking out. He had come so close – so close to doing it. He felt a sudden sickening revulsion. It was the Gorgon. She was evil. *Toxic*, that was the word – something that worked unseen, undetected, poisoning everything. He had come within a few seconds of just such a deadly outcome, and the thought made him tremble.

Yet he still had the Gorgon's head. It was still

under his control, stashed away in the cellar, primed for destruction. It was madness to keep it, but where could he possibly get rid of it? And anyway, it had been sent to him. The Gorgon's head was his – his to do with as he saw fit. Even if he had known how to dispose of it safely, he couldn't just let it go. There must be a reason for its arrival at his door, and he was determined to find out what it was.

CHAPTER 10

There was an item on the local news about Hannah's dad. There had been an accident on a bridge over the canal, and a forty-six-year-old man had been taken to hospital with head injuries. He was in a critical – but stable – condition. A police spokeswoman praised the men from the pub and said the victim probably owed his life to their quick reaction. No foul play was suspected: it had been an accident, pure and simple. Two or three local residents were interviewed about the fact that they'd been complaining about the bridge parapet being dangerously low for years. Now perhaps something would be done about it. Marcus was glad there was no call for witnesses, and he decided not to tell Uncle Frank he had been there, nor that the injured man was Hannah's dad. When Uncle Frank expressed his agreement about the danger of low parapets on the old bridges, Marcus just nodded and hoped the topic would fade of its own accord.

Of course, that meant making up a new site for his fishing expedition, which led to further fabrications. He obviously had to choose somewhere they seldom went and where there wouldn't have been people Uncle Frank knew. He thought of a pillbox a mile or two down the canal in the other direction and said he'd been there.

'Any good?' Uncle Frank asked.

Marcus was on safer ground with the actual fishing, and was pleased with Uncle Frank's praise for his catch.

'Shame I wasn't there. Still, I made good progress on the patio. I've decided I'm going to text her, just to let her know how it's going.'

'Good idea, Uncle Frank.'

'Glad you agree,' his uncle replied with a broad smile. Marcus had to keep remembering that though he knew Aunt Hester was never going to come back, Uncle Frank didn't. Sending a text would obviously make Uncle Frank happier, and Marcus could concoct a reply – the shorter the better – to help maintain the lie and manage Uncle Frank's expectations. But what was going to happen when that expectation died? Facing Uncle Frank when the truth came out was going to be unbearable. His lies would seem such a betrayal of trust. He didn't think he could face it. Perhaps he could run away?

He went up to his bedroom feeling depressed. Before going to bed he checked his aunt's phone. Sure enough there was a text from Uncle Frank: 'Dear Hester, I hope you are having a good break. We are missing you, but getting on fine. Good progress with patio. M sends his love. As do I, Frank.' He'd reply in the morning, he decided, switching the phone off and climbing under his duvet.

Although he was tired to the point of exhaustion, he fought against sleep, dreading what his dreams might bring.

A dim light shimmered from a distance, and then gradually grew stronger. It was as though a lighted torch were being carried towards him down a long corridor or tunnel. As it came closer he could make out a shape at the centre of the light, and soon he realized it was Medusa's head, hovering in the darkness, surrounded by the luminous nimbus of her snake-hair.

Well, Marcus, that was a lucky escape.

A vision of Hannah's dad falling off the bridge flashed briefly. It hadn't been *that* lucky. But perhaps lucky for Marcus.

Broken bone – better than stone. A knowing smile played over the Gorgon's cracked lips.

It was harsh, but Marcus saw what she meant.

Yes, Marcus: there was harm, there was blame, there was punishment.

Medusa's face began to harden. The usual half-life drained away completely. For a moment Marcus gazed at the carved plaque with its crude approximation – wide eyes, pillar-box mouth, blunt nose – and then simply at featureless stone.

After the night he'd had, even the prospect of church seemed welcome. But first he had to reply to Uncle Frank's text, so tapped out a terse message: 'Frank, having a good break with Megan. Glad you are coping. Hope Marcus catching up on school work. H.'

Uncle Frank was ecstatic, and took great delight in reading it out. He didn't seem disappointed by the tone or by the fact that Aunt Hester hadn't mentioned the patio. Although it made Marcus feel a complete fraud, it had worked perfectly – and gave Uncle Frank an easy response to the barrage of questions from Mrs Prewle, who just happened to be lingering in the road as they set off for church.

There were more polite enquiries from other members of the congregation. Though they were surprised she hadn't mentioned her trip, everybody seemed pleased that Hester was having nice holiday with her sister in Wales.

But even though the text had worked wonders, Marcus felt very uneasy. His usual tactic for surviving the service – submerging himself like a submarine in the depths of his own thoughts – didn't work as it normally did. This was largely because his own thoughts were the one thing he wanted to escape from: the lie about Aunt Hester's holiday in Rhyl; Hannah's father lying in a critical condition in hospital. And shadowing everything, there was the picnic hamper and its contents hidden at home, ticking away like a time bomb.

When Marcus came up for air, the service wasn't much of a help. There were the usual mumbled prayers, a rousing hymn or two. Marcus managed to drift through these on autopilot – though he did notice that Uncle Frank's responses were more fervent than usual, as if he were really pleading with God to bring Aunt Hester back to him. 'God is everywhere and sees everything,' the vicar reminded them; but Marcus did not draw any comfort from that. It meant that God knew about the Gorgon's head and how Marcus had planned to use it. And if there were any doubts as to what God might think of that, they were resolved when Mr Tenby, one of the stalwarts of the choir, got up to read the lesson. He stood at the big bible, cleared his throat, and began:

'Dearly beloved, avenge not yourselves, but rather give place unto wrath: for it is written,' – and here Mr Tenby's fine bass voice seemed to get even deeper – '"Vengeance is mine: I will repay, saith the Lord".'

Mr Tenby looked up, and by chance directed his gaze at the pew Marcus was sitting in. It was probably only for dramatic effect, but Marcus felt the attention of the whole congregation focused on him. No one – apart from God – could possibly know about Marcus's plans for vengeance. But guilt made you paranoid, he thought as he shuffled on the hard pew.

Mr Tenby continued mellifluously through St Paul's advice to the Romans, but Marcus closed his mind to any further consideration of God's knowledge, intentions and judgements, gazing idly at the procession of saints in the transept win-dow. Eventually Mr Tenby announced: 'Here endeth the lesson,' and strode back to his place in the choir.

Mrs Prewle walked home with them after the service.

She mentioned Marcus's offer to produce the posters to find Decimal, and congratulated Uncle Frank on having such a thoughtful nephew before quizzing him about Aunt Hester's holiday, and then asking how they were coping on their own.

'Are you eating properly?' she enquired.

'I think so. What do you think, Marcus?'

Marcus thought of the bangers and mash they had agreed would make a good Sunday lunch, and said Uncle Frank was a good cook.

'I'm sure he is,' Mrs Prewle replied. 'But if you should need any help, you must let me know.'

When they got in Uncle Frank brought up Mrs Prewle's cat.

'It's most odd: he's been around for as long as I can remember and never went missing once.'

Marcus was getting Uncle Frank's beer out of the fridge.

'I wonder if it might have wandered down the embankment,' his uncle said as he put the bottle on the table.

'Oh, no,' Marcus said, far too quickly.

'No?' Uncle Frank looked sharply at him.

Damn, he thought.

'Oh, I don't know. It's just all brambles and nettles.'

'Have you been down there?' Uncle Frank asked. 'You know you're not to go down there, don't you?'

'No I haven't.' Marcus kept his head down as he pulled the top off the bottle and concentrated on pouring the beer into Uncle Frank's glass.

'Well, don't. It's a nasty slope.'

Uncle Frank picked up the glass and took a pull at his beer.

'Ah that's good,' he said, adding: 'It's kind of you to do those posters for Mrs P.'

'It's the least I can do.'

Hannah wasn't back in school in the morning.

Rose found Marcus at break, and he faced a breathless torrent which consisted mainly of 'Isn't it terrible?' and 'How does she cope with it all?' There were some nuggets of actual news buried amongst the exclamations of sympathy, which Rose had gleaned from a Sunday spent gossiping with her friends. Hannah's dad was definitely alive, but not conscious.

As it had said on the news, his condition remained critical but at least it was stable. The key thing was when he would regain consciousness. Marcus quickly extracted himself from the conversation, if you could call it that, having established that Rose couldn't say when Hannah would be back in school.

Marcus wanted to see her very badly. Should he go round? What if she was still showing signs of the thumping her dad had given her? She'd hate him to see her if she were. Now her dad was out of the house he could phone her. But the chances were that her mum would answer, in which case what would he say? Even though he had done nothing to cause Mr Yarder's accident or make it worse, there was no wriggling away from the fact that he had been there and seen it – and then simply got his bike and shoved off home.

He thought about writing a note and dropping it through the letterbox. But what would he write? It would be like English homework, only worse. It would just come out all wrong, he knew it. He scowled at the photograph of Decimal as he photoshopped it in the Art department. Without really thinking about what he was doing, he ran off thirty copies of the poster and slipped them into his school bag. He couldn't go another day, he decided, without seeing Hannah – or at least trying to. After school he'd walk over there. He wouldn't knock on the door, but just walk past the garden gate. He might see her at a window. He needed a sign that she was all right.

'Walk me home?'

Rose was suddenly beside him in the rabble at the school gates.

Marcus looked down into her earnest face with its would-be-winning smile. Why not? Rose was only a few streets away from Hannah's house.

'Sure,' he said. 'Meet in the park?'

Rose evaporated into the crowd. Marcus was glad she seemed to understand that he didn't want them to be seen together. He hated being the centre of any kind of attention, and was determined not to give the gossips anything go wagging their tongues about. As for Rose herself, she could be annoying, but she was definitely useful. And a bit of kindness didn't cost anything, Marcus reflected, as he picked his way through the crowds towards the park.

'You don't half walk quick,' Rose said a few minutes later when they were heading out towards

Hannah's end of town.

Marcus made a deliberate effort to slow his pace, giving Rose the chance to talk.

'It must be awful, knowing he could die at any minute,' she said.

'I thought you said he's stable.'

'Oh, he is, but all the same, he could still – you know. And then there's what happens when he comes round.'

Marcus looked questioningly at her.

'Well, you know, if he's – if he's not right. In the head. He might be a vegetable or something. Wouldn't that be terrible?'

It was all terrible.

Marcus thought of Hannah and her mum in the hospital. They would walk down the long corridors reading the signs until they got to the room where he was. They would peer through the window, waiting for a nurse or a doctor to say they could go in. And there he would be, with tubes coming out of his arms and a plastic mask over his face, his eyes open but unseeing. And Hannah would lean over the bed and kiss his forehead and talk very gently to him.

'It's not fair,' Rose said. 'I know he's not been perfect—'

Marcus bunched his hands into fists. *You could say that again.*

'—But he was good as gold before his brother died.'

'His brother? I didn't know Hannah had an uncle who died.'

'Yeah,' Rose said. 'Ten years younger than her dad – the baby of the family. Turned into a right little tearaway, my mum says. Anyway, he always got what he wanted, and what he wanted was a motorbike. So they got him a motorbike. And then he had a crash.'

Marcus slowed and looked at her. 'When was this?'

'A long time ago now. But Hannah's dad never got over it. It was him that taught his brother to ride the bike, you see. He was devastated. And that's when he took to drink. He blamed himself.'

Where there is blame, there must be punishment, Marcus thought, walking on in silence.

'Perhaps I shouldn't have told you,' Rose said after a while.

'No, it's all right.' Marcus reassured her. 'I just didn't know, that's all.'

'Don't tell Han I told you, will you?'

'Of course not.'

They reached the end of Rose's street, and

stopped for an uneasy moment at the corner. Marcus forced his face into a smile.

Rose's smile was genuine, though there was a look of uncertainty in her eyes.

Marcus put a reassuring hand on her shoulder.

'Bye, Rose. See you tomorrow.'

Marcus was thinking so hard about what Rose had told him that he only noticed the man lounging at the end of Hannah's street at the last minute. He was big, wore a donkey jacket and a woolly hat, and was reading a tabloid paper folded up into a square. He might have been a builder waiting for a lift after his day's work. Whoever he was, Marcus was annoyed. Lounging at the corner, keeping an eye on the house, was exactly what he'd been planning to do. Instead, he had to walk on past, as though bound for another house in another street.

He went to the next corner and stopped by a telephone box, which provided good cover from which to watch the man at the corner.

He was concentrating so hard that he didn't notice the limousine that quietly drew up next to the telephone box until the driver hailed him.

'A lovely piece of work, isn't he?'

Marcus almost leaped in surprise, taking in the

man's ferrety features, and pencil moustache, which twitched in an ambiguous smile.

'That's George, that is, and he's waiting for me. Oh look, he's seen me.'

The lounging man had pushed himself off the wall he'd been leaning against and was now shambling down the road towards them. He didn't look best pleased to see Marcus.

'George is my associate. Not to everyone's taste, but he grows on you,' the ferrety man said. He smiled again, but all that did was lift his upper lip away from his fang-like teeth. Not a good look, Marcus thought.

'What's your name?'

'Mind your own business,' Marcus told him.

'Mind my own business. But that's exactly what I am doing – what George has been doing. But by the look of things I'd also say he's got his towel on the beach first. Am I right, or am I right?'

George was nearly upon them now, and Marcus could see his forehead furrowed by an angry frown.

'What is it, boss? Who's this?'

'Ah, that is currently a mystery, George. But he's been giving you the eye all right.'

'Has he now?' George loomed above Marcus. 'He better watch out, that's all I can say.'

The ferrety man laughed. It was an unhealthy laugh, somehow cracked and insincere.

'What's his game?' the big man scowled.

'You better ask. I couldn't get a word out of him.'

'We'll see about that.' George looked fiercely at Marcus, who stepped back, glancing over his shoulder to check his escape route.

'Now, now, George; that's not our way is it? I'm sure this can be resolved perfectly amicably.'

'What can be resolved amicably?' Marcus challenged. 'I don't know you – either of you. I don't know what your business is. And I don't care.'

Marcus stood back, taking in the quality of the car and the natty clothing of its driver, who in turn was subjecting him to close scrutiny.

'And we don't know what your business is either, young man,' the driver said. 'But I would hazard a guess it concerns the same party – or parties – as ours does.'

Marcus bristled. What could the ferrety man and his hulking sidekick have to do with Hannah and her mother?

As though reading his thoughts, the driver said: 'Let me guess, you're interested in a young female, pretty, still at school – perhaps at your school. Father

184

just had a nasty accident. Which is perhaps why you've walked all the way out here to see her, and console her maybe?'

Marcus hated the fact that the ferrety man had got it so right. He took a step forward, but George took an even bigger step forward, towering over Marcus like a troll.

Refusing to be intimidated, Marcus said: 'So what do you want with them?'

'Ah,' said the ferrety man. 'Our interest – well, *my* interest, to be accurate, though George here is the guardian of my interests generally – is in the other party, also female, who likewise is distressed by the terrible accident suffered by her husband.'

Marcus didn't like either man, or the fact that they were there and intending to call at Hannah's house. The situation was frightening, but he was more angry than scared.

'You leave them alone,' he said. 'I don't see what business it is of yours that Hannah's dad—'

'Fell in the canal and cracked his skull?' the ferrety man finished for him. He went on: 'I do like a bit of fire in a boy. Reminds me of my younger self. But don't be too hasty, young man. I have a perfectly legitimate reason for visiting your girl's ma, I assure

185

you, and I'm sure neither she nor your girlfriend would want a bad situation made worse by a misplaced – and, I should say, futile – exhibition of schoolboy gallantry.'

'She's not my girlfriend,' Marcus insisted. 'Not that it's anything to do with you. Who are you, anyway?'

'I'll tell you – though you wouldn't answer the same question when put to you nice and civil five minutes ago.'

At this point the driver opened the car door. George held it open for him, and he climbed out onto the pavement.

Marcus found himself looking at a showily dressed man of small stature.

'Desmond Darke – at your service.'

He gave a little mocking bow and clicked the heels of his highly polished shoes together. Marcus couldn't remember when he'd last taken such an instant dislike to someone, and pointedly ignored the small hand that was extended towards him.

'You may not want to shake my hand,' Mr Darke said, 'but for the convenience of all concerned, it would be useful to know your name.'

'Marcus,' Marcus said rudely.

'Marcus. I don't think we know a Marcus, do we George? We do get to know a lot of people, so we come across a lot of names. But Marcus? No, I can't recall a Marcus.'

'Why would people want to do business with you?' Marcus asked.

'Why indeed, Marcus? But they do. Oh yes, in surprising numbers. They seek us out. Well, they seek *me* out. To do business. Sometimes after we've done business, we have to seek *them* out, don't we, George?'

George grunted a humourless laugh.

'George tends to do more seeking out than me. He has a natural gift for it. But sometimes we do the seeking out together. Which explains why you find us here, in this quiet corner of our little town. And I think' – here he looked at his watch; a very large watch, Marcus noted – 'as time is getting on, we should go and make our visit. And I don't see why we shouldn't all go together, seeing as we're all going to the same address, and I'm not sure we've convinced our latest acquaintance of our bona fide and legitimate purposes.'

Marcus didn't know what was going on, but he knew he didn't like it. He also didn't like the idea of turning up on Hannah's doorstep unannounced, but checking out Mr Darke's intentions seemed more important.

Darke was watching his face closely.

'I see you've seen sense, young man. You can hop in the limo if you like.'

'I'll walk.'

'Please yourself. You hop in, then, George. See you in a tick.'

Marcus set off up the street, but the car soon overtook him. Mr Darke gave him a twinkly little wave, while George scowled at him from the passenger seat.

They turned right into Hannah's road and Marcus quickened his pace. Whatever they were up to, it was clearly no good. No good at all.

CHAPTER 11

Marcus didn't know what he was going to do when he got there, in fact he felt totally out of his depth, but he was damned if he was going to let Mr Darke and his horrible henchman terrorize Hannah and her mother.

As he turned the corner he saw Mr Darke's limousine already parked outside the house. It looked out of place amongst the other vehicles in the street. Marcus recognized Hannah's mum's car – he saw it on Saturdays when she dropped her daughter off at orchestra. The paintwork was tired; there was a scratch down one side and a strip of rubber had peeled off the windscreen wiper. It looked exhausted, defeated. Mr Darke's by contrast looked arrogantly superior. Marcus frowned disapprovingly. It all came down to money in the end. But what was Mr Darke, who obviously had loads of the stuff, doing with Hannah's family?

He walked up to the garden gate which had been left open. As he went through he heard a cry: 'There he is!' Mr Darke was pointing at him from the open front door. 'Come on in, young man. She's here, your princess. And she looks as though she could do with cheering up.'

Marcus felt his face going hot and red. *Princess!* He hoped Hannah hadn't heard that. Mrs Yarder was standing in the doorway next to Mr Darke. She was a small woman. Marcus remembered her as pretty, but now her good looks were drained by stress. Her eyes jumped around nervously, and her voice, when she spoke, came out as barely a whisper.

'Hello, Marcus. Do you want to come in? I'm sure Hannah would love to see you.'

Marcus was anything but sure about that, but he had no option but to walk awkwardly up to the door.

'Mr Darke said he'd met you on the street coming over to see her. Come in. She's upstairs. I'll call her down. Hannah!'

Marcus wanted to stop her, but it was too late. And anyway, he felt he was right to be there, though he had no idea what he could possibly do to help if anything happened.

'Hannah, love. Come down. There's someone to

see you,' she shouted again as they all squeezed into the tight little hallway – George seemed to fill so much of it.

Marcus looked expectantly up the narrow stairs with their threadbare carpet and ancient-looking wallpaper. There was a pause, then a door opened. Marcus couldn't see Hannah, but he could hear her all right.

'I don't want to see anyone. Tell them to go away.'

'It's Marcus, love. Walked all the way out to see you.'

There was an even longer pause. The bedroom door shut.

'She'll be down in a moment, Marcus. Just wants to brush her hair, I expect.'

Hannah's mum gave him a quavery smile. Marcus hoped she wasn't going to burst into tears.

'You better come in here,' she said to Mr Darke and George. 'Can't stand around in the hall all afternoon, can we?'

With that she ushered them into the front room.

It was clean but tatty. And Marcus noticed how bare it was. Apart from a sofa which had seen better days and a sagging armchair next to a rickety-looking coffee table there was no furniture. There were no lamps, just the bulb hanging from the ceiling. And there was no television. There was a radiator under the window, but the heating wasn't on.

While he was registering the depressing details of the room, Marcus was really listening out for sounds that Hannah was coming downstairs. Mr Darke lowered himself gingerly into the armchair, as though he half-expected it to collapse under him, while George flung himself onto the sofa without a care. Marcus certainly didn't want to join him, so stood awkwardly near the door.

That's where Hannah found him when she came into the room. She didn't look at all pleased to see him. But she was even less pleased to see Mr Darke and George, though Marcus could see that – like her mother – she knew who they were.

'Hello, Hannah,' Marcus said woodenly. 'How are you?'

She looked dreadful, her skin pallid, her eyes puffy with crying. She deliberately kept her head at an angle, but Marcus was pretty sure he could see the shadow of a bruise above her left eye.

'Why did you come?' she asked fiercely.

'To cheer you up, darling,' Mr Darke said with one of his creepy smiles. 'Very nice of him, we thought, didn't we, George? We just happened to be coming to visit at the same time. One of life's little coincidences.'

'And what do *you* want?' Hannah demanded sharply of Mr Darke.

Marcus was surprised at the hardness in her voice. She sounder much older, as though taking an adult part in the proceedings.

'Now, now, miss. Don't take that tone with me. We have a little business matter to discuss with your mother – don't we, Stella?'

Hannah clearly hated his use of her mum's first name, but as though to cut off any reply, Hannah's mum said: 'It's all right, love. We've just got one or two things to sort out. I'll put the kettle on,' she added, going through the alcove to the kitchen beyond the lounge. 'Would you two like some squash?'

Marcus and Hannah stood uncomfortably apart, not looking at each other. Marcus felt he'd made a terrible mistake in coming here. But there was nothing he could do now. He was here. All he could hope was that he didn't make things even worse.

'Hannah, fetch a couple of chairs through.' Hannah did as she was told. Marcus made a move to help her, but a burning glance was enough to stop him in his tracks. Hannah came through from the kitchen and almost dropped the chair on his feet, then turned and went to fetch a second, which she placed as far away from his as possible.

Marcus caught Mr Darke's expression as he looked on, and felt a spasm of rage at the man's obvious enjoyment of the embarrassment his visit was causing.

The kettle came to the boil and Hannah's mum made the tea and two weak glasses of orange squash.

'Here we are.' She put the tray down and looked around for a chair. Hannah quickly surrendered her own and went to get another, which she placed even further away from Marcus.

'Sugar?' Hannah's mum enquired as she handed out the cups of tea.

Mr Darke gave his head a little shake, but George reached forward with a heavily-tattooed hand and started helping himself.

'Thank you, Stella, very hospitable.' Mr Darke raised the cup to his lips and closed his eyes briefly. 'Mmm. You can't beat a nice cup of tea, as my dear old mother used to say, before she passed over. God rest her soul.'

As if to show his complete agreement, George drained his tea in one long gulp, and banged the cup down on the coffee table.

Mr Darke replaced his cup gently in his saucer, and then said: 'Perhaps we should talk business, Stella. I don't know whether our young friends might like to step into another room?'

'I'm not going anywhere,' Hannah said; 'but Marcus can go.'

'I rather think the young admirer would prefer to stay to give moral support,' Darke said. 'I also think he might learn something, understand the situation better, and thereby allay his understandable, but unnecessary, concerns.'

'I'm sure you're very welcome to stay, Marcus,' Hannah's mum said.

Avoiding eye contact with Hannah, Marcus mumbled 'Thank you' into his orange juice and sat tight.

'Good,' said Mr Darke. 'Let us proceed.'

He reached into the inside pocket of his jacket and produced a document which he unfolded and looked at briefly.

'Now, Stella, you know what I've come for.'

'But I haven't got it, Mr Darke.'

'Desmond, please, Stella.'

Mr Darke smiled amiably. At least, that was clearly his intention. Unfortunately his thin smile only exposed his teeth, making him look more than ever like a predatory animal.

'I haven't had a chance, what with my husband's accident. And the car was more than they said it would be.'

'That's the trouble with those old bangers, isn't it? Once they get the bonnet up, there's no knowing what they'll find. Still, a stitch in time, as my old mother used to say.'

Marcus was getting tired of Mr Darke's old mother. But he was beginning to see what the score was between Mr Darke and Hannah's mother. She had borrowed money from him, and was now having difficulty paying it back.

Without asking permission, Mr Darke got out a packet of cigarettes and lit up.

Hannah's mum seemed not to notice, but Marcus saw Hannah stiffen. He watched the bluish cloud of smoke hovering above their heads like a conqueror's flag.

Hannah's mum sat with her head bowed. Suddenly she started to speak: 'I borrowed a bit from—'

'From a friend, yes,' Mr Darke completed the sentence for her. 'And what are friends for, if not to give a little helping hand here and there? As my dear old mother used to say, A friend in need is a friend indeed. And how right she was, how right she was. But then, friends need repaying, don't they, Stella? That's where the trouble starts.'

Marcus noticed Hannah's hands clenching. Mr Darke's dear old mother was obviously testing her patience as well.

'I was going to use it to repay you, but I had to give it to the garage instead.'

'I quite understand, Stella. Needs must. We see it all the time, don't we, George?' Darke shook his head in mock sorrow.

'We do, boss,' the huge man said. ''eart-breaking, 'ow one thing leads to another.'

'Indeed. But although I couldn't be more sympathetic, Stella, we all have to abide by our legal liabilities, don't we?'

'Can't it wait till next week?' Hannah's mum pleaded.

'Unfortunately it can't, Stella. Because by next week you'll owe the same again. Plus interest. It's all here in the agreement.'

Mr Darke held up a document.

'And there, down at the bottom, there's your signature. It's a legally binding agreement freely entered into, Stella.'

'But I only wanted it for a few days, so that I could get the car fixed. And we need the car even more, now we've got to get over to the hospital. We were just about to go when you called.'

'I understand, Stella. That's why I lent you the money in the first place. Just to be helpful. So it's really only fair that you pay back what you've agreed to pay. You have to understand that. We provide a service – and a very good service, I like to think – so when you need money, up front, in your hand, "on the nail", as my dear mother used to put it, we're counting out the notes on the office table within the hour, aren't we?'

Hannah's mum nodded. Marcus noticed her hand moving up to her face and thought she was wiping away a tear.

Mr Darke drew heavily on his cigarette, knocking off the ash into his saucer.

'But, of course, we have to have our due returns, we have to reap the rewards of our generosity and the risk we take. Because you'd be astonished at how many people forget their obligations. And that's why we have to be constantly reminding them. George does the reminding generally, but in a special case – like you, Stella – I like to come along and do the reminding myself.'

There was a silence

'I'm afraid, Stella, what we need from you is . . .' here he drew a calculator from his pocket and tapped in some numbers.

'That is quite a bit, now I come to look at it. But then that's the APR for you. I did warn you. 1368 per cent APR – it soon mounts up. Which is why we advise people to pay their loans back as soon as they can. Because, of course, by next week, once we add the APR to the original sum . . .' Again Mr Darke's fingers glided over the calculator. Then he sucked in his lips. 'Ooh, that is a lot. But that's numbers for you.'

'But what can I do?' Hannah's mum made a gesture with her hands. 'As you can see, we haven't . . .' her sentence tailed off hopelessly.

'Much to offer,' Mr Darke agreed. 'No, I do see that. All gone down to the pawn shop has it, to keep your old man in liquor?' Marcus caught a movement from Hannah. She was tensed, like an animal ready to spring.

'It's a shame. We see it so often, don't we, George? Man of the house runs down the portable assets – a mirror there, an armchair, perhaps – the telly – all for the sake of a few drinks or a flutter on the horses. Always ends in tears. Tears shed by the women and children mainly, while the men abandon ship.'

'My dad hasn't abandoned anyone! He's in hospital fighting for his life!'

Marcus knew it was coming, but even so, he was surprised by her ferocity when Hannah confronted Mr Darke. He loved the way her eyes flashed, though he was worried that her fury would only trigger more trouble.

'Well,' Mr Darke said, looking her up and down, 'if he's got half as much fight in him as his daughter, he should be all right, I'd say. Wouldn't you, George?'

George gave a guffaw. Then he got up, looming above Hannah in a way that seemed to make the whole room shrink. Marcus got up too, and Mr Darke also pulled himself out of the armchair, dropping his cigarette into his cup, where it gave off a soggy hiss.

'Now, we don't want to spoil a pleasant social occasion by a show of ill-temper, do we? I'm all for a bit of spirit, especially in the young. But when it comes down to it, business is business. And the trouble is, Stella, you don't have a lot to do business with, do you?'

He looked around the bare room, and his eyebrows arched meaningfully.

'Unless, of course, you've got a few treasures stashed away upstairs?'

George made a move for the door.

'Don't bother,' Mr Darke said, having seen from Hannah's mum's face that it would be a wasted journey.

'Cleaned you out, good and proper, did he? Jewellery, the lot?' He shook his head ruefully. 'But sometimes, just sometimes, they keep something back.' His wolfish smile returned.

Stella's mum clasped her left hand with her right.

Mr Darke nodded. 'I'm right, aren't I, Stella?'

'No,' she said.

'Come on, Stella. Show us what you've got.'

Mr Darke took a step towards her.

Hannah bristled, but George blocked her.

No one seemed to notice Marcus was still there. He was hating every moment of it, but there was no escape. He could hardly walk out at this stage. But he also knew that Hannah hated his being there even more than he did. It would take her a long time to forgive him for what he'd witnessed – if she ever could.

'Come on, Stella: hand it over – and the other one, if you've still got that.'

Hannah lunged forward but George caught her in one of his huge arms.

'Let me go! Leave her alone! Get out of our house!'

'All in good time, young lady,' Mr Darke told her, never once taking his eye off her mother's hands.

'Come on, Stella. Let's not prolong the agony. You know you're going to have to hand them over, so why make a difficult situation worse?'

Slowly, very slowly, Hannah's mum unclasped her left hand. Gleaming dully on her finger were two rings. One was a thin gold band; the other had a gem on it.

'Not bad, by the looks of it. I'll get them properly valued. Honest. We always play fair, don't we, George?'

George gave a horrible grimace and slightly shifted his grip on Hannah, who pressed feebly against his arm.

Her mum was crying now, and put her right hand up to wipe away the tears.

Mr Darke stood in front of her, waiting. Hannah's mum started to twist the first ring off her finger.

She placed it in Mr Darke's hand.

Mr Darke kept his hand out, and Hannah's mum twisted off the second ring and handed it over. Marcus just glimpsed a little band of lighter flesh near the base of her ring finger, before she clasped her hand again, as though to cover up its nakedness.

Mr Darke briefly held up the second ring, and gave it a slight nod of approval.

'There, that wasn't so hard, was it?'

Mr Darke pocketed the rings, and prepared to leave. George relaxed his grip on Hannah, and she stepped back from him, her eyes blazing.

'As I say, I'll get a valuation, Stella, and take it off the total. Then I'll let you know what we need next week. I do hope you can get someone to give you a hand, because I'd hate to have to take the car off you after you've gone to so much trouble to keep it on the road. Of course, if you do find someone to help you, you know where to find me.'

He laid a business card on the coffee table.

'I'd rather not have to come over in person, if it can possibly be avoided. And I'm sure George feels the same, though it has been a pleasure, and we're very grateful for the refreshment. But now' – his wrist snaked out of his cuff to expose his expensive watch – 'we must be off. We've got a couple more calls to make this end of town, haven't we, George?'

George grunted. Then he slowly, horribly, cracked each of his knuckles in turn. The noise made Marcus think of small, defenceless necks snapping.

Turning to Marcus, Mr Darke said: 'What are you doing, young man? Staying here with the delightful young lady?'

'He's going,' Hannah said, flatly but firmly.

'Well, there's my answer,' said Mr Darke. 'I hope you've learned a bit about business today, young man. I wouldn't want you getting yourself – and other people – into trouble through a misguided sense of how the world ought to work, as opposed to the way the world actually does work – if you get my meaning, catch my drift?'

He gave Marcus a humourless smile.

'We'll let ourselves out.'

George opened the door for him, and then slammed it with unnecessary force behind them.

The three of them were left standing in the most uncomfortable silence Marcus had ever experienced.

He didn't know where to look, and he certainly didn't want to meet Hannah's eye.

Hannah's mum was fighting back tears. She busied herself collecting the tea things and taking them back to the kitchen.

'Satisfied? Seen enough, have you?' Hannah came close to him and hissed the words in a ferocious whisper. 'Why did you come? Why couldn't you leave us alone? There's nothing you can do. Nothing.'

'Hannah, I didn't want to – I couldn't leave you, not with those two.'

'And how much help were you? Standing gawping while they stripped the rings off my mum's fingers.'

Now Hannah was crying.

Marcus wanted to put his arm round her, but thought better of it.

'You see – you think you can fix things. But you can't. You can't fix anything.'

She looked into his face. Her own was dark with fury and pain. She was trembling with the effort to control herself.

'Go. Just go. Go away.'

She stamped her foot on the threadbare carpet, turned and walked away from him.

Marcus looked at Mr Darke's business card lying on the coffee table. He slipped it into his pocket before letting himself out of the house.

He was relieved to see that Mr Darke's car was gone, and that Hannah's mum's car remained by the pavement. Mr Darke had threatened to take it off them, but that wasn't going to happen. Marcus wasn't going to allow it to. Hannah said he couldn't fix things but he could. And he would.

CHAPTER 12

When Marcus got home he went upstairs to his room, took the business card out of his pocket and read:

D. W. Darke & Associates
Bailiffs & Debt Collection Services

No mention of loan sharks, Marcus thought; and 'associates' was rather a grand name for George. He made a mental note of the address and then stowed the card safely away.

He felt a calm resolve. Although he was boiling with anger at the way Mr Darke had treated Hannah's mum, and felt a flush of embarrassment at the way Hannah had reacted to him, in his innermost being he was utterly focused. He might have had doubts about using the Gorgon's head on Mr Yarder, but he had none about turning her powers on the odious Mr Darke and his huge henchman. *Where there is harm there is blame* – and there was no doubting either the harm or the blame here. So there must be punishment. And this time, he would have to carry it through. He couldn't see either Mr Darke or George falling conveniently into the canal.

The weather suddenly turned unseasonably hot. It was as though it had given up on the last long dreary days of winter and skipped to the very end of spring almost overnight. Marcus had to stop and take off his jumper before he'd got even halfway to the school gates. Other pupils had their blazers over their arms, and the entire mood was good. Marcus didn't share in the general lifting of spirits. His own were leaden with thoughts of Hannah, and dark with the tunnel-vision of his intentions. But he knew what had to be done.

Hannah was in school, but made it very clear she wanted nothing to do with him. Rose managed to give him a nodding, eye-rolling 'Sorry-but-what-can-I-do?' look at break, but Marcus could tell she was quietly relishing the new situation. The rest of the day passed in a dull blur of lessons until the relief of the final bell.

He allowed himself to be jostled along in the stream of pupils heading down the main corridor, but instead of breaking away at the earliest opportunity, he hung around the school gate to see Hannah's mum drive up and collect her for their trip to the hospital. After watching the car pull out into traffic, Marcus set off into town. It was quite a long trek to the street he was looking for, and the afternoon was still warm, so he was tired and hot by the time he found it.

The office of D. W. Darke & Associates was a meagre two-storey building lurking in the shadow of a much more handsome townhouse. There was a peeling sign above the window repeating the words printed on the business card. Down the side of the building a potholed drive gave access to a yard. From what Marcus could see from the street, Mr Darke's car was not there, which suggested he and George were out on their rounds. Marcus shivered at the thought of George looming in a doorway, Mr Darke right behind him smiling his little insincere smile, and wringing his hands at the 'unfortunate necessity' of a personal visit. They were like Arran and Digger – one small, nasty, vicious and scheming; the other pure sadistic muscle – only on a much bigger scale. But Marcus had the power to see them off, and for Hannah's sake, and her mum's, that is what he was resolved to do.

With a look up and down the street, he slipped into the yard. At the back of the building there was a door at ground level. Below some rusty old railings there was a flight of stone steps leading down to a door into the basement. A large cardboard box, surrounded by litter at the bottom of the steps, suggested that the door to the basement wasn't used very often. The window above the steps was barred, and Marcus didn't fancy the chances of anyone trying to break in. Although the glass of the window was filthy, you could just see through. Marcus screwed up his eyes and made out what looked like some sort of store room. There were piles of things heaped untidily – television sets, stereos, domestic appliances. These were obviously the 'portable assets' Mr Darke and George had taken from their 'clients' in lieu of payment. Marcus remembered Mrs Yarder's rings and felt a hot wave of anger.

He was still standing in the yard, wondering how exactly he was going to get the rings back, when he heard the noise of a car being driven slightly too fast and realized that it heralded the return of George and Mr Darke. He froze in panic. What if they found him here? Marcus looked around for an escape route, or at least a place to hide. The wall that divided the yard from the neighbour's was tall and topped with broken glass, but lined up against it were three wheelie bins. Marcus managed to leap behind them as the limo squeezed down the narrow drive and pulled up. Peering round a bin, he could see George getting out of the driving seat and coming round to open the passenger door for Mr Darke, who got out and walked over to unlock the back door of the premises.

Meanwhile George threw open the boot of the car. Mr Darke returned to inspect the contents. He nodded in quiet satisfaction at their haul, then said: 'How's your hand?'

'Bit sore,' George admitted.

'You shouldn't have hit him so hard.'

'He needed a slap.'

'If you'd given him a slap, you wouldn't have hurt your knuckles, would you? I don't know why you thought you had to punch his lights out.'

'He was thinking about doing it, boss – getting his retaliation in first. I know that type. Big blokes. Think they can take you. Anyway, we got the telly without any trouble after that, didn't we?'

'Go on, then,' said Mr Darke. 'You got it: you take it inside.'

George leaned into the boot and then stood up, holding a very large television set.

Mr Darke looked at it appreciatively.

'What do you think, £350?'

'At least. Maybe four-fifty.'

Mr Darke cocked his head. 'Anyway,' he said, 'we'll tell them three hundred.'

George gave a humourless laugh, and made his way over to the door. He had to turn sideways to get the television through it. Mr Darke loaded up an armful of lighter articles, and followed him.

Marcus wondered if he had time to race across the yard and back onto the street, but while he was still trying to decide, George and Mr Darke came out again.

'Did you get those rings valued, boss?' George said conversationally.

Marcus's ears pricked up.

'I did,' Mr Darke said.

'And?'

'Not bad. Eighteen-carat gold. And a real diamond'

'How much?'

'Two hundred and twenty the pair. We'll tell her one-forty. I didn't let him keep them.'

'Why's that, then, boss? She'll never have the money.'

'You're right there,' Mr Darke said, with a dry little laugh.

'So?' George's question came from behind a microwave.

Mr Darke blew out his breath from between pursed lips.

'There's more to life than money, George, as my dear old mum used to say. She's an attractive woman, Stella is. Or at least, she would be if she could only stop crying.'

'You're not going soft on me after all these years, are you?' George sneered.

Mr Darke laughed.

'I'm not going soft on *you*, George. Certainly not.'

Marcus felt himself prickling with anger again – and glared out at Mr Darke through the gap between the wheelie bins. He could just see him, standing by the boot of the car, with a framed picture under one arm, his face split by a nasty grin.

'Clear out the rest of this rubbish,' Mr Darke said. 'And then, talking of rubbish, put the wheelie bins round the front. Bin men in the morning.'

Marcus had been concentrating so hard on how

much he hated this man, that it took a moment for Darke's last words to sink in. When they did, he thought his heart had stopped. Getting cornered by George was not part of his plan, especially after what he'd just overheard. Marcus looked about him desperately. He had his back to the wall – in both senses. The wall itself was no use to him. The best chance would seem to be the steps down to the cellar, so he inched along to have a look. Although the basement door was set back in a kind of porch, it wouldn't provide sufficient cover for him. The only possibility was the abandoned cardboard box. It would be horrible to be trapped down there, but it was that or make a dash for it, and that was really high-risk too. Even if he escaped capture, they'd recognize him, and that would make the mission he'd set himself almost impossible. He had to make his mind up quickly. George was already lumbering across the yard with what looked like the last armful from the car. As he disappeared through the doorway, Marcus flung himself down the steps and crept into the cardboard box.

His arrival disturbed a couple of woodlice who scurried into one of the box's corners. Marcus felt an ancient spider's web across his face, and tore it away in disgust. The box smelled really unpleasant. It had obviously been there for a long time. Marcus prayed this wasn't going to be the day Mr Darke told George to put it out for the bin men.

He heard heavy footsteps in the yard, and the big car's boot was slammed shut. Marcus braced himself as George branched off towards the wheelie bins, horribly aware that not all of him was inside the box, and that should anyone look directly down over the railings they would see the back of his trousers and his shoes. He wished he'd brought the snake head with him. As it was, he was defenceless.

There was a grunt from above as George yanked at the first wheelie bin, turning it round and then dragging it off to the front of the building.

Marcus held his breath, trying to stay calm as he waited for George to come back for the second bin. The heavy boots returned, and he heard the big man cursing as he manoeuvred the second bin. Marcus heard it trundle away. Now that there was only one left, he was most at risk from George looking down and seeing him. His heart pumped. He felt like a rat in a trap. Then he heard another set of feet in the yard.

'Come on,' said Mr Darke as George came back. 'How long's it take to put three bins out?'

His next sentence nearly made Marcus throw up with fear.

'And how long's that box been down there?'

Marcus was convinced they'd be able to hear his heart thumping. He imagined the two of them, hulking George and dapper Mr Darke, standing at the top of the steps. In just a few seconds he could be yanked to his feet and hauled into the office – for what Mr Darke would doubtless call a bit of 'business'.

'Why don't you get it if it's bothering you?' George replied, lugging away the last wheelie bin.

'Oh, another day won't hurt, I suppose,' Mr Darke said. 'I'll get the kettle on and make some tea.'

Marcus's whole body seemed to go limp. His school shirt was damp with sweat. But inside he was whooping with delight. He'd got away with it. In a moment he would be free – free to slip out of the yard and escape back into the safe streets beyond. He was about to crawl out of the box when a noise from behind the basement door made him freeze. What if Mr Darke had decided to remove the box after all? He crouched like a sprinter waiting for the starting pistol. At the first sound of a key being turned or a bolt drawing back he would be off.

He heard voices. They were both down there. Which meant they would probably hear him if he did a runner. He would have to sit tight a while longer.

Marcus couldn't make out what they were saying, and wasn't particularly interested anymore – he just wanted them to get out of the basement so he could make his break for freedom. He heard objects being moved around – by George, he imagined.

Then there was a pause until Marcus heard Darke say: 'Don't stop now, George. I want to get home.'

'It's me hand,' George said.

'As I said,' Mr Darke continued, 'if you just gave them a slap, instead of punching their lights out, you wouldn't cause so much grief – to all parties. Come on, I'll give you a lift. Let's get this blessed crate moved and then we can both get home.'

There was silence, broken by the occasional grunt of effort. Marcus imagined them: one huge, the other tiny, wrestling to move the crate. But the comic picture didn't distract him from his own situation for long. He was playing for high stakes, and he couldn't afford to get caught. After a final grunt, he heard Mr Darke say: 'OK, that'll do. Let's lock up. It's nearly five.' Their voices moved away.

Nearly five? Marcus had lost all track of the time. He had to get home before Uncle Frank came back from work. Hoping it was safe, he pushed the cardboard box to one side, placing it carefully in its original position, and then slipped up the steps to the yard.

At the top he crouched so he couldn't be spotted through the back window, tiptoed past Mr Darke's car and then flattened himself along the side wall. The sound of a toilet flushing gave him a shock as he crept under the frosted-glass window, but then he was back on the street, and without a glance behind him, walked away as fast as he could.

Marcus made it home before Uncle Frank and had a chance to shower and change.

'Thought I'd better smarten up before I took the posters round to Mrs Prewle,' he explained.

'Well done. Good lad,' Uncle Frank said, with a slightly half-hearted smile.

His uncle had the post in his hand, some of which, Marcus had noticed, was addressed to Aunt Hester. He was glad he'd got the excuse of the posters to get him out of the house. Not that a visit to Mrs Prewle was a treat.

She was genuinely grateful for the posters – which had come out well – but still wanted to have a lengthy, and one-sided, conversation about what could possibly have happened to Decimal. He managed to get away eventually, keeping a few of the posters to pin up on telegraph poles and trees on his way to school in the morning.

Marcus and his uncle ate their tea in the lounge. Frank had taken to watching the evening news. Marcus was glad to find Hannah's dad had dropped off the list of stories covered.

CHAPTER 13

'Digger?'

The large boy swung round slowly.

'Break. You know where.'

Digger frowned with concentration, then his face broke into an ugly smile. But before he could speak, Marcus simply said: 'Be there,' and hurried away to his class.

On the surface life had to go on as normal. School carried on being school. Hannah carried on avoiding him. If it was possible, she seemed to avoid Marcus even more pointedly than before. He could see the stress she was under, and her mum looked worse every day when she drove up to school gates – in the car that Mr Darke would presumably soon be taking as a contribution to her mounting debt.

Which was why Marcus was working with steely concentration on his plan. Surely Hannah would renew their friendship if he could make everything OK for her and her mum?

* * *

'What's up, boss?'

Marcus flinched slightly at this echo of George, but at least it showed that Digger was on side and ready to be useful.

'I need your mobile.'

Marcus had considered using his aunt's mobile, but dismissed the thought immediately. He would rather rely on Digger keeping his mouth shut than risk making a traceable connection with Mr Darke.

'You're up to something.'

'None of your business. Give it to me.' Marcus put out his hand.

'You're not going to get me into trouble, are you?'

'Why would I want to do that, Digger? Now hand it over.'

Digger dug into his pocket and produced the phone.

'And to turn it on?'

The one school rule that was enforced with total consistency was that pupils' mobiles should be turned off throughout the school day.

Digger pressed a button and keyed in his pin.

The screen glowed.

'When do I get it back?'

'End of lunch. And, Digger?'

'Yeah?'

'Thanks.'

'OK, boss.'

The time between break and lunch dragged. Marcus must have run through what he was going to say to Mr Darke a hundred times. What if Darke just laughed?

Somehow, Marcus thought he wouldn't. He probably would laugh, but the chances were that he would be interested as well. And, as Marcus would point out, he'd have nothing to lose. Mr Darke could still climb into his big car and drive round to Hannah's house with George in tow if what Marcus was offering didn't come up to scratch.

Finally, the bell rang. Checking the phone was in his pocket, he made his way against the flow heading for the canteen and found himself a quiet spot around the back of the sports hall. Despite his palms having become annoyingly sweaty, he tapped in the numbers he had memorized. *He won't be there*, he told himself. *I won't have to speak to him.* But then suddenly the familiar creepy voice purred in his ear.

'Darke and Associates. How can we be of

assistance?'

'Oh, Mr Darke,' Marcus just managed to get out.

'Yes?' Mr Darke's voice sounded cautious.

'Um – you may remember – we met last week?'

'Who is this?' Mr Darke's tone was suddenly sharp. 'I hope you're not wasting my time.'

'Oh, no, not at all, Mr Darke. It's Marcus. If you remember. We met at Hannah's house.'

'Marcus!' Mr Darke's voice had a forced friendliness to it that was more unnerving than his cross voice. 'How nice to hear from you, young man. Of course I remember you. It was a pleasure. Now, what can I do for you?'

'Well, you know the – er – Mrs Yarder's – er—'

'Debt, yes. No point in not calling a spade a spade, is there, young man? I do recall the debt. And, if I'm not mistaken, the next repayment is due in twenty-four – or is it forty-eight? – hours. I do hope you're not going to embarrass us both by making a well-meaning, but perfectly futile attempt to intervene.'

'Oh, no, not at all,' Marcus gasped.

'I'm so glad. I did try to explain the way business works, didn't I? There really isn't anything you, or anyone else, can do about it – except pay, of course!'

Mr Darke gave an unpleasant chuckle, before asking, 'Do you happen to know whether that's a possibility?'

'No . . .' Marcus began.

'No, I thought not. Ah well, another outing for me and George, I suppose.'

'No,' Marcus said more firmly.

'No? Do you have an alternative, young man?'

'Yes. At least, I might have.'

'Really?'

'Yes.'

'Tell me more, young sir, tell me more.'

'Well, I've got something—'

'Nothing catching, I hope?'

Mr Darke's laughter in his ear was horrible but he carried on.

'No: it's something I think might be valuable – something that might be of interest to you.'

'How fascinating. And what manner of thing is this "something"? Is it an antique, for instance?'

Medusa's head – yes, you could call it an antique, Marcus thought grimly.

'Yes – yes, it is.'

'And what is it, though, Marcus?'

'Well, I don't exactly know.'

'You don't exactly know? Forgive me for sounding sceptical, but it's beginning to sound like something you've dreamed up to help someone you care about – a very laudable ploy, but utterly, utterly futile, I'm afraid.'

'No, no, listen. It's – it's – well, I think it's to do with an ancient myth. It's certainly very old.'

'I hope it's not mythical in the sense of you having made it up, Marcus.'

'Oh no, it's real enough, I promise.'

'All right. So where did you acquire this asset, Marcus?'

'It belonged to my parents.'

'But doesn't it still, Marcus?'

'They're both dead.'

'I'm sorry to hear that, Marcus; I genuinely am. So the piece is definitely yours?'

'Yes. I found it only recently. And it just looks – as though it might be, you know . . .'

'Valuable? Yes, yes, I see. And what is your proposal exactly? Would you like me to see it – to see if it is indeed worth something?'

'Yes – but I'll bring it to you. It's a bit awkward, because . . .'

'I think I understand. Your current guardian might

not approve. My middle name is "Discretion", young man: I'm known for it.'

'And I wouldn't want Hannah – or her mum—'

'To know. Yes, I see that. Very noble. Very noble indeed.'

There was a pause. Mr Darke was obviously thinking about it. Marcus could see him calculating that he might have something really valuable which he could offer a derisory amount for.

'When can you bring it in?'

'After school. Tomorrow. About four?'

'All right, young man. But you know that's the day I need payment. I'm afraid if your little offering doesn't come up to snuff, I'm going to have to drive round in the car and see Stella. You do understand that, don't you, young man?'

Marcus said he did and let Mr Darke give him directions.

'Thank you, Mr Darke,' he said. 'I'll find it.'

'Good man. We'll see you around half four. I'll tell George to put the kettle on.'

That was tomorrow. In the meantime, Marcus had plans for the afternoon ahead. They hadn't included talking to Rose, but she ambushed him again on the way home.

'I'm so sorry, Marcus. I don't know what's going on. But she really does seem – you know – angry with you. What's happened?'

Marcus didn't answer. The memory of that awful visit was going to stay with him for a very long time.

Despite his black look, Rose carried on: 'I keep telling Han how much you care about her. Really I do. But she just looks away or changes the subject.'

'How's her dad?'

Marcus thought he might as well get whatever news there was.

'Same as,' Rose told him. 'I can see that's what's keeping her down. But like I say, you only want to help. And where's the harm in that? It doesn't make any sense.'

Then she stopped, making Marcus stop too.

'But I think there's something else, Marcus.' Rose's eyes were big with speculation. 'I know it's all terrible; but there's something more than just her dad. I know there is. Like today, yeah, I said something about her mum coming to pick her up, and she said, "Well not for much longer". It just slipped out; I know she didn't mean to say it. I mean it could have meant she didn't think her dad was going to pull through, but that's a weird thing to say. Anyway, she's really down, Marcus. I don't think she's sleeping. She looks terrible.'

She paused, and then looked Marcus in the face.

'And you don't look so great, either. Have you looked in a mirror recently? You've got terrible shadows under your eyes.'

She touched his arm.

'You've got to look after yourself. You mustn't worry. She'll come round, I'm sure she will. And if she doesn't – well . . . there'll be other people interested, Marcus. Remember that.'

Marcus mumbled something that he hoped wasn't too ungracious and escaped. He walked away rapidly, passing one of his Decimal posters as he approached Brunel Street. Once home, he changed, and without stopping to give himself time to chicken out, went straight down the cellar steps and got the hamper from its hiding place. Everything in life needed practice. You couldn't just pick up your clarinet and play it perfectly in a concert. And you certainly couldn't handle something as dangerous as the Gorgon's head without rehearsing every last move. As before, he took the hamper down to the bottom of the garden and set up the mirror at the base of the tree.

It was another blazing-hot day, and the air was

humming with insects startled into life by the accelerated spring. It was the sort of afternoon you could lie on the grass and gaze up at the cloudless sky. Marcus felt a pang of regret that such a simple pleasure was so far out of his reach as he steeled himself to unlatch the hamper and deal with the horror it housed.

Marcus, the voice was gentle but immediate, matching the smile in the mirror. *Marcus . . . you brave boy . . . you brave hero.*

Although her lips moved, Marcus felt sure the voice was actually in his head. Had anyone else been present, he was certain they wouldn't have heard anything. If they happened to catch the Gorgon's eye, they wouldn't hear anything ever again, he reminded himself. But just for the moment, all seemed calm. The snakes writhed, and the king cobra reared – but there was none of the frenzied hostility he had experienced before.

As though answering his thought, the voice began again: *Yes, Marcus; the creatures are subject to my will. But let us focus on you. Your mission is a valiant one, and I will play my part.*

The smile in the mirror looked positively winning. Again, Marcus could see the ghost of the beauty that had once made Medusa famous throughout the ancient world.

Suddenly her face was clouded with a frown. It was as if his thought – the thought of her lost beauty – had struck home.

Marcus . . . Marcus, dear boy. I was lovely once, you are right. But not just lovely. She let her eyelids droop. *I was kind . . . I was generous . . . I had friends as well as suitors. Friends . . . true friends. True friends whose eyes I could meet openly and honestly . . .*

The voice was beguiling, and the expression on the ruined face was disarming. Perhaps, Marcus thought, Medusa had been misjudged; certainly her punishment seemed terribly disproportionate to her 'wrong' which, after all, was only the sin of vanity.

Marcus . . . you understand so much . . . Let us be friends, Marcus . . . Let me feel the trust of another heart, the faith of another soul . . . after all these years, all these years of stony suffering, an eternity of loneliness.

Time weeps stone years

Stone face weeps stone tears.

It sounded like a poem, or a fragment of one. *How sad,* Marcus thought. *How very sad.*

Yes, Marcus, it is sad. So terribly sad. Listen . . . listen to me, Marcus . . . we can help each other. I can help you – oh, how I can help you. And all I ask in return is a little tenderness, a little trust . . . Put aside the mirror, Marcus. Let not a sheet of glass stand between us . . . look at me, Marcus . . . look me in the eye, dear boy . . . brave boy . . . brave, brave boy . . .'

He was transfixed by the once-beautiful face, now washed of its characteristic malice and fury, the lips slightly parted, the eyebrows raised in supplication. All he had to do was turn the hamper round and look directly into those innocently wide eyes . . .

Yes, Marcus . . . friends . . . We would be the closest friends imaginable . . . And I have so much knowledge to impart to you . . .

Marcus felt his hand reaching out. The king cobra was completely still, its black eyes focused on his outstretched fingers. Around him the other vipers formed a coronet, like strangely coloured asparagus. Marcus switched his gaze back to the mirror. Was Medusa sincere? Could he trust her? He thought of the relief he'd feel if he could, the strange joy her friendship and her power would give him.

Fluttering round the tree came a butterfly – a surprisingly large butterfly – released by the trigger of the early summer heat. It flickered briefly in the sunshine, distracting him from the Gorgon's face. He looked back in the mirror just in time to see Medusa raise her eyes. Instantly, the butterfly dropped from the air – like a stone. Medusa darted a look at Marcus. She saw his horror in an instant, and everything changed. Her face stiffened into its familiar malign contours, and as it did so, Marcus thought he caught a glimpse of defeat or frustration in her eyes. The king cobra puffed out his hood, and the brood around him leaned forward together, baring their fangs in unison at Marcus.

Marcus backed away, trembling at how close he'd come, once again, to submitting to the Gorgon, how close he'd come to giving her the satisfaction of victory. He felt sick. His legs were weak. He squatted in an ungainly heap away from the hamper, breathing hard. After a moment he forced himself up and, shaken, advanced once more on the picnic basket. Up went the front panel and down came the lid, despite the furious resistance. The wickerwork rattled with rage, but with the latches fixed, he knew he was safe. He reached down and picked up the mirror. On the grass beside it was the butterfly – or a perfect stone replica of it. He picked it up carefully, as though it were the finest porcelain; the wings were no thicker than they had been in life, but when he tested them between finger and thumb, there was nothing brittle about them: they were as strong as flint. Likewise the antennae: two steel pins. The butterfly was exquisite, lying heavy in his palm, like a precious piece of jewellery.

It had saved his life. It would be his lucky charm.

As for you . . . he thought, as he heaved the hamper onto his shoulder. *You'll serve your purpose, and then . . .* Judging from the frenzy inside the basket, the Gorgon had read his mind.

And he was in more danger than ever.

That evening Marcus said he had a lot of homework and went up to his room straight after dinner. With a pile of A4 paper in front of him, he sat writing for long time, then folded the two letters he'd been working on into separate envelopes. He left one in the top drawer of his desk and put the other one into his schoolbag.

They said you shouldn't fight fire with fire, but that's exactly what he was going to do.

CHAPTER 14

The first thing Marcus did when he got to school was place the envelope addressed to Mrs Faversham in his locker where it couldn't be missed. Walking away, he put his hand up to his shirt pocket and felt the hard sharp lines of the stone butterfly. He was going to need all the luck in the world to get through the day ahead.

And what a long day it was. Marcus moved through it in his own bubble. In so far as he noticed anything, he registered Hannah avoiding him, Rose attempting to make some sort of eye contact, and Digger giving him a knowing grin. He might have been vaguely aware that everybody else seemed to give him hasty glances before speeding away along the corridor, but being left alone was all he wanted. He had a lot of things to think about. Apprehension and impatience kept him on tenterhooks – he cursed the slow-moving hands on the classroom clocks, and yet every time they jumped another quarter of an hour, the dread at what he had to do gripped his heart.

And then it came: the last lesson of the day. Mr Hillsborough was 'on a course,' so the class was taken by another incompetent supply teacher. It was chaos, but Marcus was happy to hunker down while paper pellets flew and pens 'accidentally' rolled across the floor.

When the bell finally rang the classroom looked like a battlefield. The pupils pushed through the door, yelling in triumph, leaving the teacher slumped like a defeated general, surveying the chairs that should have been put up on the desks, and what looked like a wheelie bin's worth of litter scattered over the floor. Marcus helpfully put his chair up and dropped a juice carton in the bin as he went out. 'Bye, sir,' he said, but there was no response.

He took his usual position within sight of the school gates to see Hannah's mum drawing up in the car. She looked worse than ever – this was the afternoon the money was due and she didn't have it. Hannah got in and gave her a peck on the cheek. Her mum brought a hand up to her eye. It looked as though she were trying to conceal a tear. Inside, Marcus was boiling. If things went well over the next three hours, the Yarders would never have to fear George's knock on the door again.

Once home, he ran up to his room and changed quickly. He took the envelope out of his drawer and placed it prominently on the desk top. He wrote 'Uncle Frank' on the front and stood back contemplating it for a moment. After that he rooted out his pencil case, and could tell from the response inside it that the severed snake head was still fit for purpose. He gave the elastic bands that contained it a snap before slipping the box into his coat.

Patting his pocket to check he had the stone butterfly with him, Marcus went downstairs again, his pulse already racing and his mouth dry. He went into the kitchen and got himself a drink, but was hardly able to swallow the weak squash. Then he went into the hall and approached the basement door, standing with his hand on the latch while his heart hammered against his ribcage. But this was no time for hesitation. Heroes don't hesitate: they act.

Yes, Marcus, they act, echoed the voice in his head. Having Medusa talking to him was scary – very scary – but it gave him a turbo-charge of confidence. He couldn't wait to see the look on Mr Darke's face when he revealed his 'antique'.

*   *   *

Marcus had decided to go by bus. Sitting near the back – the hamper on the seat next to him, concealed by a coat – Marcus watched the nondescript streets go past. There was nothing remarkable about the day at all. The steam clouds from the food factory rose doughily into the air as usual, getting lost in the general ordinariness of the sky. And there was certainly nothing extraordinary about a boy sitting on a bus with something box-shaped on the seat beside him.

Marcus intended to keep within the zone of ordinariness for as long as he possibly could. He knew it couldn't last long. When he rested his hand on the wickerwork beside him, he felt the telltale stirrings under the lid. The snakes knew something was up. They were like restless soldiers on the eve of battle. Marcus felt like a very raw recruit about to face the horrors of war for the first time. He wished the bus would hurry up. Then he wished the bus would never get there. But it did. Suddenly they reached his stop, and Marcus leaped out of his seat. In his hurry, he caught another passenger on the shoulder with the picnic basket.

Marcus looked back and saw a large woman

rubbing her shoulder and looking reproachfully at him. It was too late to say sorry, so he just stumbled off the bus as quickly as he could, cursing himself for his clumsiness. The bump had disturbed the snakes, and the picnic basket was now vibrating like an over-revved engine. It felt as though it could blow up at any moment. Although Medusa had not communicated with him since yesterday, Marcus felt her vengeful spirit emanating from the hamper, and a dark exhilaration at the power he had boxed up under his coat. Here he was, walking through the unsuspecting crowds carrying a lethal weapon. What would happen if he simply stopped, pulled off the coat, and opened the basket?

Who would be the first to catch the Gorgon's eye? The slow old woman with her shopping bags? The smart young man in his suit, marching along the pavement as though the world were at his feet? Possibly the old fellow selling the *Big Issue* outside the stationer's. Yes, sitting there, he could well be the one to freeze into stone first. Him or his dog. And the others would follow. Everybody would want to see what was happening and what was causing it. It would take a moment for people to cotton on. Then there would be screams and panic. But that would bring even more people to stop and stare – and to stay, stopped and staring: for ever. And after that all the footsteps would be going in the other direction as the crowds ran away from the town centre, leaving him alone, surrounded by the uneven rings of silent stone shoppers, peering, gaping, gawping in his direction, a hand flung up here, a face half-turned there. Just like Aunt Hester.

'Oy, look where you're going, lad. You can't go bumping into people like that.'

The man was glowering at the basket, which Marcus quickly covered more adequately with his coat. *You'd make a fine statue*, he thought, looking at the man, before mumbling an apology and shuffling on. *Where did that violent thought come from?*

He shook himself. The man may have been unpleasant, but he was right. Marcus couldn't go wandering around town in a daydream of annihilation. He had to get out of the main thoroughfare. He wasn't far from Mr Darke's office, and it would be easier to approach via a less crowded side street where he could calm down and get his mind right for what he had to do.

The faded sign was exactly the same. The single

239

window with the frosted glass was exactly the same. The front door with the peeling paint was exactly the same. The only difference this time was that Marcus was going to knock on that door.

It was George who opened it. He wore a stripy shirt which was at least a size too small for him, making his enormous hands look even more enormous.

''Ello, Marcus. Come on in,' he said with a horrible leer. Marcus noticed he hadn't shaved for a day or two. George ushered Marcus into a dark hall, lit only by one dim central light. There were doors ahead, and to the left and to the right. And, Marcus noticed, a large trapdoor set in the floor.

'Wot you got in there, then? The crown jewels?' George pointed at the hamper. He laughed. It was not a pretty sound.

'I do 'ope you're not wasting our time. You know what Mr Darke says: "Time is money". And 'e doesn't like people wasting 'is precious asset.'

'That Marcus, George? Show him in.' Mr Darke's voice came from behind the door to the left.

George did what he was told, swinging the door open for Marcus.

Mr Darke was sitting at a sizeable desk, on which

were spread a mass of papers – tallies of debts, Marcus guessed. The wall behind him was shelved floor to ceiling, and the shelves were crammed with box files. Darke's reach was obviously extensive.

The ferrety man looked up from his calculator and dismissed George with a wave. He smiled at Marcus, sending his tiny moustache bristling along his upper lip and exposing his wolfish teeth. It was not a reassuring smile.

'Give me a moment, Marcus.' He pecked away at the calculator, and then scribbled a figure at the bottom of a long column of numbers on a small notepad. The figure, Marcus could see, was a big one.

'There.' Mr Darke threw down his biro. 'They won't pay it, of course, but one has to do the maths nevertheless. Legal requirement. Now, my boy: let's see what priceless treasure from antiquity you have so kindly brought for me to view.'

Marcus slipped the coat off the hamper onto the chair next to him and then felt for the catch securing the lid. He was glad there had been no preamble; that things had come so easily and quickly to a head.

'Go on, then; let's see,'

Mr Darke's tone was lightly dismissive, but his face

was lit by the unmistakable glow of acquisitiveness.

Marcus released the catch, and flung back the lid of the hamper. Even though he knew what to expect, what happened was more spectacular than Marcus had bargained for. In an explosive burst of spitting fury, the king cobra forced his way through the wicker hole, his hood ballooning and his fangs yawning. Darke flung himself backwards, his hands scrabbling against the wall of box files behind him.

'George, George!' he cried out in terror, as the cobra strained towards him, lurching this way and that like an attack dog at the full extent of its chain.

'George! Help! George! Get that thing away from me.'

It was too late for Marcus to advise against calling George. He heard heavy steps coming across the hall, and the door to Mr Darke's office flew open. George seemed to fill the doorway, but he got no further than the threshold before he saw the cobra and stopped in his tracks.

'George! Do something!' Mr Darke screamed.

'Stay where you are,' Marcus ordered.

'Get him, George!'

George's eyes swivelled between his terrified employer, the king cobra, which had now craned round to take in this new presence in the room, and Marcus.

'He's just a kid, George. You can't be frightened of a kid.'

That did it. George lumbered into life. But only for a second.

Marcus had been prepared for this. He swivelled the basket round to face the door, releasing the latches to the front panel as he did so.

George had taken only one step across the room when he met the Gorgon's terrible gaze. And from then he remained motionless, a long arm extended towards Marcus, a look of astonishment carved onto his face.

'George! George? Oh my God, oh my God, oh my God . . . What have you done to him? What in God's name have you done to him?'

'The same as I'll do to you if you try anything.'

'George? *George?* He's turned to stone. I don't believe it. This can't be happening. I'll wake up; I'll wake up . . . Oh, my God . . . What you got in there?'

'I'll show you.' Marcus inched the hamper round a little.

'No. No, no, no. I don't want to see. George . . . George?' Mr Darke's voice had turned into a defeated whine. He slumped back in his chair, shielding himself with his arms, his terrified eyes staring out over the sleeve of his coat.

Marcus got out the mirror. Mr Darke cringed and began to whimper: 'I don't want to see; I don't want to see. Don't show me.'

Marcus ignored him, and held the mirror to the side of the hamper.

Mr Darke turned his head.

'Look,' Marcus said. 'Look at it. You better know what you're up against.'

Marcus had seen the deadly face enough times to know that however many times you saw it, the electric terror you felt never lessened. You could never get used to it: the ruined beauty of the Gorgon's features, the malice of her eyes distilled to venom over centuries of lonely bitterness.

Marcus slowly turned the mirror. Mr Darke had no option but to see. His cry was the most abject sound Marcus had ever heard: horror and despair blended together in a wail that petered out into a sobbing sigh.

'Oh my God, oh my God . . .' was all Mr Darke seemed capable of saying.

'You see?' Marcus said.

'I do see,' Mr Darke croaked. 'The Gorgon . . . An antique . . . indeed . . . yes, yes . . . I do see. Put the mirror down, Marcus. Thank you. *Phew!* Yes, very clever. Very clever. Clever, cunning . . . who'd have thought it? A lone boy. Turned George to stone. Poor old George. Probably never heard of the Gorgon. Classics not his strong suit. Not sure that he had one – a strong suit, that is. Except *being* strong. Yes. Didn't do him much good, though, did it? No defence against that. Oh, no. Just blundered forward as usual. Didn't know what hit him. Oh God, oh God. What are you going to do to me? You're not going to turn me into stone, are you? Not your clever, friendly, helpful Uncle Desmond?' Mr Darke wheedled. 'You wouldn't do that to me, would you? You're a good boy, you're a nice boy . . . a clever boy . . . with a bright future. Oh yes, oh yes, I think so.'

Mr Darke had turned to nodding now. He looked like a ventriloquist's dummy whose puppeteer was having a nervous breakdown. His arms had started flapping uncontrollably, and his Adam's apple was bobbing up and down, reminding Marcus of a fishing float on the canal.

'Maybe we can sort something out, Marcus,' Mr Darke said, when he was calm enough to speak clearly again. 'You know, you scratch my back, I scratch yours. That kind of thing?' He giggled nervously.

In reply, Marcus moved the hamper round a bit further.

'No, no, quite. I understand, Marcus. You've got all the trumps. Of course you have. You call the shots. What do you want, Marcus? Tell me what you want. You can have it. Anything, anything at all. Anything at all within reason.'

Marcus nudged the basket round another inch or two.

'Anything at all,' Mr Darke gabbled, his eyes bulging. 'Absolutely anything at all – without qualification. Just say what you want, Marcus. It's yours, my boy. And happy to let you have it.'

Mr Darke had his hands together and was wringing them in front of his face. Marcus could see tears forming in his eyes, eyes that flickered between Marcus and the mirror. Marcus let him sweat for a moment. He looked at the man's face, which was twitching with fear. His smarmy, threatening charm was rather threadbare now. And, he realized thankfully, Mr Darke seemed to have forgotten all about his 'dear old mother'. *The man is a fraud, through and through*, Marcus thought.

246

Then he said: 'All right. To business, as you would say.'

'Yes, yes, I would, wouldn't I? To business. Exactly right. You are a good boy, Marcus. I see a lot of potential there, really I do.' Mr Darke smiled. Or tried to. The result would have made a good ghoul mask for Halloween.

'You couldn't – just as a favour – you couldn't shut that thing, could you?'

'This?' Marcus said, deliberately nudging the hamper round a little more.

Mr Darke threw up his hands with a little shriek.

'No, no, I quite understand. It's your bargaining chip. I do see that. And quite a bargaining chip it is too. I really wouldn't like to see what you could do with a nuclear warhead, young man. I just hope you know what you're doing. I really do hope that.' He stopped blathering and looked uncertainly at Marcus.

'Perhaps, perhaps if you're not going to close the lid – and I fully understand, young man, probably a very sensible decision, but fairly unnerving to the person on this side of the desk I don't mind admitting – I wonder if you would mind awfully if I had one of these?'

Here he reached for a packet of cigarettes on the desk.

'You didn't ask Hannah's mother permission last week did you?'

'No, no, Marcus I didn't, and it was very remiss of me, and I regret it, I'll regret it to my dying day, which' – again he broke into an awful smile – 'which I very much hope will not be for many a long year. I apologize. It was wrong. It was a terribly, terribly bad decision. As was, I now realize, inviting you along in the first place. I must have been mad. What was I thinking? Oh my God, oh my God – please let me have a cigarette.'

Marcus didn't want to negotiate with someone having hysterics, so he nodded permission.

'Thank you, thank you, young man. You don't indulge yourself, do you? I know a lot of youngsters do.'

Marcus shook his head.

'Good. Good, good, good. Very bad habit. Very bad for you indeed. But there are occasions, there really are occasions when it can be very helpful. Very helpful. But to business. Yes. Terms and conditions apply. *Phew.* Is it me, or is it really rather hot?'

He loosened his tie and undid his top button, before pulling deeply on his cigarette. The king cobra didn't seem to like the smoke, and started moving his head menacingly.

'I think I'd put it out if I were you,' Marcus said, nudging the basket a further degree round.

'Just say the word. Just say the word, young man.' And with one last inhalation, Mr Darke stubbed out the cigarette. 'Oh, my giddy aunt. Where were we? Terms and conditions . . . yes. Just tell me what you want.'

'I think you know,' Marcus said quietly.

'I've got it here.' Mr Darke said groped among his papers. 'Look – *Stella Yarder*.'

He held it up for Marcus to see.

The cobra craned and peered at it as though interested in its contents, and Mr Darke whipped his hands back, well out of range.

Then he ripped the loan agreement into shreds.

'OK?'

'Now let's have the money.'

'She borrowed that! I didn't make her.'

'All of it.'

'But she was desperate. I knew Stella was a bad bet, but she begged me. Marcus, I was doing her a favour.'

'And then, when she couldn't pay it back, you

started charging her ridiculous amounts of interest –
and intimidating her.' Marcus looked him straight in
the eye and moved the basket round a couple of
centimetres.

'You're a fine one to talk about intimidation . . .
All right, all right!' Mr Darke put up his hand. 'I'm
not condemning it. I'm not. You'd have *some* career
in business, my boy, I'm telling you that for free.'

Darke opened a drawer in his desk and produced
a large wad of bank notes. Giving Marcus a
penetrating stare he started counting them out onto
the desk.

'How much? And I can check.' Marcus said.

'Do I look stupid? Five hundred and twenty-five
pounds. I can show you the figures.'

He threw a last five pound note on the pile and
reached for a brown envelope.

'And the rings,' said Marcus. 'You were going to
cheat her on those as well . . . Except you had other
plans, didn't you?'

Mr Darke stayed silent.

'Didn't you?'

Marcus put his hand on the basket.

'Don't. You're a very perceptive boy for your age,'
Mr Darke said.

Marcus didn't think he needed to know he'd been hiding behind the wheelie bins.

There was a pause.

'All right,' he said.

Mr Darke opened one of the drawers in his desk, and produced a cash box. This he unlocked with a key he produced from the top pocket in his jacket.

The cash box was full to overflowing with jewellery.

Mr Darke picked out two of the many rings, identifying Hannah's mum's easily. He added them to the wad of notes which he placed in the envelope.

Then, with a very bad grace, and keeping well clear of the picnic basket, he pushed it across the desk.

Marcus reached carefully to retrieve it. Slipping it into his pocket, he said:

'And now all the others.'

Mr Darke nearly leaped out of his chair.

'What? What are you talking about?'

'I'm talking about all the other loans. All of them.'

'You're mad. You can't just come here and – you'll ruin me.'

Marcus put his hand on the basket again.

'Oh, God.' Mr Darke collapsed back into his chair. 'This is criminal. That's what this is. You coming in here, using threats, making me do things I don't want to do. That's gangsterism, that's what that is. It's seriously out of order. It's against the law.'

'Why don't you ring the police, then?' Marcus asked.

There was silence in the little room. Mr Darke glared at Marcus but said nothing.

'How many people's lives have you ruined over the years? What would they want me to do if they could choose?'

He gave the basket another little nudge.

'You're frightening, you know that?' Mr Darke said sulkily. 'Who do you think you are – Robin Hood? Robbing Hood, if you ask me.'

'I wasn't. Now get those contracts out and start ripping them up. And then we'll have to deal with George.'

With a venomous look at Marcus, Darke swung round and pulled down a box file marked CURRENT which he thumped on the desk. It was crammed to overflowing. Just like the cash box. Marcus looked on as Mr Darke gloomily ripped each sheet of paper to pieces. From time to time he stopped to look at one; some obviously caused him more pain to destroy than others.

'These' – he held up a sheet – 'these could pay. I know they could. They've got a stash somewhere. George would have got it out of them.'

Marcus glanced across to the frozen figure in the middle of the room. Mr Darke followed his gaze. Admitting defeat, he tore up the contract with particular ferocity.

'I got to live,' he muttered as he got nearer the bottom of the pile.

'You've got lots of ways to make a living,' Marcus said. 'What's it say on that sign out there? Bailiffs, debt collectors . . .'

'Oh, so we do believe in people being made to pay their debts after all?' Mr Darke said sarcastically.

'Of course,' said Marcus. 'But that's different from you finding the people who are in trouble and then putting them in even worse trouble by sharking them loans at sky-high interest they'll never be able to pay.'

'Gordon Bennett!' Mr Darke surveyed the heap of shredded contracts on his desk. 'You may as well have the shirt off my back while you're about it.'

Marcus looked at the garment in question. It was drenched in sweat.

'You can keep your shirt,' he said. 'But what you can do is help get rid of George.'

'Close that up then, son.' Mr Darke indicated the hamper.

'No funny business,' Marcus ordered. 'I've left a note at home – about where I've come. And if I'm not back by half five my uncle will read it – and he'll be round here in a shot.'

'I'm not going to try any funny business, boy.' Mr Darke looked done in. 'He's going to be a bit of a handful,' he said, nodding at George. 'In death as in life.'

Marcus flipped up the front of the hamper.

The voice in his head said: *Nicely done, Marcus, nicely done. But watch him. He's a slippery one.*

Marcus noted that Mr Darke's mood improved with the closing of the hamper. He let out a sigh and mopped his brow with his handkerchief before giving Marcus a watery smile that looked more like a leer. Yes, he did need watching, Marcus agreed – very, very closely.

'And the bloomin' snake,' Mr Darke said.

Marcus looked at him once more, trying to work out whether he really had accepted defeat.

'OK. But I warn you – I've got something else up my sleeve if you try anything.'

Mr Darke waved away the suggestion with both hands. 'I've seen enough already, lad. You win. End of.' He spread his hands in submission.

In return, Marcus slowly lowered the lid, forcing the cobra into the hamper amidst much hissing, and secured the front catch.

Mr Darke let out his breath in a long sigh.

'Have you got a trolley?' Marcus demanded.

Mr Darke nodded. He got up slowly and edged round the desk. Marcus watched him, keeping his hand on the top of the picnic basket. The Gorgon's head was the most fearsome weapon, but it was awkward to use and he didn't want to give Mr Darke the chance to rush him.

Marcus waited for him to take the lead. He looked at George's eyeballs, bursting from their sockets as the flash of shock and surprise hit in the last second of consciousness. He had been the greater physical threat, but Darke was cunning. As Marcus followed the little man into the lobby, he felt for the pencil case in his pocket and eased off one of the elastic bands. He could feel the snake head vibrating with anticipation. 'There's a trolley through here.' Mr Darke opened a door into a vestibule which led out to the yard. After moving one or two of the things strewn about the place, Mr Darke emerged with an ancient-looking porter's trolley.

'What are we going to do with him? Assuming we can shift him at all.'

'You tell me,' Marcus said. 'The basement?'

Mr Darke looked at him balefully.

'If you want him down there, we'd better open the trap up, hadn't we?'

The trapdoor opened in the middle. Rings were inset in metal mountings on both halves of the door. Marcus and Mr Darke stood on either side, each waiting for the other to go first. In the end Mr Darke lunged forward and pulled his half of the door open. Marcus followed suit, but for a moment he felt uncomfortably vulnerable. Mr Darke made no move to take advantage of him, but it was a reminder to stay super-alert.

There was a pile of goods below the trapdoor – the large television had made its way down there, along with a nearly-new vacuum cleaner, a big cardboard box with a picture of a microwave on it, and an electric heater.

'I'll just go down and clear a nice big space,' Mr Darke said.

Marcus looked at the clock hanging over the door to the vestibule. It was already after four-thirty.

'There isn't time. I've got to get home.'

'But you're not suggesting we just tip him? There's a couple of grand's worth of goods there. He'll smash them to pieces!'

'Tough,' said Marcus. 'You don't want my uncle reading that note.'

'Mad, you are,' muttered Mr Darke. 'All that good stuff – smashed . . .'

Shaking his head, he skirted the open trapdoor and pushed the trolley roughly back to the office door.

Marcus got into the office first. He wasn't giving Darke a chance to get his hands on the hamper.

'OK,' he said. We'll try to rock him forward so you can get the plate under.'

Marcus took George's raised hand and pulled, and Mr Darke pushed the trolley's plate under George's heel.

'Now backwards,' Marcus instructed.

'Steady now,' Mr Darke said. 'I don't want to be crushed to death by my own right-hand man. God knows how heavy he's going to be.'

George turned out to be very heavy indeed, and Marcus had to rush to Mr Darke's assistance as soon as he'd tipped the stone figure backwards.

Mr Darke grunted with the strain. With Marcus's support, he managed to stay standing, but only just. Slowly they staggered back, guiding the trolley into the lobby and towards the gaping hole of the trapdoor.

The little trolley wheels squeaked in protest, but eventually they got George to the edge of the trapdoor. They stopped, taking the strain together. Out of the corner of his eye he could see Mr Darke's face, sweating and twitching.

'He's too big to tip,' Darke said.

'We'll just have to send him down on the trolley,' Marcus said.

'Oh my giddy aunt; that'll make an even worse mess,' moaned Mr Darke.

Marcus ignored that. 'It'll be easier if we turn him round. Then we can push him.'

With a lot of effort they swivelled the trolley so George was facing the trapdoor.

'OK,' said Marcus: 'One, two, *three!*'

There was a final squeak from the trolley wheels

and a grunt from Mr Darke.

Then George rolled over the edge and disappeared. There was a mighty crash from below. Marcus felt his whole body relax with the relief of finishing the job.

The moment lasted barely a second. With a cry of fury, Mr Darke hurled himself at Marcus, grappling to get his hands around his neck.

CHAPTER 15

Marcus flung his hands up and grasped Mr Darke by the wrists, as they teetered on the brink of the trapdoor.

'You toxic little vermin,' Mr Darke hissed at him. His face was horribly near and his moustache was writhing like a caterpillar. To make it even worse, his breath smelled foul.

Marcus lifted his elbow sharply and caught Mr Darke a cracking blow under his chin. For a second the man's grip relaxed, but then it tightened again, even more ferociously. The wiry little man was stronger than he looked. Marcus brought his knee up firmly. Mr Darke grunted in pain and his grip slackened again.

'You want to fight dirty, do you?' he spat. 'I'll give you dirty.'

He removed his hands from around Marcus's neck, and produced a flick-knife, whose blade shot out of the handle at the touch of a button. Then he began waving it to and fro, just like the cobra swaying its head, waiting to strike.

Snakes.

If that's the way you want it. Marcus reached into his pocket and brought out the pencil case. He could see Mr Darke's eyebrows rising, and then his face cracked open in a sneer.

'You'll have to do better than a pencil case, young shaver!' he cackled. 'Ha! I'll have you – I'll have you on toast.'

The little man advanced. Marcus retreated, edging round to the other side of the trap in the floor. He glanced down briefly to see George's form now resting on the broken TV. Mr Darke also glanced down and the sight seemed to inspire him to new heights of fury.

Marcus continued to back away. If he could get round the trapdoor and make it into Mr Darke's office once more, he could turn the Gorgon's power on his enemy and that would be that.

'Oh no you don't!' Mr Darke cried, rapidly retracing his steps and getting between Marcus and the door. 'I see your little ploy. You want to turn me into stone as well, don't you, you maddening, meddlesome little . . .'

It was now Mr Darke's turn to start backing away, as he tried to get into the office first. Marcus couldn't allow that. He launched himself at Mr Darke, who wasn't expecting such a reckless assault. Marcus hit the little man in the stomach, knocking him to the ground, and then threw himself on top of him, grappling for his wrist at the same time. Mr Darke struggled violently, his knife hand twisting like a hooked fish.

Marcus saw his moment, flicked off one of the elastic bands and planted the pencil case against Mr Darke's ear. He felt the cold blade of the knife against his skin. 'I've only got to push,' Marcus heard Mr Darke gasp.

'And I've only got to open this box,' Marcus replied.

Mr Darke's eyes swivelled to take in the pencil case. 'What you got in there, then? A compass? A pencil sharpener?'

'It's better than your knife,' said Marcus, thrusting the box closer to Mr Darke's ear.

Mr Darke tried to get his head away, but Marcus kept the box close. He felt Mr Darke's left hand scrabbling at his elbow.

'I wouldn't do that,' he said. 'If that lid slides back,

you're gone.'

'Take it away.'

'Take the knife away.'

'That's not how it works. We know I got the knife. Don't know what you got in that box.'

'Listen, then.'

Marcus pressed the pencil box harder against Mr Darke's ear. He could feel Mr Darke flinch, but he kept the box in place.

'Hear it? Hear it hiss?'

'What is it? What you got in there?'

'Look.' Marcus let the pencil box lid slide back.

'Oh, my God, oh, my God. More snakes. I can't bear it.'

'Two minutes. Two minutes of agony. Then you're gone.'

'I'd kill you first.' Mr Darke said. He was trying to sound tough, but his face had turned completely white; his forehead was damp with sweat; and his eyeballs bounced around like trapped mice, flicking from Marcus's eyes to the pencil box.

'But you don't want to kill me, do you, Mr Darke? My uncle gets home in less than half an hour. And if he reads my note . . .'

Marcus could feel the pressure on the knife ease.

'You're a devil, you know that? You're an absolute little devil.'

'Drop it,' Marcus ordered. 'Drop the knife.'

Reluctantly, Mr Darke withdrew the weapon and a moment later Marcus heard it clattering onto the floor.

'Don't kill me,' wheedled Mr Darke. He was trying to look away from the snake head, but at the same time not wanting to let it out of his sight.

The snake hissed as its tongue shot out, making Mr Darke squeal.

At his moment of triumph, Marcus heard Medusa in his head. *Oh brave boy, warrior-boy, you fought well. Now despatch him, as he deserves.*

Marcus could feel the crook wriggling under him. It made him feel sick. Mr Darke repulsed him. He was a mean, despicable, vile, backstabbing runt of a man. *Kill him, Marcus, kill him. Where there is blame, there must be punishment. Do it, Marcus. Do it!* The voice was getting stronger, like a wind blowing up. It would be so easy . . . so easy to do what she wanted.

He glanced at Mr Darke. There was a dribble of saliva running down his chin. His whole body was limp. It was like lying on a half-deflated lilo.

Marcus couldn't stand it any longer and rolled away from him.

'Turned out my pencil case was better than your knife after all, didn't it?'

Mr Darke nodded his head, and started to pick himself up.

'You won. Game, set and match.' He dusted down his jacket. 'I can't argue with that. I won't fight you anymore. Can't fight a devil, can you?'

Marcus had also got to his feet, picking up the flick-knife as he did and putting it in his pocket.

They watched each other like duellists. But the duel was over. Marcus had won.

Mr Darke got out his handkerchief and mopped his face.

'I gotta have a cigarette,' he said, and felt for his packet. But it was still on his desk. He looked at Marcus, who in turn looked at the clock on the wall. It was past five.

'I've got to go.' He pushed past Mr Darke to reclaim the hamper from the office.

Darke opened the front door for him as he left.

'You really are a most remarkable boy,' he said. 'But you better know what you're doing, my young friend, or you will end up in trouble. Serious trouble. I'm warning you.'

Marcus made it home before Uncle Frank but decided not to risk going into the basement in case his uncle caught him down there. Instead, he took the hamper straight up to his room and spread some homework on his desk; but the life and times of Charles Dickens was a meaningless blur of blacking factories, coach journeys and workhouses. All Marcus could think about was the ordeal of the previous couple of hours. He couldn't tell whether he was more shaken by what had happened to George or by the thought of what had nearly happened to him at the hands of Mr Darke. The flick-knife's blade had grazed the skin, and when he felt it under his shirt, his finger came away with a little red smear. What if Mr Darke had actually stabbed him? Or, worse still, if he had got to the hamper, so that in addition to a statue of his henchman, he would have had a life-sized statue of Marcus as well?

Reaching into his pocket for the brown envelope, Marcus pulled out the grubby used banknotes and tipped out the two rings. He started to feel better. He had achieved what he'd set out to achieve, however close to the wire he'd gone. He was just counting the notes when he heard Uncle Frank's key in the door, and shovelled them guiltily back into the envelope. He felt anxious going downstairs, because he still felt shaky, but Uncle Frank was tired. They had a simple supper, then watched a bit of television. It was good to be back in the normal world, good to be back sitting on the sofa with Uncle Frank. Though it was weird not to be able to tell him about the extraordinary afternoon he'd had, just looking into his uncle's face made it all seem impossible. Looking at Uncle Frank also made Marcus feel ashamed – ashamed of the rage and aggression he'd shown. He remembered the powerful urge he'd felt to exact full retribution on Mr Darke. Even though he'd done a good thing – and not only for Hannah and her mum, but for dozens of other people he would never meet – he knew, if he were honest, that he'd enjoyed the power he had had over Mr Darke.

He had to get Medusa's voice out of his head. She had served her purpose, and now it was time for her to go. He would decommission her. That's what you did with obsolete or unwanted weapons systems: you decommissioned them, either by making them harmless or destroying them. There was no way to make the Gorgon harmless, so she would have to be destroyed.

He yawned, exhausted, and when Uncle Frank suggested he should have an early night, he was quite happy to go to bed. The wound on his ribcage was visible in the bathroom mirror, but in truth it was only a scratch. Mr Darke had done more damage to his shirt, but only someone with Aunt Hester's laser eye for rips or marks, however slight, would notice it.

Back in his room Marcus looked at the clothes piled up beside his wardrobe, the pile which now concealed the hamper. Aunt Hester would certainly have had something to say about such a mess, but Uncle Frank probably wouldn't notice it. Marcus felt confident it could remain there until he got back from school tomorrow. He put his head close to the pile, but all was quiet. He continued getting ready for bed, and when he came back from the bathroom, slipped under his duvet to try and read a page or two of his book before turning off his light. He heard Uncle Frank clattering about in the kitchen, and listened to his heavy tread up the stairs. His bedroom door was pushed ajar, and the last thing he heard was a whispered 'Goodnight, Marky.'

* * *

Marcus . . . Mar . . . cus . . . the voice was sweet, persuasive. Marcus struggled to block it out, but it was impossible. Just as it was impossible to resist looking into the face that hovered in the middle distance, glowing against the darker background. Even though he knew it was safe to look at her in a dream, he still felt a rising terror as the approaching light sharpened into the Gorgon's head.

Marcus . . . brave, foolish boy . . . Medusa was smiling at him, but with her mouth turned down to suggest disappointment.

He was caught off-guard. He'd assumed that the next time the Gorgon spoke to him she would have been furious, but her tone was sorrowful rather than angry. She looked at him with large eyes. He began to feel uneasy, guilty, even.

Yes, Marcus: you plan to cast me off – cast me off, like all the rest – like everyone I've ever known. Rejected, cast out – that is my fate. That is the fate the Gods decreed. But I forgive you.

There was a pause to let this sink in. Forgiveness? From the Gorgon?

Marcus began to feel uncomfortable. But he had to stay firm. He had to get her out of his life – for ever.

269

I know that's how you feel, Marcus. I have helped you release the one you love: Yes, love, Marcus. Even though it takes me to make you acknowledge it. And why not? She is a lovely girl – though only a girl . . .

Marcus felt a charge of emotion run through him. It was mainly fear – fear at the ease with which the Gorgon could get into his mind. But behind the fear, there was a spark of something else, a hint of elation. He had battled for Hannah, he had released her and her family from Mr Darke's clutches. And beyond that, he had to admit that what he felt for Hannah was something more than friendship.

The thin lips moved again: *Oh yes, Marcus. The heart is my domain. You can have no secrets from me. And so I know you want me gone. I understand. But what you don't know is how much more help I could give you, if only you would let me – with the mysteries of your own life, Marcus.*

There was another pause. Marcus wondered what she could mean.

I mean, Marcus, that though I am happy to help you help those you love, I really want to help you.

This must be a trap, he told himself – an attempt to win him over, cause him to change his mind.

How suspicious you are, Marcus. But that's good –

good that you ask questions. Here's a question for you, Marcus – or perhaps for your uncle: who killed your mother?

What did she mean? Marcus was suddenly agitated. No one killed Mum: she died in an accident.

Medusa pounced on the thought. *She was killed, Marcus. It might have been an accident, but harm was done – terrible harm – to her – to your father – to you. And where there is harm there is blame . . .*

And where there is blame there must be punishment, I know, thought Marcus. But no one had ever mentioned there being someone to blame.

That may be, Marcus, but have you ever asked? Of course not. Ask now, Marcus. Ask your uncle. After all, harm was done to him: he lost his sister. Ask him, Marcus, who killed his sister.

The question seemed to explode in his head. All through his life, his mother's death had been a fact: the central fact of his existence. But because it was a fact, it was never talked about, it was never revisited, it was never questioned – not in the way that Medusa was questioning it now. Yes, Marcus knew his mother had died in the car accident; yes he knew that his father had been exonerated of all blame.

271

So, Marcus, if your father was not to blame, who was?

Marcus's head spun with confusion, but this soon distilled into something else – an unfocused anger which seemed to have been bottled up for years and years.

Yes, Marcus. You are right to be angry, and you are right to ask who to direct your anger towards. Now I have asked the question you won't rest until you've had the answer, Marcus. And why would you not want that answer? To know your mother's killer – that is your destiny . . .

And then she was gone.

He cried out for her to stay, but all he heard was an echo of her last word, destiny, carried on the wind as he awoke.

Marcus burrowed into his pillow, trying to chase the dream. But the Gorgon had gone, leaving him to a succession of other dreams. In these he saw fleeting fragments of destruction – petrified groups, single figures frozen in stone, all with faces stricken with terror. And then, as a grand finale, came a longer, more coherent scene.

The hamper was at the foot of his bed, the lid slowly rising. The king cobra forced it right back, and there was the snake, with its darting eyes, the bold zigzag of its markings, and the magnificent hood which spread out from either side of its head. The head and the hood which slowly to and fro, like seaweed drawn this way and that by the current.

He wasn't frightened.

It seemed perfectly natural to be sitting up in bed watching a king cobra gently swaying barely a metre away. The cobra showed no sign of anger or hostility. If anything, it seemed positively friendly, almost domesticated.

This impression, Marcus suddenly realized, was greatly enhanced by the fact that the cobra had a pipe in its mouth. Again, that seemed perfectly natural – a pipe-smoking king cobra, nodding its head at him in the friendliest way possible.

Marcus was entranced, his eyes locked on this weird but wonderful sight. The more he gazed, the more he began to discern the snake's true features. The dark, beady eyes – which never left his – had something around them. Glasses! Wire-rimmed spectacles; and if you looked really closely at the cobra's hood, you could see that it actually formed two human ears. And below the smiling mouth, with its pipe stuck at a jaunty angle, there was a tie, a rather busy tie, certainly, with its zigzag pattern, but a tie nonetheless.

Marcus felt his pulse quicken. He wanted to say something, to ask for confirmation. But before he could he saw that the side catches of the picnic basket had been released and the front flap was beginning, very slowly, to drop.

He braced himself to meet Medusa's ruined face, but as the forehead was revealed, there was something about the skin there that surprised him. The graveyard green had gone, replaced by a much more natural colour. The texture of the skin there too had changed. It looked healthy, a little tanned, definitely human – and living. And the broad unblemished forehead led down to a pair of thin but handsome eyebrows.

Marcus wasn't interested in the rest of the face. All he could do was to gaze into the eyes – and these too had changed completely: in place of the dead eyeballs smouldering with an unquenchable lust for destruction, here were two living blue eyes, whose depths spoke only of love and compassion. Somehow Marcus felt as though he had known them all his life. He forced himself to break eye-contact and take in the whole face.

And as he did so, his heart contracted. It was as though a hand had reached inside his ribcage and squeezed it. He cried out in a bittersweet combination of pain and the greatest joy. Because there, instantly recognizable from the photo on the lounge mantelpiece; the photos in the photograph album; and the little scuffed passport photo he always carried in his wallet, was his mother, smiling at him.

Marcus kicked and clawed at his bedclothes in an attempt to reach her. He would have given anything to touch her, to kiss her, to claim her as his after all the years of loneliness and grief. And now there was his father, nodding and beckoning him, his pipe rising and falling in encouragement.

'Mum!' he shouted as he finally launched himself towards her.

And then he was falling.

He came to sitting on the bedroom floor. In the throes of his dream he'd flung himself out of bed. He just hoped he hadn't disturbed Uncle Frank.

The landing light didn't go on, and he heard nothing from the bedroom across the way, so he climbed back under his duvet, hoping that that was the last visitation of the night.

He fell asleep almost immediately; but it was not a peaceful sleep. Images kept floating through his head, each one more disturbing than the last. He seemed to be able to avoid seeing them in too much detail only by flying on to the next one.

It was a relief when Uncle Frank came in and drew the curtains the next morning.

His bad night obviously showed.

'Are you all right, Marky?' his uncle asked when they were both downstairs in the kitchen. 'You're looking peaky, as your aunt would say.'

'I'm all right, thanks.' Marcus toyed with some toast.

Uncle Frank looked at him over his cup of tea. 'I'm worried about you, lad. Is something bothering you? You seem to have the weight of the world on your shoulders.'

Without looking up, Marcus said: 'I want to know who killed Mum.'

CHAPTER 16

'Hello, Marcus.'
     'Hello, Rose.'

He forced a smile and asked: 'How's Hannah?'

'Strange. You know . . .' She tossed her head slightly.

'No, I don't know. Which is why I'm asking.'

Rose frowned.

'Well, she's a lot better than she was. Lots better. Her dad spoke to her yesterday.'

'Her dad's conscious again? What did he say?'

'Nothing much. Just "Hannah", I think she said. But she was pleased about it. She knows he's sorry.'

'Of course. That's brilliant.'

'She seems much better, actually. It's as if something has changed, suddenly. Though she's still very nervy.'

That made sense. Mr Darke had not gone round to the house yesterday demanding the latest impossible instalment, nor would he. But Hannah wasn't to know that. She would still be worrying that he could come knocking at any time.

'That's great, Rose. Really great.'

'No it's not. I mean, about – you know – you and Han.'

'What about us?'

'She's still mad at you, Marcus. I can tell. What I'm saying is, I wouldn't, you know, count on her coming back to you. I know it sounds harsh, but I don't want you to get hurt.'

Rose had moved closer to him now.

'Anyway, like I said the other day, you wouldn't need to be on your own for long.'

Here she put her hand playfully on his chest, right over his pocket with the stone butterfly in it.

'What's that?' she said as her fingers felt it through the material.

Marcus gently took her wrist and pulled her hand away.

'I know what it is, Marcus: it's your stone heart. That's what it is!'

She turned away with a dramatic sweep.

'Come on, Rose, don't be like that. You've been brilliant. You really have. And I'll never forget it.'

'Do you mean that, Marcus?' She swung round

and gave him what he could see was meant to be a winning smile.

'I do. And,' he added, 'there's one more thing you can do for me which would be the most helpful thing yet.'

'What is it?'

'Well, it's a way to stop Hannah worrying once and for all.'

'Really? You know what's been bothering her?'

'I think so, but I can't tell you. And now it's going to go away. And you are going to be part of making it go away.'

'Me?'

'Provided I can trust you.'

'Of course you can trust me, Marcus. You know you can.'

'What you have to do is put this' – here he produced the brown envelope from Mr Darke's office – 'in her bag. Can you do that?'

'What, when she's not looking?'

'That's right.'

'Not just give it to her?'

'No. I want it to be a surprise. She'll probably know it's from me, but I don't want you to just walk up and say, "This is for you, from Marcus".'

'Why not?'

'Rose. Just do it. All right?'

'All right, Marcus.'

'Thanks. You're a star.'

'Really?'

'I wouldn't say it if I didn't mean it.'

'Thanks, Marcus.' She grinned. But he was already walking away.

Marcus thought that perhaps he should try to resume an interest in his school work. His marks had been falling steadily and one or two teachers had commented about overdue homework. He didn't want Uncle Frank getting notes asking why his performance had dipped so badly. His uncle had made clear just how anxious he was at breakfast when Marcus had brought up his mother's killer. Uncle Frank had peered at him as though it were the weirdest question he could ever have asked.

'I wouldn't have thought this was the time to talk about Jilly,' he'd said.

Did he mean breakfast time wasn't right, or generally? Marcus wondered, but Uncle Frank was obviously in no mood to continue the conversation. He cleared his plate off the table, picked up his briefcase and left the house with a short goodbye, leaving Marcus to get himself ready and make his way to school.

'Marcus? Yes, you at the back.' Mr Edwards was giving him one of those quizzical teacherly smiles that indicates you've been caught out. 'I know it's a warm day,' he went on, 'and because of that some people may not be following as closely as I'd like. So, just for those people, Marcus, I'd very much like you to repeat the five major causes of the Great War that we've been talking about for the last ten minutes.'

Marcus opened his mouth, but managed only a vague gulping noise. This was soon drowned out by the rest of the class's laughter.

'Thank you everyone, that's enough. I think I have made my point, Marcus. Stay behind at the end of the lesson and we can discuss your detention. Now, as I was saying, The Schlieffen Plan . . .'

It was hopeless. Marcus simply couldn't concentrate. He'd just have to work really hard to catch up when this was all over. But when would that be?

He looked up at the classroom clock. He was counting down the hours till Uncle Frank came home, wondering whether he would be any more forthcoming about his mother's accident. Because Medusa was right. Now she had raised the question, Marcus wanted an answer.

'They look far happier now, don't they?'

Rose had sidled up to him as he watched Hannah run to her mother's car.

'Did you get the envelope into her bag?' he asked.

'Of course I did,' Rose said. 'But I don't know whether she found it. We're not in the same classes after lunch.'

'Thanks anyway.'

'That's all right, Marcus. Walk me home?'

Marcus should have said OK. He had nothing else to do, and it would help fill the time before he could talk to Uncle Frank again.

But somehow he just wanted to be alone. He made some excuse about homework and said good-bye. He turned and looked back from the other side of the road outside the school. Rose was walking purposefully along the opposite pavement, her head up, staring straight ahead of her.

Damn, thought Marcus. *I shouldn't be so mean.*

He paid for it.

He was just approaching home when Mrs Prewle dashed out to intercept him.

'Marcus?'

Marcus could have kicked himself for not taking the back route, but he'd been so lost in his own thoughts.

Mrs Prewle was looking at him with a sort of eager desperation.

'I haven't had any calls about Decimal.'

'I'm sorry,' he said.

'It's not your fault. The posters you did are splendid – thank you.'

'Not a problem, Mrs Prewle.'

'By the way, how did your art project go? It sounded very interesting.'

What art project?

'With the squirrel and the mirror?' she prompted.

Oh, that art project.

'It was fine, thank you. They seemed to like it, though I haven't had the assessment yet.'

Actually, he'd been quite pleased with the way that had worked out. He had added to the tableau – a few sprigs from the garden to suggest a rural setting – and given it the title "Art: the Mirror to Nature". It was going to be in the school exhibition the week before half term, and he was confident it would get him a good mark. Every cloud . . .

'The things you children do these days. It wasn't like that when I was at school. Art meant studying the old masters and writing essays on them.'

Marcus couldn't think of anything to say in response, so he fished his house key out of his pocket as obviously as possible. But he wasn't going to get off as lightly as that, apparently.

'And how are you both? I see your uncle coming and going – and I've heard the noise he makes working on the patio. It must be nearly finished.'

'It is. Very nearly.'

'Well, I look forward to seeing it – perhaps when your aunt comes back. Have you heard when that's likely to be?'

Marcus shook his head. 'She seems to be having a good holiday,' he said, thinking another exchange of texts wouldn't go amiss. Should he have messaged Mrs Prewle, too? He pushed down a familiar, rising panic.

'I'm sure she is, especially if they're getting the same wonderful weather as we are,' Mrs Prewle said. 'Such a strange thing for her to do, though: just to up-sticks like that. Like Decimal.'

Marcus tried to keep his face blank.

'Well, I'm sure she didn't kidnap the cat and take him with her to Wales,' she added with a smile, and then went back up her little garden path, allowing Marcus to walk briskly up to his own front door.

Uncle Frank was tired when he got in, but the impatience he'd shown at breakfast had evaporated. Marcus met him in the hall, where his uncle dropped his briefcase and put his hands on Marcus's shoulders. 'I wish I knew what was up with you,' he said. 'You look all done in, lad. Do you think we should take you to the doctor?'

'No, I'm fine, Uncle Frank,' Marcus managed. But he found himself unable to hold his uncle's gaze.

'Well, that's for you to say; but if you asked me, I'd say you were either ailing or carrying some burden that's crushing the joy out of your life. But if you don't want to share it with me, that's up to you. You know I'm here if you need me.'

He released Marcus's shoulders, picked his up briefcase and went into the kitchen and put the kettle on.

Marcus followed him.

'I'm sorry – about this morning,' he said lamely.

'What about this morning?'

'Asking about Mum.'

Uncle Frank took off his jacket and loosened his tie as he made himself a tea.

When he'd done that he indicated the kitchen table and they both sat down.

'It's all right, lad. It just came a bit out of the blue – especially the way you put it.'

'But she was killed, wasn't she; and it wasn't Dad's fault?'

'No, it certainly wasn't. There was a suggestion that he wasn't used to English conditions, driving on the left-hand side and all that, because he was abroad so much, but every witness said he'd done nothing wrong. All the blame lay with the other driver.'

And where there's blame, there must be punishment.

'So who was the other driver?'

Uncle Frank sighed.

Marcus worried that he was going to become impatient again, but he was wrong.

'I always said we should tell you as soon as you were old enough to understand. But your aunt insisted there was no point in upsetting you, that you were settled now, so why would we stir it all up again when it wasn't necessary. I left it. But I was right – you are asking questions and, of course, it's only proper that you get some answers. It's just, coming at the present time, with your aunt' – he hesitated and a look of pain flashed across his face – 'with your aunt away, and my worrying about her, it caught me on the wrong foot, if I can put it that way.'

'I'm sorry, Uncle Frank.' Marcus might have added: *It's all right, I don't need to know now.* But he didn't say that. He couldn't.

'It's all right, lad. And maybe it's better talking about it while your aunt is away. Not that she'd tell you any different to me; but it's something she feels very strongly about. Not that I don't – of course I do. But I've been more successful in putting it behind me, I think it's fair to say. Your mum and dad were over in England for a break. They were travelling around, seeing lots of people, and they stopped with us for a couple of days. The accident was bad luck; pure bad luck. A bit of reckless, stupid driving, and bang, smash: I'd lost a sister and you'd lost your mum – just like that. Philip and you were damned lucky you weren't killed too. The other car came in on the passenger side, which was why Jilly died. Your dad climbed out of the wreckage with a few cuts and bruises . . . and you . . .'

Here he stopped. Marcus looked up and saw tears in his uncle's eyes.

'You were unharmed and, given what the car looked like, that was little short of a miracle.'

Uncle Frank suddenly got up and went to make another mug of tea. With his back to Marcus, he continued: 'It was terrible, of course. There was the funeral, and then the court case, and then everything else that needs to be done when someone dies. Philip and you stayed with us, although he sometimes had to go off and meet people about his work. But we were happy enough looking after you. You were a delight, a lovely little boy.

'Obviously your dad had to completely rethink his life, having you to look after on his own. But that's what he was going to do: he was absolutely committed to it. Only he really needed to get back and finish the job before the current dig came to an end. You only get a licence for a certain amount of time, you see, and the licence had nearly expired. There wasn't much time, and it was a once-in-a-lifetime opportunity. He looked into getting a nanny out there, but in the end we agreed it would be best if you stayed with us for the couple of months or whatever it would be so that he could go back without distractions.'

Uncle Frank sighed.

'We never saw him again.'

'What happened?'

Marcus knew that his father had disappeared abroad, but had never been told any of the details.

It turned out there weren't any.

'No one knows what happened. He just vanished. After a while it was assumed he'd died, though they never found him,' Uncle Frank said.

'He'd taken to working very late all on his own. They were excavating some temple, buried in the sands for two millennia, and the colleagues he was working with said they thought he was onto something, but he didn't say what it was. They said he was acting strangely, working obsessively. But they put it down to his loss and thought it was best to leave him be. Of course afterwards they realized that had been the wrong thing to do. But by then it was too late.'

Marcus stared at the kitchen table.

'So there were no clues?'

Uncle Frank shook his head.

'He could have been attacked, he could have wandered out into the desert and got lost in a sandstorm. We just don't know. It's a tragedy.'

He opened his hands, to show that that was all he had to offer.

'So within a few months you lost your mum' – (to

a reckless murderer, Marcus thought, though he didn't want to interrupt Frank's rare moment of openness) – 'and your dad.'

'You'd settled in with us, by that stage, and as there were no other family members in the frame we decided to bring you up ourselves.'

There was an uneasy pause.

'Hester obviously can't be a real mother to you, but she does her best. I know you don't always see eye to eye, but she's a good woman, and only wants what's right for you. We couldn't have children of our own – some couples just can't – and we'd accepted that. You aunt didn't have the happiest childhood herself; she was sort of settled in her own mind that she wouldn't have a family to look after, that it would just be the two of us. So you were a bit of a shock to the system. That's all.'

Uncle Frank took another gulp of tea.

'I'd been more disappointed about not having children than she had, so it worked better for me. I've loved having you. And not just for you, but because I see so much of Jilly in you.'

Marcus noticed his uncle's voice getting a bit croaky. He felt a lump forming in his own throat too.

'You've been brilliant, Uncle Frank. You both have.'

Uncle Frank pushed his chair back. The moment was over.

'Well, all this chat won't get supper on the table.'

'I'll help.'

'Good lad. Let's get some potatoes peeled.'

It was the best evening they'd had together for a long while. It had been good to clear the air, even if Marcus knew it had been very one-sided. Uncle Frank could tell him about the things that mattered to him; but he couldn't tell his uncle anything about Aunt Hester.

After supper, Uncle Frank went into the front room and Marcus heard him pulling open a drawer in Aunt Hester's bureau. He came back into the kitchen with a large brown envelope in his hand.

'Here,' he said. 'Press cuttings about the accident. I think they're pretty accurate, if a bit sensationalist.'

Marcus took them up to his room and sat at his desk with the envelope in his hands and thought of Medusa's words. Harm had been done, terrible harm, and who was to blame? He held the answer to the question in his hands. Slowly he opened the envelope and tipped the contents onto his desk. There wasn't much: a few letters relating to the court case – where and when it was to be held; a few notes in

291

what he recognized as Aunt Hester's handwriting; and some newspaper cuttings. These were yellow with the passage of time, and came from three newspapers – the local town paper, the countywide weekly and the county's daily tabloid.

WIFE OF VISITING ARCHEOLOGIST KILLED IN ACCIDENT, announced the local paper on its front page. Below the headline it said: HUSBAND AND THREE-YEAR-OLD SON SURVIVE. The weekly was similarly constrained, but the tabloid went with TODDLER'S MIRACLE ESCAPE FROM ACCIDENT CARNAGE!

The photos were pretty dramatic. The car had been shunted right across the road and had keeled over onto its side. It did look as though he and his father had had a miraculous escape. Looking at the pictures Marcus couldn't relate them to the accident he'd experienced from inside the car. He couldn't remember it accurately, but the sensations were vivid still. There was the squeal of tyres, and his mother's scream – the only memory of her voice that he had. And then there was the terrible collision, followed by the world flipping upside down. When it gradually all stopped spinning, there was silence and the smell of scorched metal and spilled petrol. Suspended the wrong way from his seat in the back, he had been vaguely aware of his mother's body hanging like a rag doll from her seat belt.

The silence hadn't lasted long. Soon the air was filled with shouting and sirens, and the shattering of glass as strong hands reached in to rescue him. There were policemen, and paramedics, and the *nee-naw* helter-skelter ride in the ambulance up the hill to the hospital, with his mother on a stretcher and his father holding her hand and leaning over her.

Although the breaking story had presented the newspapers with sensational front pages, it was the account of the court case that was most revealing.

Local man, Barry Ambrose, 24, ran a red light at Waverley junction and collided with a hire car driven by archaeologist Dr Philip Waldrist. Dr Waldrist's wife, Jilly, was pronounced dead on arrival at the Hopefield Hospital. Dr Waldrist suffered abrasions and shock, and the couple's three-and-a-half-year-old son miraculously survived unscathed.

Police said that Mr Ambrose, who himself escaped with minor injuries, had been drinking and had more than twice the legal limit of alcohol in his blood when breathalysed. The hearing continues.

The papers eked out more column inches the

following week, though they were confined to the inside pages by this stage. Mr Ambrose pleaded guilty and was sent to prison for what seemed to Marcus a very short time.

He looked from the cuttings to the photo of his mum and dad in its frame on his desk. It was taken against a backdrop of a sparkling blue sea, and breathed the freedom and adventure of the lifestyle they had chosen. His dad was dark and handsome, his arm round his wife's shoulder. In his other hand he held his pipe. As for Marcus's mum: she was beautiful, her hair slightly blowy in the sea breeze, her face lit by a warm smile as she looked up at his dad.

They didn't deserve to die. He didn't deserve to lose them. And the few months Mr Ambrose served in prison – how could you call that justice? It couldn't possibly weigh against the harm he had done. But now, with the power he had waiting to be unleashed in the cellar, Marcus could put that right. *There was blame* – Mr Ambrose had even admitted he was guilty – *so now there must be punishment*.

CHAPTER 17

Hannah was at school the next morning. Something about her – the way she moved, having a laugh with those around her – showed that she had found the envelope Rose had put in her bag. She was unburdened. The shadow had lifted. But she still showed no sign of being pleased to see Marcus, and made no move to approach or thank him. She must have known he was behind getting Mr Darke off their backs, even if she could have no idea how he managed it. Instead, she stared uncomfortably at him, as though looking at him for the first time and wondering who he was. Marcus was relieved when she turned away, back to her group, and walked off with his hands in his pockets. Whatever thanks he got for it, he'd done what he had done and wasn't sorry for it. He was now concentrating on what he was going to do next, and for that he needed Digger's mobile phone again – and Mr Darke.

Mr Darke was anything but pleased to hear from him.

'You've surely plagued me enough, young man. You've nigh-on ruined me. I can't see what's left for you to take.'

Marcus said: 'I don't want to take anything from you. I need you to do something for me.'

When Mr Darke tried to wriggle out of it, following Marcus's explanation, Marcus used his best tool of persuasion. 'But tracking people down is what you do, isn't it? And now you've got a bit of time on your hands . . . I can't see what the problem is. Do you want me to come round to your office again?'

'No: once was quite enough, thank you. Who is this Mr Ambrose, and how has he reached the top of your Most Wanted list?'

'Just find him,' Marcus said. His head thumped, but he felt a thrilling, dangerous resolve. 'And if he's still living in the town, text his address to me on this number.'

Then he rang off.

Hannah wasn't at orchestra in the morning. Marcus struggled on alone.

'Do we know when Hannah will be rejoining us,

Marcus . . . ?' Mr Bishop posed the question after a particularly reedy little interlude from his lone clarinet, which had set off a wave of sniggers among the violins.

Marcus shook his head. 'But her dad's regained consciousness.'

'That's very good news. Hopefully that will speed up a return to normality. We are going to need her back soon. I went to a lot of trouble to find a piece for *two* clarinets.'

He turned a page of the score with a flourish and raised his baton again. Marcus watched the hands of the hall clock creep on towards the hour.

'Baked potatoes all right?' Uncle Frank stuck his head out of the kitchen when he heard Marcus come in. 'How was orchestra?'

'Fine,' Marcus said unenthusiastically.

'What's the matter?'

'We haven't got much time before the concert, and there's a new piece – and without Hannah . . .' He shrugged unhappily.

'Don't worry about Hannah, she'll pick it up in no time. You just have to concentrate on your part. You're good enough. Your only trouble is you don't believe in yourself.'

Marcus shook his head. It was kind of Uncle Frank to try to cheer him up, but it wasn't working.

He took his clarinet upstairs to his room. The day was beginning to feel oppressive. There was nothing to do, but lots and lots of time to think. This was a very bad combination.

He stared at himself in the bathroom mirror. Could he really be going to set out on another revenge mission? It seemed madness, especially after the close shave with Mr Darke. Marcus only meant to persuade him, but the little man could have killed him. What if Mr Ambrose was a muscle-bound six-footer? But then the thought of Mr Ambrose – long released from prison – simply getting on with his life, as though the accident had never happened, made him angry. He deserved to be punished. And Marcus was going to see that he was.

Marcus . . . Mar . . . cus.

Medusa was there again, her face hanging like a sallow moon in the drab dark of the cave where she held her audiences.

You see? She was killed. Your mother's life was taken, so the taker's life is forfeit. You have chosen well, Marcus. Use me one last time. I will be the instrument of your revenge, and I will guide you. You will let me guide you, won't you Marcus? Let me help you find the peace that comes when a wrong is wiped away – by justice: true justice.

The ghastly face was split by a thin smile.

What do you say, Marcus? Shall we work together? Say you will, Marcus . . . I will not let you down, Marcus . . . Mar . . . cus . . .

Marcus struggled to respond. He was drawn to her, to her power, to her implacable purpose. There were no half-measures with her. Again, his head banged as he tried to push his thoughts above the sound of her voice. Where there is blame . . .

Yes, Marcus, yes! You have learned well.

Medusa's eyes gleamed with a tarnished conviction.

I may seem cruel, Marcus. But life is cruel. You have experienced its cruelty, just as I have – I, who was punished by the goddess Minerva, punished so harshly that I became a terror to the world. And I have punished in my turn, without hesitation, without mercy. I was made a rod for mankind's back, and I have not stinted.

He felt awed, flattered even, to think that she was putting her power at his disposal – to right a private, insignificant wrong.

No wrong is insignificant, Marcus. Certainly not yours. Just let me lead you, Marcus, and we will taste the greatest vintage – revenge.

How could he refuse?

You cannot, Marcus; you cannot.

With that, the glow that lit her face began to dim, and gradually she faded back into the darkness, leaving Marcus with his usual nightmares.

Sunday was dreadful, as only Sundays can be. The weather stayed bleak, church was boring, and Mrs Prewle insisted on escorting them there and back as though they were prisoners on parade. There were more pointed questions about how long Aunt Hester was going to be away, and a noticeable amount of nodding and staring on the part of other members of the congregation.

'God is working His purpose out as year succeeds to year,' they sang. Marcus thought the timescale unrealistic. He had to work his purpose out straight away, possibly even tomorrow. He wasn't sure it was compatible with God's, and tried a prayer apologizing in advance, though he soon gave it up as the hypocritical sham it was. Next to him, Uncle

Frank was as fervent as he had been the previous week, and behind them Mrs Prewle mouthed the responses as though leading an elocution class.

It was a relief to get home, but the Sunday routine lacked something. It seemed as though they were just going through the motions. Even their small pork roast turned out to be disappointing.

'Sorry, Marcus,' Uncle Frank said with a wan smile. 'Not my greatest attempt, I'm afraid.'

'It's all right.' Marcus had to stop his effortful chewing to say it, and shortly afterwards got a bit of rubbery crackling, which didn't crackle, horribly stuck in his teeth.

Uncle Frank cleared away with a sigh.

'I'm going to finish off the French windows, and then that's pretty well job done. And if we haven't heard by the middle of the week, I'm just going to ring and say it's finished. If she's mad at me, she's mad at me; but that can't be worse than not hearing a thing from her all this time.'

That set alarm bells ringing, but there was nothing Marcus could do about it. It was out of his hands. All he could hope was that he would have time to finish his mission before the day Uncle Frank discovered the awful truth. And for that he had to rely on Mr Darke.

He sat in his room, listening to the buzz and whine of Uncle Frank's drill downstairs, wondering how Mr Ambrose was spending what was likely to be his last Sunday. He looked at his homework schedule and groaned: geography, history and French. In the vain hope of finding something to distract him, he randomly pulled open drawers in his desk. Chewed biros, age-hardened rubbers, paperclips clustered around a magnet, the scratched lens of a magnifying glass . . . Why did he keep such rubbish? He rootled around, letting the useless objects tumble through his fingers.

And then he stopped. Under an old notebook with a rip across its cover, Marcus found an envelope. As he pulled it out, a very distant memory started to stir. His hair stood on end.

It was addressed to M. *Waldrist Esq.* . . . and the handwriting was the same as that on the label of the box containing the Gorgon's head. His father's.

He sat staring at it. How could he not have recognized it when he saw it the other day? He pulled out the postcard inside the envelope. It showed a great ruined temple set in desert sands, and on the other side there was a simple message:

My dear Marcus,

Daddy thinks about you every day and will be home to see you very soon.

All the love in the world.

Marcus would have been far too young to read it for himself, maybe too young even to understand it when Uncle Frank or Aunt Hester read it to him. But he had kept it ever since, even though he hadn't looked at it for years. What connection could there be between the Gorgon's head and his father? Marcus sat staring at the short message, a message of love and hope. There was surely no way it could be associated with the horrors in the cellar. And yet there somehow had to be a link. Staring at the postcard was like staring at a stone wall and expecting it suddenly to split apart and let him through.

He put the card back in the drawer and willed himself to get through the remainder of the day on autopilot.

Monday morning was rainy and windy, making the walk to school even less appealing than usual. Although school was better than moping around at home, it didn't lift Marcus's spirits much. At break he went and sat in the 'office'. For a while, he gazed at the cracks in the wall, wondering when – if – Hannah would ever speak to him again. Why didn't he have any other friends? He was now estranged from the only two people he was close to in the whole world. He felt resentful about Hannah – after all he'd done for her – and he felt guilty about Uncle Frank. How great it would be to have a mate he could go and kick a football around the park with.

He heard a key in the lock, and the door opened.

Although Mr Jarrold had told him it was fine for him to use the room, Marcus still stood up when he came in. The caretaker wasn't having the best of Monday mornings either, apparently. He was carrying two toilet seats. 'Bloody little 'ooligans,' he said as he threw them down on the floor.

Marcus saw they were both cracked.

''Ow do you do that to a toilet seat?' Mr Jarrold pointed at them. 'Not with your backside, that's for sure!'

The caretaker shook his head as the bell went.

'And now I've got to spend the next hour on my knees fitting new ones. If you happen to find out who did it, I'd be more than grateful for a name or two,' Mr Jarrold said gruffly as Marcus eased past him.

He nodded and joined the tide of pupils in the main corridor.

There was no way he could concentrate on lessons. All he wanted was to hear from Mr Darke via Digger. Then all the wearisome waiting would be over, and he could swing into action. He felt a buzz of excitement at the thought.

He saw Hannah again in the distance. This time he decided to walk over to her. After all, if things went spectacularly badly this might be his last chance to speak to her, ever.

'Hello, Hannah,' he said, aware that the girls around her, Rose included, had stopped talking and were watching as though this was the key scene in a play.

'Hello, yourself,' Hannah said. What was it about her voice? Marcus wondered. It didn't sound hostile; but it didn't sound particularly friendly either. Just neutral. Which was more unsettling than outright anger would have been.

'How's your dad?'

'Better, thanks. He's sitting up and talking now.'

'I'm really pleased.' Marcus took a step forward,

hoping to coax Hannah into leaving the group so they could talk alone. But she stood her ground, waiting patiently, politely even, to see if he had anything else to say.

'How's your mum?'

'She's fine, thanks.'

There was an upbeat note to that, he thought, and maybe a wider expression of gratitude, an acknowledgement that he had been responsible for freeing them from George and Mr Darke.

'Great,' he said. Out of the corner of his eye he saw two of the onlooking girls catching each other's eye. His embarrassment was proving entertaining.

He was struggling to think of anything else to say. 'I didn't know you had an uncle who died young in a motorbike accident. I'm sorry', clearly wasn't a possibility, but looking at Hannah as she stood demurely in front of him, he did begin to wonder if he had only imagined that they were close friends.

And then Hannah did speak.

'How's it going with you, Marcus?'

'Fine,' he said. But it came out half-strangled. He had so much going on in his life, so much terrifying stuff which was too dreadful to tell to anybody – certainly not Hannah, not on school premises in front of an audience of half a dozen girls who would spread even the tiniest titbit of gossip around the entire school by the last bell of the day.

'I'm glad,' said Hannah. But the penetrating look she gave him made it obvious she wasn't remotely fooled. It seemed as though she knew intuitively that his life was in meltdown, but there was nothing she could do for him unless he let her into his terrible secret. Which, of course, he never could. She'd be horrified with him.

'See you,' he said, putting on as brave a face as he could.

Walking away he definitely heard an ill-supressed laugh, and another girl going: '*Shhhh!*'

He felt the tips of his ears burning, and the look he gave to a couple of loitering Year Sevens made them give him a very wide berth as he walked fast across the yard.

Fortunately he was distracted by Digger jogging across to him.

He gave Marcus his lopsided psychopath's grin and thrust his bony thumb in the air to show he'd got the text from Mr Darke.

They found a conveniently private spot and Digger proudly held out his mobile.

'Just got it,' he said.

'Let's see.' Marcus took the phone from him and looked at the screen.

24 Crackendale Close. Two numbers and a few simple letters.

Marcus feasted his eyes on them.

''Oo lives there, then?' Digger asked.

'Doesn't matter,' Marcus replied.

'D'you want me to reply?'

'No. Thanks.'

'So that's it? Done and dusted?'

'Done and dusted,' Marcus confirmed, his face set like stone.

For the first time in days Marcus didn't wait to see Hannah being picked up by her mum. He was impatient to find out where Crackendale Close was, and that was the first thing he did when he got home. He fished a map out of a drawer in the kitchen and spread it on the table. It took him a while to find it, but eventually he put a triumphant finger on the spot. It was on one of the relatively new estates on the other side of town.

Like their street, Crackendale Close backed on to the railway line. In fact, it was probably only a couple of miles up the track. Marcus had vague memories, from one of the very few train journeys he'd ever been on, of a steep bank leading up to the new houses. Aunt Hester had made some disparaging remark about 'little boxes', and Uncle Frank had said something about people probably saying the same thing about the houses on Brunel Street when they were first built.

He forgot, now, where they had been going – a rare trip to a museum in London, perhaps. He couldn't have guessed how close they were passing to the home of the man who was responsible for throwing them together in the first place.

Marcus stared at the map for a while, working out his best route. Then he folded it up and put it in his pocket. There was a lot to do, including writing another letter to Uncle Frank in case anything went wrong and he didn't make it home.

He set out the whole story as simply as he could, and finished with a lengthy apology. It was the best he could do. Uncle Frank wouldn't believe a word of it – until he walked down to the embankment just to check the impossible was impossible. And at least that way, when the police called to say that Marcus had been found turned into a statue, his uncle would know he wasn't the victim of some bizarre hoax.

After he'd finished the letter, Marcus decided he would take a final look at Aunt Hester. He wasn't sure why. A gesture of respect perhaps, and to remind himself of the power at his disposal, of the utter finality of stone. He pushed through the broken gate and kicked through the undergrowth to the great mound of brambles where he had dumped her. Even from a few yards away he could see her legs sticking out. As he approached, he made out a latticework of snail- or slug-trails over his aunt's stumpy calves. There was bird poo on her back and several spiders' webs reaching from her outstretched hands across to her waist. What a sad and shameful end, he thought as he surveyed her indestructible remains. He wanted to apologize, but how could you say sorry to a block of stone? A corpse, even a badly damaged one lying in the morgue, would be enough of the real person to say a few words to. But there was nothing he could say to Aunt Hester's stone back.

He retraced his steps up the garden, admiring Uncle Frank's work on the patio and French windows. It really was finished now, with just a few bags of rubbish waiting to be shifted to the recycling depot. All ready for Aunt Hester to admire when she came back.

Poor Uncle Frank. There was nothing Marcus could do for him. Now he had to steel himself for one last, monumental effort. He couldn't afford to be distracted by feeling sorry for anyone, not even his uncle. Perseus had unleashed the power of the Gorgon without pity or mercy – and so would he.

That night the Gorgon dominated his dreams again.

Ah, Perseus, dear Perseus . . . You remind me of him, Marcus, you do. Of course, you're only a boy, and he was – well – the son of Zeus, a demigod, a hero, sweeping towards me through the sky, with wings on his sandals . . . I had such hopes for him, Marcus: such a valiant figure, flying over mountains and seas, to me . . . to me . . . to save me from my dull existence sitting at the entrance to the underworld with those crones. Oh what hope I had for him, what expectations . . . For why would he be winging his way to me, if not for love; if not to fill the void in my heart, after all my suitors turned to statues? Not one of them had the brains to win me round. No: they were all fools. Enter, sweeping bow, one shy peep – and that was that. Another statue for the gallery.

But Perseus had brains, Marcus. He had his polished shield; he had his hovering heels. I smiled at him; I welcomed him. I thought that we could make a match: the two of us against the world, righting wrongs and wreaking vengeance. And as I smiled, I closed my eyes. I trusted him, Marcus. I thought we understood one another.

Here Medusa led her eyelids fall, and her lips pushed forward slightly in a wistful pout. Then her eyes opened, and her mouth dropped.

You know the story, everybody knows my story – but you cannot imagine my surprise, Marcus. Instead of a kiss – yes, a kiss: I was inviting him to kiss me, unscathed. But instead of a kiss, instead of the warmth of human fingers on my neck, Marcus, I felt the touch of steel.

Oh what a blow that was – a double blow. The pain of the blade was nothing to the pain of his betrayal and the anger I felt at falling for his trickery.

Playing with my heart, Marcus, he had deceived me. And all for love. Oh, yes, his whole insane quest was all for love – not for love of me, alas, but for his mother, held by that ogre of a king who kept her captive, just waiting for the news I'd killed Perseus so he could force her into marriage.

Which is perhaps why you remind me of him, Marcus: because you have brains, you have tamed me, you have bent my power to your will – in service of the ones you love: the girl, and now your poor innocent mother whose death you must avenge. And you will, Marcus. With my help, which I freely give, you will succeed. You will succeed . . . We will succeed together . . .

The Gorgon's face slowly faded. Marcus was back in a place he knew, and there at the end of the bed was the picnic hamper. Slowly the lid lifted, and the king cobra writhed into sight. This time, instead of sporting a pipe, its mouth was clamped around a clarinet. And as it moved it played – a horrible, squeaky tune, slow and mesmeric.

The front flap started to descend. Marcus tried to turn away, but it was no use, he had lost all power to move. The first snakes appeared, all writhing in time to the cobra's ghastly tune. Marcus steeled himself for the face below, but as the flap dropped steadily down, he did not see the forehead he expected, but a strange, brown, leathery shape. Then, as the flap finally descended, all was revealed.

Marcus found himself staring at Aunt Hester's handbag, suspended from the fangs of a dozen demented vipers.

Marcus felt beads of sweat forming along his hairline. He tried to draw up his legs to form some sort of barrier, but they might have been sawn off for all the response he got from them.

Gradually, the reedy wail increased in tempo. The cobra's head tilted with an increasing fury which was picked up by the swaying vipers below. The handbag was tugged around more and more violently. The snakes were buffeting it from both sides, and it was pummelled in and out like a bellows, or an accordion played by a maniac.

Stop it! he cried out in his head. *You'll rip it!*

He was too late. The strain on the handbag became too much, and it split down the middle like a grotesque Christmas cracker, scattering its contents all over the bed. Lip salve, paper hankies, keys, notes and cards cascaded out of the torn bag.

Marcus watched the avalanche of possessions, but his eyes were soon drawn back to the picnic basket. At first, where the Gorgon's face should have been, he could see only writhing tendrils of smoke. Gradually, out of the swirling darkness, a shape began to form, a shape now recognizable as a face, a face with craters for eyes, burning with molten intensity, and a great crevasse for a mouth, open like a furnace door.

The face became more familiar, even though he

fought against what he was seeing. But there was no putting off the moment of recognition. Aunt Hester stared at him, her eyes as severe, as reproachful, as judgemental, as they had ever been in life.

To Marcus's horror, he noticed that the face was getting bigger – closer. It was pulling away from its moorings in the picnic basket, straining to float free – with all the vipers still attached to it, writhing and reaching for him.

And the king cobra played on, increasing the tempo, increasing the volume, until Marcus could bear it no more. He had to cry out, to move, to make one last almighty effort to save himself, as the burning blackness yawned to envelop him.

His back arched as though he had been electrocuted, and he felt his legs kicking in a spasm that somehow threw him clear at the last second . . .

Awake, he lay in his pyjamas soaked with sweat. And yet he was shivering. He clutched himself for warmth and waited in a sort of numb trance till the light began to steal in under his bedroom curtains.

CHAPTER 18

This was the day. Marcus got ready for school, as usual. Except there was nothing usual about this particular day. On this particular day, he was planning to exact retribution. He was going to wipe the slate clean, and draw a line. After today it would be over. He would be able to move on with the rest of his life.

He walked to school thinking about it. He sat through lessons thinking about it. There was nothing else to think about. The plan was straightforward: he would take the Gorgon's head over to Crackendale Close and leave it at Mr Ambrose's door. Mr Ambrose would take it into his house and open it. And then Medusa would deliver her part of the bargain – as she always did. There was a part of him that wanted to confront Mr Ambrose face to face, to let him know about the family he had torn apart. But he knew that he couldn't. What if Mr Ambrose tried to argue his way out of it? Pleaded for mercy? Or turned aggressive? The fight with Mr Darke was still fresh in Marcus's mind. Anyway, the beauty of delivering the box and walking away was that it would limit his responsibility. Marcus would simply deposit the head and leave Mr Ambrose to his fate.

He had thought long and hard about how it should be delivered. The simplest way would be to take it in the hamper. But the hamper was distinctive, and people might remember it. There were already enough people who had seen it when he took it through the town to Mr Darke's office. Whereas a boy with a nondescript box should be able to travel round the back streets without anyone paying him much attention at all. The original box had been trashed by Aunt Hester's assault on it with the Stanley knife. Marcus would need to replace it. Still, the school must have dozens of boxes delivered to it every day containing everything from loo rolls to marker pens. He'd find one somewhere – or even ask Mr Jarrold.

At break he let himself into the 'office'. There, on a high shelf, was exactly what he was looking for. It contained a few old cleaning products and a few rags that had dried hard through disuse. He couldn't imagine Mr Jarrold missing it. He put it back on the shelf. It would do.

At lunch time he saw Hannah, keeping her usual distance, but he knew there was no point in approaching her, and indeed, the minute she saw that Marcus had seen her, she melted away into the crowd.

Two lessons left.

Some early spring sunshine broke through the clouds and bathed the back row of the French class. It was pleasantly warm again, and if you closed your eyes you could almost imagine you were in France, as Miss Springfield went through a typical French menu which she'd written up on the whiteboard.

But Marcus was incapable of concentrating on the *plat du jour*. All he could think about was getting home, getting the Gorgon's head out of the picnic basket and into the box, getting it over to Crackendale Close, and getting home again in time for tea. He had about three hours, which had been long enough – just – to sort out Mr Darke and George. But although he had time, there were still a lot of things that had to go right. His main worry was transferring the Gorgon's head from the basket into the box. Just thinking about it made his palms go sweaty.

'*Et Marcus, attendez-vous?*'

Miss Springfield was asking everybody what they wanted to order.

With a panicky reference to the whiteboard, Marcus stammered out: '*les frites et . . . les languoustines,*' which made everyone laugh, though he couldn't see why.

'*Merci,* Marcus,' Miss Springfield said in her singsong voice. '*Et puis?*'

Marcus felt himself blushing, but managed to mutter '*Fromage . . . s'il vous plait.*'

There was more laughter, but mercifully Miss Springfield didn't prolong the agony, passing on to ask someone else what they would like for lunch.

Eventually the bell went, its high, metallic drilling noise sounding an ominous summons.

If going to school in the morning had been weird, walking home felt even stranger. Marcus couldn't help thinking that everyone he passed would notice his rucksack bulging with the cardboard box he'd emptied and flattened in Mr Jarrold's cubbyhole. He was convinced people were looking at him suspiciously. He told himself he was being paranoid, but still had to fight the urge to look over his shoulder at regular intervals. He deliberately walked past Mrs Prewle's house to get home. For once he did want her to notice him. She would provide his alibi, should he need one.

He let himself in, and stood for a moment with his hand on the door. The house felt cool – almost cold – and the silence seemed to gather in the hallway. He could feel the sweat running down inside his shirt, and shivered. But there wasn't time to let fear over-take him. He had to get on. Quickly, he ran upstairs to his room and changed.

He had decided to transfer the Gorgon's head in the dining room. The wall mirror would again be a help. He had to be sure that he didn't fall victim to his own lethal weapon on the last occasion he used it.

The dining-room table had been moved back to its proper place in the middle of the room – nearer the wall mirror. There were still dust sheets folded up in a corner and Marcus shook one out and spread it out to protect the table top. Then he got to work on the box.

He taped the two sides, but left the front open. Like the first time, he would use Uncle Frank's spade to transfer the head from the basket to the box. It was the single most dangerous thing he had to do, and he was dreading it. He felt for the stone butterfly. It reminded him of the power he had at his disposal. It made him feel invincible. Then he fetched the spade and went through a Gorgon-less rehearsal. Doing everything the wrong way round in the mirror was awkward, and with one ill-judged stab of the spade, he knocked the box onto the floor. In his frustration, he looked round. *Dead. Stone dead. That's what you'll be if you do that when the flap is down,* he told himself. Spill the Gorgon's head and he could forget about delivering it to Crackendale Close. He tried again, and again. How long could you practise something before you knew you could get it right? The clock on the mantelpiece reminded him he couldn't put it off for ever. Ready or not, he had to do it now.

For the last time, Marcus went down the basement stairs. For the last time he stood in front of the pile of junk that hid the picnic basket. And for the last time he stared at it, an old, slightly quaint, relic from the past – the sort of thing you'd see in the window of a junk shop, or as a prop in a period drama on TV. Only he knew what explosive horrors it contained.

He leaned over to grasp the shoulder strap. Normally when he picked up the basket, the snakes began to stir, their movements setting up a hateful vibration which made carrying it like transporting a hive of bees. Very angry bees. But this time there was nothing – no movement, no sound. It was so eerie that Marcus put his head to the basket to listen. Still nothing. Except . . . very faintly, almost the echo of an echo, the distant whispering of that desert wind he'd heard so many times in his dreams.

The cellar suddenly seemed very small – a horrible place to be trapped with a cargo of malice from the ancient world. He clamped the basket to his side and stumbled up the wooden stairs to the hall.

Marcus put the hamper on the dining-room table and placed the box on a chair at what he hoped would be the right angle. He rested the spade on the table and looked at the hamper in the mirror. And then, with trembling fingers, he undid the latches. He whipped his hands away, expecting the lid to burst open as usual, the king cobra sticking up like a periscope to see what was happening. But this time there was nothing.

Gingerly Marcus flicked back the lid himself. The snakes were still there, but they remained nestled down, with the cobra lying prominently at the top.

The front of the hamper fell.

Marcus looked in the wall mirror.

Good day, Marcus.

There was Medusa, smiling at him calmly.

I'm so glad you have stayed faithful to your vision, Marcus.

Again the voice was in his head, Medusa moving her lips in time with the words like a pop star on a music video.

The voice was friendly, as if designed to soothe away his doubts.

Then her eyes swivelled and she caught side of the spade.

Oh, Marcus. No. No, no, no – please not that horrible instrument. It's bad enough having one's neck cut without being reminded of it by being shovelled around like something horrid on a farm. Could we not, please, try something a little more civilized?

Via the wall mirror, Marcus looked her in the eye. What could she mean?

I mean, she answered him, *the proper way. Lift me as Perseus did – by my hair.*

Here the snakes that were her hair writhed slightly. There was no way he was going to plunge his hand in amongst them.

Trust me, Marcus . . . trust me.

She smiled winningly.

Fetch the gauntlet then, she said when she saw he still doubted her.

Marcus looked across to the big leather glove by the fireplace.

Go on. You must have courage, Marcus. You have shown bravery – extraordinary bravery – already. This is a new challenge, but one that will give you such confidence, such pride. You will feel as Perseus did – you will feel like a conqueror!

Under the pressure of that intense stare, Marcus moved across to the fireplace and picked up the gauntlet. Once he'd slipped it on, he reversed towards the table, always keeping his eye on the wall mirror.

Oh, Marcus. Can I not win your trust? Perhaps when you have me in your grasp you'll feel differently. Come, take the plunge and pull me up. I want to see you in the hero's role, like Perseus at the tyrant king's court. Oh how we blazed forth then – rank after rank of courtiers caught in their last pose, the gasps and cries choked in their throats. Help me relive my finest hour, Marcus!

There was such vehemence in her voice, such command in her eyes, that he obeyed. Hardly daring to think what he was doing, he thrust the gauntlet down among the snakes.

What had he expected? A stab of fangs through the leather?

No such thing. Instead his fingers folded round what felt like a couple of snake necks, and then he pulled.

The head was heavy, but it lifted easily out of the hamper and hung in mid-air at the end of his arm.

And Medusa was right: although he had never been more frightened in his entire life, he had also never felt more alive, more elated. There he stood in the mirror just like Perseus in so many of the pictures he'd seen on the internet – their two heads on a level, the Gorgon's at the end of his outstretched arm.

Yes, Marcus; yes. You see . . . you really are a hero. For all your tender years, you hold in your hand more power than any but the chosen few have ever been given to wield. Let us go closer, Marcus; take us closer to the mirror.

Marcus shuffled forward. It was extraordinary having her at the end of his arm, looming on his peripheral vision. Although he was concentrating on keeping his eyes locked onto the glass, the presence of the real Medusa – right there, so close – was an almost irresistible pull, tidal in its strength.

Her face became more animated.

You are a handsome boy, Marcus. And what will you become – a suitor fit for the greatest beauty in the world? Oh yes, Marcus, you're quite a man – just like your father.

Marcus nearly cricked his neck jolting it back from its instinctive lurch to the right.

Your father, Marcus. Yes. He found me. Haven't you worked that out yet? That's why I'm here. He sent me.

He hadn't wanted it to be true. 'What happened?'

He came looking for me. He knew he'd find me. Tap-tapping, night and day. He had worked out where I was. Clever, Marcus. Like you.

'But I don't understand. If he found you, how come you didn't . . . ?' Marcus couldn't bring himself to say it.

I was in disguise, Marcus.

'In disguise as what?'

Myself, Marcus, as myself! Look:

And there in the mirror her face stilled, the eyes lost their penetrating power; the mouth was set in a carved grimace. He was looking at the stone image of the Gorgon which he had seen in his dreams. And then, just as quickly, the process reversed, and Medusa was smiling at him once again.

He was looking for an archaeological treasure, Marcus. Which he found. I could study him, as he chipped me out, as he brushed the grains of ancient dust from my eyes. And such a man of sorrow I never saw, Marcus, not in hundreds of years. I pitied him; I suffered with him, and I burned with rage for him. For he had loved. I knew. I knew the secrets of his heart. I watched him writing in his notebooks night after night by the light of his little lamp; and I could read him more easily than the written word.

Marcus was trembling. His arm was aching. This was unbelievable. And yet . . .

'How did he send you to me?' he suddenly blurted out. 'And why did it take so long? And what happened to him?'

He was going to smuggle me out under the guise of a present to you. Each night he chipped my stone head out of the temple wall where it was set, telling none of his colleagues. I think he was obsessed with me, Marcus; I really think so. One night he came so close – as close as we are now, Marcus, as close as we are now. He stared into my eyes, my harmless stone eyes, and raised his finger to my cheek – not with a brush or a cloth, to wipe some grain of dust away, but simply to touch my once-lovely cheek, as he once touched your mother's. I have seen into many men's hearts, Marcus, and your father was pure, but passionate. A true lover. He came so close, I almost thought he was going to kiss me. But, of course, I was only stone to him − a trophy. Whereas to you, Marcus, I am so much more than that.

There was something so melodious, so mesmerizing in her voice; the weight of the head pulling down his arm was making it feel numb.

Marcus, dear boy, dear heroic boy, come closer. That's right, bend your arm a little, turn your head, yes, yes, like that, a little more. I'll close my eyes, and we can seal our partnership . . .

Marcus felt so drowsy, it was easier to do what she asked than to resist, and he was just about to turn his head completely, when a brisk rapping sound to his left made him snap out of it.

'Marcus!'

He swung round. Mrs Prewle was peering through a pane of the French windows.

Oh, no, what on earth could she want? was his first thought. His second was simply: *Oh, no,* for there, leaning forward at an awkward angle, her hand raised for a brisk tap she would never deliver, was a perfect statue of the retired librarian.

Suddenly everything changed. Marcus was shocked out of his trance. His first instinct was to throw the Gorgon's head away from him. But that would be to lose control over it, which could prove as fatal to him as it had to Mrs Prewle. Instead he shot his arm out as straight as it would go, keeping Medusa as far away from him as possible. The snakes started moving and hissing, doubtless reflecting the Gorgon's change of mood. He expected fangs to scrabble at the gauntlet at any moment, and immediately stepped backwards, avoiding eye contact in the mirror and concentrating only on the waiting box.

As the head approached it, the snakes became even more restless, but obviously the Gorgon's patience just prevailed over her temper; he was able to drop the head unceremoniously into its latest home.

Oh, Marcus, why so rough? A little more respect surely?

In answer, Marcus folded down the lid and taped it firmly shut. Then he flung up the front of the box and taped that in place too. He kept on taping, strip after strip, until he was sure the head was secure.

Then he rested, falling into one of the other dining-room chairs. He didn't dare look at the terrible form of Mrs Prewle at the French windows. He simply stared at the box on the chair, his skin crawling with fear and panic. He had been so close, *so* close to disaster.

All along Medusa had been messing with his mind. She was driving him mad. And now, with her latest flash of power, she had landed him in a situation from which there was no escape. He couldn't face trying to haul Mrs Prewle down the garden to rest in the brambles with Aunt Hester. He felt drained of energy, drained of willpower. At least the head was boxed up. He would just sit there until Uncle Frank came home. It was all beyond him now.

Nonsense, Marcus, nonsense. You mustn't let misplaced pity deprive you of the prize of justice.

'What justice did Mrs Prewle have?' He spoke listlessly out loud.

A foolish, interfering old fool, Medusa hissed in his head. *Always busying herself with other people's business. Well, she won't do that anymore. That was her fate, and who are you to challenge the gods' decisions? Who knows what lies hidden in her past? We must move on. We have our mission, Marcus. Come along.*

He looked at the spade. He wanted to pick it up and then smash it through the box, slicing through the snakes and battering the skull. There she was, boxed in, defenceless. If he went round behind the table, he wouldn't be in any danger. He could smash and smash and smash, until he had destroyed her.

But that would leave our work undone, Marcus. Surely you can see that. Look at your parents – here Marcus looked up at the photograph on the mantelpiece *– you're not going to fail them them are you, Marcus? All that happiness stolen; stolen from them, stolen from you . . . Harm was done: you're not going to let it go unpunished, are you, Marcus?*

The pressure built and built, until it was simply easier to give in. He imagined her staring dead eyes, wide open in the box's darkness, concentrating hard on his every spasm of thought, so that he could be channelled to her will.

Yes, Marcus, I know what you are thinking. But it is your mother we seek to avenge . . . your mother, Marcus. As your father would have wanted.

She was right. Even though the fact that she had been found by his father astonished and fascinated him, leaving so many questions unanswered, Marcus could feel the urgency of the situation. If he was to wreak revenge on Mr Ambrose, he had to act – now. He felt a bit like a robot being moved around by remote control. There were things that had to be done – though tidying up the dining room while Mrs Prewle stood stooped in stone at the French windows was pretty pointless. He did it anyway.

Once the hamper had been taken back to the cellar and the fire glove returned to its place beside the grate, there was just the ordinary-looking box, sitting on the chair. One Gorgon's head, ready for delivery. Now all he needed to do was write the label.

CHAPTER 19

Giving the stone butterfly in his shirt pocket a quick touch for luck, Marcus let himself out of the side gate and pushed his bike up Brunel Street.

Marcus decided he'd prefer to push his bike, with his deadly cargo secured in the not-quite-big-enough basket, rather than actually ride it. He was worried that the box might fall off onto the road if he got up any speed. He could ride like the wind once he'd made the delivery. He covered the box with his hoodie, but then felt exposed himself. He tried to act casually, but felt anything but relaxed. In addition to worrying about people remembering him, he was haunted by the suspicion that he was being followed. But every time he turned, the road behind was empty.

Nerves, he told himself.

Marcus pushed on up the hill, grimly focused on the pavement ahead of him.

He thought of Aunt Hester. He thought of George. He thought of Mrs Prewle's cat and now

Mrs Prewle herself. He thought of how close he himself had come to being turned into stone. He was determined that all the death, danger and fear was not going to go to waste.

Marcus pulled up at a corner to check the map. It wasn't far now: only a few more streets. He was near the crest of a hill, and would soon be wheeling his bike, with its terrible load, down towards Crackendale Close.

In the distance he heard the harsh wail of a train, heard the clatter of its wheels as it rushed down the track just below Mr Ambrose's street. Looking at his watch, he hurried on. Time was even tighter now he had the additional problem of Mrs Prewle to deal with. Other worries crowded his brain. What if Mr Ambrose wasn't in? What if his house didn't have any sort of front garden and his front door opened straight onto the street? And then there were the fears that he had been pushing to the back of his mind for weeks: what if he got caught? What if Mr Ambrose came to the door too quickly and made him come in and open the box with him?

The top of the hill provided a great vista of the town: the multi-storey car park, the big shops grouped in the middle, a church spire or two, the factory, blowing out its writhing plumes of steam. Everything just as quiet and ordinary as it always was.

The descent was steep, and Marcus had to keep a firm grip on his bike. Although he'd studied the route, he wasn't quite confident of the last part, and had to stop and look at the map again. There was a turning to the left, then a road to the right before the final turn into the close. A car was drawing up, and a man got out and went into one of the houses. He didn't give Marcus a second glance. All the same, Marcus felt conspicuous. A boy with a box in the basket of a bicycle. People might remember that when the police came calling to interview them. Something made him turn back and sneak a glance up the street behind him. Nothing – apart from a cat making its way unhurriedly across the road. There was so little noise Marcus could hear his bike wheels ticking as he pushed it along the pavement. He felt like a secret agent behind enemy lines, anonymous, undetected, invisible, yet only a moment away from being the focus of a whole community's fear and hatred. He felt his legs go jerky, and the handlebars suddenly swung out towards the road. He had to fight to keep the bike on the pavement. How could the simple task of wheeling a bicycle along a street have become so hard?

Then he was there.

Crackendale Close was a cul-de-sac: two terraces of houses facing each other with two more blocking off the end of the street. A footpath between them led to a bridge over the railway line.

He was pleased to see that the houses all had small front gardens, and that most had a porch like a sentry box, which would make the box less conspicuous.

The first house on his left was number 1. Next to it was number 3. That meant number 24 would be further down on the right. He stayed on the left-hand side of the road, pretending to be casual, pretending to be invisible. All he had to do was cross the road, put the box in the porch, ring the bell and then climb on his bicycle and ride home. He'd been through it a hundred times. But that didn't make it any easier in practice.

Number 24 was just like all the other houses, with a low wall running along the pavement and a little metal gate giving access to a short path up to the front door. The gate was even open, as though inviting him in. Marcus noted all this without stopping, and decided to push his bike on a bit further before crossing. He wheeled the bike round up to the end of the close. He could still swing his leg over and casually ride it down the path to the foot-bridge. But he didn't. Instead he set off back down the street on the side with even numbers: 38, 36, 34, 32, 30, 28, 26 – 24. This was it.

Marcus leaned his bike against the wall, flicked off the elasticated clasps holding the box in place and wound them loosely round the handlebars. He whisked the hoodie off the box and tied it rapidly round his waist to keep it out of the way. Then, with his heart thumping, he walked through the gateway to the porch with the box under his arm. There was no movement or sound from inside it. It was just a box, a very ordinary box, with nothing to hint at the horrors it contained.

Marcus placed the lethal delivery on the doorstep, took a deep breath and rang the bell. He then turned, hurried back to the bike and pushed it rapidly on up the street. He'd intended getting on it straight away and riding off at top speed. But he found he had to stay and see if Mr Ambrose came to the door. He had to know. He crossed over the road to a good vantage point, and turned to gaze at the door of number 24.

Two things happened, almost at the same time.

First, the door Marcus was staring at with such intensity opened and a man appeared. Marcus hadn't any idea of what Mr Ambrose might look like, but he turned out to be a very ordinary-looking man in his late thirties, who had obviously been disturbed whilst having a nap. His shirt hung out over his trousers, and he was wearing slippers. He had dark hair, and as he bent down to look at the box, Marcus could see the beginning of a bald patch on the crown of his head.

The second thing was that just as Mr Ambrose was bending down another figure appeared – Marcus wasn't sure quite where from, perhaps behind one of the wheelie bins. It was a small figure wearing a hoodie and it launched itself up number 24's path and seized the box from under Mr Ambrose's nose.

Mr Ambrose was caught completely off-guard, but as the figure shot back down the path to the pavement he gave a yell.

The figure took no notice but kept running away from number 24 towards the far end of the close. Marcus's astonishment turned to horror when he recognized the person in the hoodie.

'Hannah!' he shouted, leaping on his bike and setting off in hot pursuit. Even though he hadn't seen her face, he was sure it was her. He'd been right: there had been someone following him. How she'd found out, indeed what she'd found out, could be addressed later. Right now he had to catch her and get the box back.

Hannah was a fast runner and she had made the end of the close before Marcus picked up speed. As he reached the pathway, Marcus had to slow down because people walking up from town were getting in his way.

'Hannah, stop. You've got to stop!' he yelled. She made no sign of having heard him and kept sprinting, zigzagging between old women with bulging shopping bags and young mothers pushing buggies up the path.

What if Hannah tripped and dropped the box before he got to her? Sweat poured from his forehead, stinging his eyes. He saw the old man with the small dog just in time to swerve violently and avoid getting tangled in the lead.

'Hannah, please – stop!' he shouted. But she simply ran faster.

Hannah looked as though she were tiring. Marcus

put his head down for a final sprint to catch her. But when he looked up a couple of seconds later, she was gone. He glimpsed a gap in the fence running along-side the path as he went speeding past it, so jammed on his brakes and skidded to a halt.

A boy of about six looked up at him from over the mudguard of his bike, while the little boy's mother stood open-mouthed. Where had *they* come from? Marcus mouthed an apology and swung the bike round to cycle back to the hole in the fence. Then he had to abandon it: the ground was far too over-grown to ride over.

Hannah was finding it hard-going on foot, but she had still put a considerable distance between them. But, Marcus realized, she was trapped: the wasteland led down to the railway track, and resumed on the other side. There was nowhere for her to go.

'Hannah, please stop!' Marcus yelled, sprinting down the slope after her. 'You don't know what you've got there! It's dangerous . . . deadly!'

She stumbled.

Oh my God, Marcus thought. It was only a card-board box. There was no guarantee it would stay intact if it hit the ground. Fortunately Hannah righted herself without losing her grip on the box.

Marcus put on a sprinter's spurt. He had to stop her.

'Hannah – it's dangerous. You could die!'

For the first time, she turned her head. He could see her face, intense, angry.

'You should have thought of that before you started playing God.'

'Hannah – please. You don't know what it is.'

'Yes I do,' she shouted back.

'You can't,' he panted.

'But I do.'

They were both slowing down now, and by an unspoken agreement kept the distance between them while they talked.

'How?'

'Remember when we swapped log-in details?'

Marcus came to a complete halt, breathing hard.

Hannah also stopped. 'I went into your account and checked your search history. And that squirrel in your art exhibition? Where would you get something like that, Marcus?'

Marcus could see she wasn't bluffing. Her eyes blazed at him and her fingers tightened on the box.

'Well, if you're right,' Marcus took a step forward, 'you'll know how dangerous it is. Give it back.'

'Give it back – to you? After what you've done with it – after what you were intending to do with it?'

'But, Hannah – you don't understand.'

She let out a noise that was almost a laugh, but it didn't contain a jot of humour.

'And I don't want to. What did you do to Mr Darke? He handed the money back – and mum's rings – and tore up the loan agreement out of the goodness of his heart, did he? Don't make me laugh. You threatened him. You threatened to take his life, Marcus. Even though he is an evil, manipulative little scumbag, you can't do that.'

Her face was flushed, partly with the running, partly with rage. Marcus took a step forward. Hannah took a step backwards. She hadn't finished.

'And that man, that man you were going to leave this for.' She held up the box with a crazy jerk which made Marcus sweat. 'What had he done? What had he done to deserve the wrath of Marcus Waldrist, may I ask?'

'He killed my mum.'

To his surprise, Hannah took a step towards him. Then another. She was staring at him.

'You what?'

'That's right: he killed my mum. In the car crash. He was drunk.'

'And for that he deserves to die? Are you seriously telling me that?'

Hannah's voice had dropped almost to a whisper, as though she were struggling to comprehend what he was saying.

He did deserve to die. You know that, Marcus. Where there is harm there is blame, and where there is blame there must be punishment.

Marcus put his hands to his head. He looked at Hannah – her lips were moving, but for a moment he was hearing only Medusa.

'You're sick, Marcus. She's put some kind of spell on you. Can't you see that?'

Hannah was closer now.

Tell her, Marcus; tell the little witch. Tell her about your father, Marcus. Get me back, Marcus; there's still a chance. Otherwise she'll ruin everything.

But before her could say anything, there was shout from gap in the fence.

'Oy, you two! What do you think you're doing?'

It was Mr Ambrose, standing at the gap in the fence, waving his arms in the air.

Hell, Marcus thought as Mr Ambrose started making his way through the groundcover towards them. Marcus could see the man's white trainers kicking through the weeds.

'Go away,' Hannah shouted at him.

'Don't you tell me to go away. You've just stolen my parcel.'

'You don't want this,' Hannah yelled. 'Honestly.'

'That's not for you to decide. Give it back.'

But Hannah was not about to do that. Turning, she continued to run down the slope.

Mr Ambrose shouted after her: 'You can't go down there; it's dangerous. Don't go near the track.'

Marcus followed her. What else could he do? Mr Ambrose was a distraction he could have done without, but whatever happened, he had to get the Gorgon's head from Hannah.

His friend continued to pick her way through the bushes and Marcus jogged after her.

'Hannah, please listen. The last thing I want is for you to get hurt.'

There was no answer. Hannah just continued to run away from him.

What was her game? There was no way out to the other side of the tracks, and the closer she got to them, the more danger she put herself in.

The ground was levelling out now and Hannah was nearly at the railway line. Mr Ambrose still shouted threats and warnings from behind him.

Marcus put on a determined sprint. It caught Hannah off-guard. She turned just as he caught up with her, a look of surprise on her face.

He made a grab for the box.

'Give it to me!'

'No.' She yanked it into her stomach.

Marcus was horrified to realize that they were now standing just a few centimetres from the railway line. *You have me now, Marcus*, the voice in his head encouraged him. *Take me from her. Take me back!*

The voice seemed to dominate. He must obey it. It crowded out everything else – Mr Ambrose's shouting, Hannah's fierce panting, even the distant noise he recognized but couldn't quite place. His entire being was focused on the box and getting it out of Hannah's hands.

'You don't understand!' he shouted. 'She saw my father. He discovered her. He sent her to me.'

Hannah looked at him, appalled.

'You're mad, Marcus! She's made you mad!'

They swung round. Marcus stumbled on a rail and

lurched backwards, losing his grip on the box for a moment.

Hannah took her chance and turned but, seeing Mr Ambrose lumbering towards them, his mouth open in a yell, she hesitated for a moment.

This gave Marcus a chance to grab the box again.

Seize it, seize it. Now! This is our chance.

'It's mine!' he shouted at Hannah. 'Dad wanted me to have it!'

'Oh, you stupid, stupid boy!' Hannah yelled back at him.

The reason they were both yelling was because the noise that had been so distant a few moments before was now growing in volume.

He could hear what Mr Ambrose was shouting now: 'Get off the track, you fools! There's a train coming!'

And sure enough, round the bend came the engine, bearing down on them like the prow of an impossibly fast-moving liner.

'Let go!' Marcus bellowed.

'No!' Hannah shouted back.

He tugged, moving backwards and feeling the other rail against the back of his shoe. Hannah came

346

with him, so now they were both on the track, the box between them.

'Don't you see?' Hannah cried: 'She killed your father!'

No, Marcus, no. The witch is wrong. Don't believe her.

'She must have done. Where is he now? If he found her, there's no other explanation!'

Now the train was looking like a cliff towering over them, and the noise obliterated everything. Marcus's eardrums were going to burst, but he was more concerned that his brain was about to explode.

Medusa . . . his father. Yes, with everything he knew, it was entirely possible.

No, Marcus: it was an accident . . . a misunderstanding. He was so handsome, I thought he wanted me . . . Hold firm . . . weakness will ruin everything.

But the spell was broken. Marcus staggered back, releasing the box, which Hannah pulled away from him.

And then like a steel avalanche, the train was upon them. Marcus stumbled on the loose stones and fell, stunned by the torrent of noise smashing past his head. The wheels of the train were like a giant demented sewing machine, dashing the afternoon into smithereens. But above the bombardment of the train was a far greater noise: a terrible scream of pain and loss.

Hannah! He felt a cry of his own welling up in his throat, and lay on the loose stones letting all the pent-up feelings of the last few weeks loose in one long howl of grief and anguish. But loud though he howled, it was nothing compared to the scream that kept going: high, piercing, insistent, a ravaging sound dismantling his entire being. He put his hands to his head. Sparks flew; the trains wheels were making a new noise; one of tortured metal. The brakes. The engine driver had slammed on the brakes.

It was far too late.

Hannah had gone. Marcus was convinced.

He lay on his back on the stones letting the screech of the braking wheels and the high-pitched scream batter him, like a tsunami of pain.

He wanted to die. He could not contain the despair that was taking over his whole being. He knew he would disintegrate under its huge weight, its unbearable pressure. It would be better just to end it all, to join all the others who he had condemned to death.

Then suddenly, as though switched off, the noise stopped. The train had passed, for all the driver's attempts, and was still moving along the line, slowing down. The scream had stopped too; instead of the awful noise there was simply the distant blowing of a wind, growing ever fainter, ever more distant.

Marcus lay spreadeagled looking up at the sky, and felt a palpitation in his chest. Was he having a heart attack? he wondered vaguely. He wasn't in pain. Perhaps his despair blotted out mere physical pain. He reached up to feel his chest.

Then he sat up suddenly. It was extraordinary, but as his fingers reached his shirt pocket they found a panicky struggle, a frustrated wing-beat, and pulling the pocket open, released the butterfly.

It was alive again.

Marcus watched in amazement as the creature lurched into the air and headed off towards the nearest bush.

It took a moment for the implication to sink in, but when it did, Marcus sprang to his feet and turned round. The first thing he saw were two figures disentangling themselves from each other on the other side of the track.

'Hannah!'

She was alive. Marcus stumbled over the railway line towards her.

'Hannah!'

She stood up, brushing the dirt off her clothes.

'You're alive. I thought you—'

'And I would have done if it hadn't been for . . .' here she looked at Mr Ambrose, who was similarly brushing his clothes.

'I'm so, so sorry, Hannah.'

'And so you should be, young man,' Mr Ambrose said fiercely. 'What did the pair of you think you were doing? Don't you realize how close you were to being killed? Killed fighting over a parcel which wasn't even yours in the first place.'

'What happened to it?' Marcus scoured the track.

'Smashed to smithereens. Whatever it was. You are going to be in so much trouble.'

Smashed to smithereens? That meant Medusa was gone, destroyed. Marcus looked along the track, searching for any sign of her, but could see none. Looking further up the line, he could see that the train had finally pulled to a stop and a door was opening.

'I've got to go,' Marcus said.

'You're not going anywhere.' Mr Ambrose reached out his hand.

But Marcus was too quick for him.

'Han – I can't explain now. Something's happened. I think it's going to be all right, but I've got to get home.'

He was running.

Hannah frowned at him.

'So you want me to clear up your mess here?'

'Please . . . just do your best. Try to keep the police out of it. We don't want it in the papers. Come round to mine later?'

And with that he was off, running as hard as he could up the slope towards his bicycle. If the stone butterfly had returned to life, he had to hope that the rest of the Gorgon's victims had as well.

He grabbed his bicycle, pushed it back through the gap in the fence and started pedalling as though his life depended on it.

CHAPTER 20

Marcus followed the footpath down towards the railway bridge. There were more people around now, trudging back to their homes after work. He dodged them as best he could, sometimes having to shout an apology over his shoulder when he clipped a shopping bag or brushed a coat. Once he crossed the bridge and got onto a proper road he was able to go faster. Ignoring the indignant car horns as he went through red lights or jumped lanes, he just kept pedalling.

He was soon out of the main road system, puffing as he went up the hill towards Brunel Street. It was only as he approached home that he began to think seriously about what he would find there. If Mrs Prewle was still a crooked stone statue looking through the French windows, all his hopes would be dashed.

Brunel Street was quiet as he raced down it, past the posters of Decimal, and came to a squealing stop by the side gate. He dismounted and pushed open the gate to wheel his bike through. As he walked down the side of the house he heard noises – unfamiliar noises.

He put the bike in the lean-to and listened.

It was laughter.

Laughter? Who could possibly be laughing?

As he advanced cautiously towards the garden he heard it again: there was no doubt about it. There was laughter coming from the back of the house.

He rounded the corner and stopped in his tracks.

There on the patio were Mrs Prewle – and, with her back to him, the familiar form of Aunt Hester, sitting on one of the garden chairs, her suitcase beside her.

Last time he'd seen them they were both statues. Marcus felt he might be about to faint.

But then Mrs Prewle saw him.

'There you are, Marcus! We're locked out!'

Aunt Hester swivelled round on the metal chair she was sitting on.

'Hello, Marcus.' She smiled.

Marcus hesitated. None of this could be happening. And yet, it was.

Mrs Prewle spoke again: 'Yes, your aunt's back – I

found her in the garden. She's lost her key. And look, Marcus!'

She lifted something from her lap. It was Decimal.

'Isn't that incredible? All our lost ones back on the same day!'

Marcus forced himself to step forward.

'Hello, Aunt Hester,' he said.

She had got up now, and looked him up and down.

Oh, no, he thought, *she's going to find fault with something.*

But all she said was: 'You look a bit hot.'

'I've been out on the bike,' he said.

'Good for you. A bit of exercise. Well done.'

Even more extraordinarily, she came forward to meet him, with her arms open. Slightly uncertainly he took another step forward into her clumsy embrace.

While his hands were behind her back, his fingers found something that felt like a twig sticking to her coat. He pulled it off and dropped it on the patio.

When the hug was over, Mrs Prewle said 'Bring up that chair, Marcus. We were just saying what a grand job your uncle's done on the patio. And your aunt's been telling me all about her holiday in

Wales – castles, beaches, stately homes. You've had a wonderful time, haven't you, Hester?'

'Yes, yes I have,' his aunt sounded vague, but there was an upbeat tone to her voice. 'I'm pleased to be home, though. Only I seem to have lost my handbag somewhere with the key in it.'

'Have you looked in your suitcase? You might have put it in there for safety on the train.'

'I can't imagine I'd do a thing like that, but there's no harm in looking, I suppose.'

Hester bent down and opened the suitcase. And there, nestled in amongst her neatly folded clothes was her handbag.

'Well, bless me!' she exclaimed. 'How extraordinary of me to forget I'd done that.'

Marcus was finding Aunt Hester's behaviour extraordinary. It was not just that she seemed to be genuinely enjoying herself – and actually seemed pleased to see him – it was the fact that she gave every impression of believing that she had been on a visit to her sister's in Wales.

'Well,' Aunt Hester said, once she'd got her key out of her purse, 'I think I'll go in and put the kettle on. Will you join us for a cup of tea, Margaret?'

'I won't, thanks, Hester. I'm going to take

Decimal home, and give him a good talking to; going off like that and leaving me so desperately worried. Decie, Decie, Decie, you naughty, naughty, naughty, naughty boy.'

The cat purred contentedly as Mrs Prewle tickled him under the chin.

'I'm so happy, Marcus. So happy,' Mrs Prewle said as Aunt Hester went round the house to let herself in.

'I told your Aunt how helpful you'd been – we must take the posters down now of course.'

'It was nothing,' Marcus said. 'So you just found Aunt Hester in the garden?'

'Yes, it was most odd really. I'd come round for something – I can't remember what.'

Just nosing around, checking on Uncle Frank's progress, Marcus thought.

'I was on the patio, looking in through the French window – your uncle really has done a wonderful job, I must say. And then, when I turned round, I saw Hester looking rather distracted, wandering about on the lawn with her suitcase in her hand.

'She didn't seem to know where she was, but when I reminded her about her holiday, it started to come back. I wonder if she fell on the way here and hit her head? She seems to have had a lovely time – a thorough break. But anyway, the next thing that happened was we heard a noise from the shed.

'I couldn't believe my ears, but it sounded like – well, it sounded like a cat – it sounded like Decimal. Down I ran, and when I opened the door, there he was – weren't you, my sweetie-pie? And you'd been trapped in that dirty, dusty old shed for all this time, yes you had, yes, you naughty, silly, curious kitty, you.'

Mrs Prewle looked up, smiling.

'I don't know how we failed to hear him before, but he seems absolutely fine. Must have got by on mice I suppose. Anyway, be thankful for small mercies. I am!'

With that, she picked up her cat and set off down the lawn towards the gate between the two gardens.

'Goodbye, Marcus.'

Marcus watched her go, shaking his head in bemusement. Everything, amazingly, seemed to be working out. He felt so very much lighter now the Gorgon was out of his head. The world was brighter again.

'We'd better ring Uncle Frank,' he said when he joined Aunt Hester in the kitchen.

'He didn't know when you'd be coming back, so there's nothing in the house. If we tell him, he can get us some supper on the way home.'

'That's a good idea. Would you like to do it, dear?'

Dear? This was so weird. But when he looked at his aunt, she gave him a wide, if vacant, smile.

He turned to the phone on the kitchen wall and got through to Uncle Frank's direct line.

'Uncle Frank? She's back!'

Once Marcus had convinced him that it really was true, he said he'd tie up a few loose ends in the office and come straight home.

'Has he missed me?' Aunt Hester sat with her cup of tea across the kitchen table from Marcus.

'Yes he has. He'll be so pleased to see you.'

'That's nice. I'll be pleased to see him too. Now, tell me what you've been doing, Marcus.'

Marcus certainly wasn't going to do that, but he managed to dredge up an account of school and other activities. He was scraping the barrel when there was a ring at the door.

'I'll go.' He jumped up.

As he'd hoped, it was Hannah. She still looked cross.

'Come in,' he said, adding in a low voice, 'How did it go?'

'All right. Well, I got Mr Ambrose to see the danger of us hanging around and being questioned by the guard. But I said you'd go round and apologize – and explain.'

'Explain?'

'Well, apologize at least. Is your aunt . . . ?'

'Through here.' Marcus ushered her into the kitchen. 'You remember Hannah, don't you, Aunt Hester?'

'Hannah? Yes, yes I think so. How are you, dear? Marcus, get your friend a squash or something.'

The conversation didn't exactly flow, but with Hannah's input, they managed to keep things going until they heard Uncle Frank's key in the lock.

Marcus ran out into the hall to greet him. 'She's in the kitchen,' Marcus said. 'With Hannah.' Uncle Frank hurried down the hall.

'Hester, you're back! What a wonderful surprise. You should have sent me a text. I could have met you at the station. Did you have a good time?'

'I think so,' his Aunt Hester said, getting out of her chair awkwardly. 'Yes, I must have done. How

359

lovely to see you, Frank. And what a wonderful job you've done on the patio.'

Uncle Frank stood with his mouth open, at a loss for words. Marcus could see he was having difficulty getting his head round what was happening.

'Why don't you show her the French windows from inside?' he suggested.

'Why not?' said Uncle Frank, and led the way.

'I'd better be going,' Hannah said.

'I'll walk you home,' Marcus replied.

'Oh, you don't have to.'

'I think I do.' He nodded firmly towards the dining room. 'Give them a bit of time together.'

'I didn't know she'd been away,' Hannah said as they walked down the road together.

There were quite a few things Hannah didn't know – and shouldn't know, Marcus thought, even though she had guessed the main secret.

'No, well, we haven't been seeing much of each other lately,' he said.

'She seemed very vague about her holiday. Is she all right?'

'Never better,' Marcus said. It was amazing: he'd never known Aunt Hester in such a good mood, especially given that she had been a stone statue for the last three weeks. Happily, Mrs Prewle didn't seem to have the first idea she'd spent a couple of hours in the same state. The petrification of middle-aged ladies was not a topic he wanted to stray onto with Hannah, but the trouble was there were also other topics to be avoided.

He decided it was best just to apologize to begin with. After all, he had exposed Hannah to the risk of falling into the same stone sleep. Gradually, Hannah thawed.

'As I said, Marcus, the Gorgon obviously had you under her spell. You were possessed. You looked so – alien. Didn't you notice everyone avoiding you at school? They were terrified of you. Once I got into your internet account and saw you'd developed an obsession with the Gorgon; well, it seemed impossible, of course, but it did fit the facts.'

'But how did you know I'd be going to Mr Ambrose's house?'

'Rose. She may be annoying but she's a good soul at heart. And she certainly has a way with people. Digger stood no chance.'

Ah! thought Marcus. That all made sense.

'Of course, I still didn't know why you were out to get Mr Ambrose, but I knew you were capable of anything, after Mr Darke. What *did* you do to Mr Darke by the way?'

'Oh, you know, once he realized what I had in the box, he soon saw sense.'

Marcus explained about his use of the mirror and how terrified Mr Darke had been.

'So you never actually used her to turn anyone into stone?' Hannah asked earnestly. 'Apart from the squirrel for your art project,' she added.

Marcus could have let her go on thinking that, but there was so much welling up in his head which he wanted to share, and he couldn't begin to do that without her knowing at least some of the truth. So he told her about George.

When he'd finished, Hannah looked at him and shook her head.

'Marcus Waldrist, you are the maddest, stupidest boy alive! What did you think you were doing? Didn't you realize how dangerous it was going to be, trying to use that . . . thing?' she asked.

'I thought I could control it,' Marcus admitted, only now realizing how stupid he'd been.

'That's the thing about weapons,' Hannah said. 'Everybody thinks they're in control of them, whether its knives, guns, or nuclear bombs. Half the people behind bars – or in the cemetery – are there because they thought they were in control.'

Marcus nodded in agreement, but what he was really thinking about was George – restored to life, like the butterfly. Marcus imagined the giant figure clambering like a Frankenstein monster out of the wreckage of TV sets and smashed microwaves. What would he do next? He might be out on the streets even now, looking for revenge.

It was a terrifying thought. He quickly told Hannah about the stone butterfly. She saw the implications immediately.

But there was more than George to think about.

Marcus stopped dead. 'Hannah,' he said, reaching out a hand to her for support.

'Marcus. What is it? Are you all right? Tell me what it is,' she said, helping him to a low wall.

Marcus could barely get the words out, the thought was so horrifying: 'If everybody she . . . you know . . . turned to stone was turned back again when she was destroyed . . . well, that would include my dad, wouldn't it? And . . . who knows where he'd come back to life!'

He leaned forward, his hands pressing against the side of his head, as though to squeeze out the awful images that were growing there – images of a man suddenly returned to life and finding himself in the stone confines of a cave or cellar where he'd lain for ten long years. It would be like waking up inside a coffin: a more horrible fate than being petrified by the Gorgon in the first place.

After a pause, Hannah said: 'Oh, Marcus . . . how terrible. But you can't know. It might not work like that – I mean surely all the people she turned to stone thousands of years ago aren't going to come back to life again are they? There must be limits – of space – and time.'

'But then, I'm never going to know, am I?' Marcus looked at her miserably.

Hannah put her hand on his. 'But at least you can hope. Hope's good, Marcus. That's all I had to hold on to with my dad. They gave him less than a fifty-fifty chance. And we sat there by his bedside every afternoon – just hoping. And we got him back. He's going to AA meetings, and coming back to us. So you might get your dad back too.'

There were tears in her eyes as she smiled at him. Marcus felt his own eyes welling up, and half to hide that and half because he just needed to, he lunged across and hugged her hard.

He felt Hannah's arm tighten around him.

And then they sprang apart as they heard a cross rapping of knuckles on the front-room window of the house behind them.

Marcus looked over his shoulder. It was the same woman who had seen him kick the plastic bottle along the pavement a fortnight ago.

'Come on.' He said, pulled Hannah up.

'About your dad . . .' she said.

'What about him?'

'How did he come across her in the first place?'

'Discovered her on a dig. He went back out after Mum's funeral. There wasn't much time left before the dig had to end, and – well, he was obviously onto something. I don't know the details, but it looks like he thought he was going to find something pretty special.'

'And it was her?'

'Well, he obviously wasn't expecting to find the real thing. But there were images of her all over the Mediterranean.'

'I know,' Hannah said. 'I read a few of the things you found on the web. But what happened when he discovered her? I suppose we can't know.'

'She told me—'

'She spoke to you?'

'Yes. In my head. In dreams. More and more. She was shouting at me when we were – you know, on the railway line.'

'My god, Marcus: you were possessed. I don't know how you've survived, I really don't. But what did she say – about your dad?'

'Well, he found what he was looking for – the plaque, set in a wall. Just a crude version of her – big mouth, bulging eyes, snakes for hair. He obviously excavated her in this stone form, but all the time she was watching him.'

'Like prey,' Hannah noted. 'And all the time she was getting inside his head like she did with you. And I guess she developed some deluded fantasy that if she revealed herself to him, he would see her for what she once was – a beautiful young woman.'

Marcus nodded. He had felt the power of that delusion; felt the power of Medusa's loneliness.

Hannah went on: 'And when she did show herself to him, his reaction was of such horror that she . . . Oh, Marcus, I'm so sorry. What a terrible fate.'

She reached out her hand for his. They walked in silence, letting the horror of it all sink in.

'But you know, there is hope,' she said after a

while. 'Dads are pretty indestructible. Look at mine. We could have him home in a fortnight. And you know, this time I really think he is going to change. He's been so good with Mum – just sitting there, hour after hour, holding her hand and looking into her face. He realizes how close he came to messing everything up – so now I think he's going to make sure he never risks losing it all again. He didn't ever want to be violent. Mum's even thinking they might renew their wedding vows. I didn't know you could do that, but apparently you can.'

'That's great,' Marcus said.

'Thanks, Marcus.' She paused to smile at him, and then went on: 'Mum and I, we're very grateful for what you did – however bad it was. You should have seen Mum's face when I gave her the envelope. She couldn't believe it. She just couldn't believe it. But even though the money was important, she was more pleased to get her wedding and engagement rings back.'

They were nearly back at her street by now.

When they got to the corner, they stopped. Hannah smiled at him, and Marcus managed to smile back.

'Whatever happened to your dad,' Hannah said,

'the important thing is that you survived. That's what he would have wanted.'

'I only survived because of you, Han,' Marcus said. 'You know that, don't you?'

She gave a little shrug.

'Better go in to Mum,' she said. 'She'll be wondering what's happened to me. I can't exactly tell her, can I?'

They shared a brief conspiratorial smile, and then Hannah was walking away, her school bag swinging from her shoulder.

Marcus watched her all the way to her house, before turning away himself and heading for home.

CHAPTER 21

M arcus tried to sit still, look relaxed. But it was hard. He felt excited and nervous at the same time. At least the clarinets weren't at the front – but, when it came to their turn, he and Hannah would have to stand up and everyone would look at them.

Beside him, Hannah was gazing up at the hall ceiling, nodding in time with the music. Marcus tried to concentrate on the piano piece that Joanna Leveridge was playing. She was sat bolt upright, her fingers gliding across the keyboard with total ease. Joanna was good, you didn't need to be told that, and everything about her suggested that she didn't need to be told it either. Life wasn't fair, but there were worse things than not being as good at music as Joanna Leveridge – a lot worse. The fact that Marcus was there at all, up on stage at the Spring concert, was amazing. That he was sitting next to Hannah, and they were just about to perform their piece together was little short of a miracle.

He stole another glance at her. She looked so composed. And yet he had seen the fire beneath that calm exterior. He'd felt her fury, but knew that he would be for ever in her debt for risking her life to save him from doing something that would have completely ruined his.

She had single-handedly put his life back together again.

Even though it had been an ordeal, Marcus was glad she'd made him go and see Mr Ambrose. He was even more glad that she'd insisted on going with him.

It was the right thing to do, but the memory still made Marcus squirm with embarrassment.

First there had been his apology – for delivering a box containing something too horrible to describe to his door. But then things became far worse when the man burst into tears and apologized to him for the car accident. Mr Ambrose said he'd thought about the accident every day of his life, and every day it made him feel bad knowing he could do nothing to atone for what he'd done.

Fortunately, Hannah had intervened to say the accident was a long time ago and that they all had to move on with their lives. She also pointed out that Mr Ambrose had risked his life to save her from the train.

'It was just a simple rugby tackle,' the man had said.

'Well, it saved my life,' Hannah had replied. 'And Marcus has forgiven you, so hopefully you can forgive Marcus.'

They had shaken hands

Mr Ambrose had also wanted to apologize to Uncle Frank, so he'd come round to Brunel Street and the two men had walked down the garden together.

And at some point someone – Aunt Hester? – had mentioned the concert, and Mr Ambrose had said he'd like to come. And so there he was, sitting a few rows back, seemingly enjoying the piano piece. In fact, it was quite an audience.

Hannah's mum and dad were sitting together on the front row, her dad looking very smart in a jacket and tie, although there was still a dressing on his head from the surgery. Further along were Uncle Frank and Aunt Hester. Aunt Hester was nodding her head in time to the music, a slight smile on her face. She smiled a lot these days, and Marcus was still getting used to it. Apparently being turned to stone was quite a transformative experience. As for Uncle Frank, he seemed to smile all the time, and hummed along to whatever he was doing around the house until Marcus wished he would stop. Except it was such a joy to see his uncle so happy, he immediately felt bad.

Mrs Prewle was sitting next to Aunt Hester. She had her 'I'm listening to classical music' face on, and Marcus wondered whether she would be able to keep that up during their clarinet piece. And right at the back, looking out of place, was Rose, who had insisted on coming even though she was clearly bored out of her head. But she had played her part in their story and it was nice that she wanted to come and support them.

And what a mad time it had been. Marcus was trying not to be too distracted by what might have happened to his father, but couldn't help worrying about George. George restored to life and hefty limb, and guided by a vengeful Mr Darke, could have been a serious worry.

But when Marcus met him, it was under very unexpected circumstances.

Marcus and his aunt and uncle were walking

through the churchyard on the Sunday after Aunt Hester returned from her 'holiday' when Marcus noticed a familiar figure looming above the gravestones.

Although he couldn't believe George would assault him in front of the entire congregation, he felt a tremor of fear as the lumbering giant approached.

''Ello, Marcus.' George extended a spade-like hand. ''Ow are we these days?'

Uncle Frank and Aunt Hester were looking at him curiously, but there was nothing Marcus could do but shake George's hand and say, 'All right, thanks. And you?'

'I'm fine, too, thank you, Marcus. An' I'm better in myself, if I can put it that way. Seemed to have strayed a bit from the straight and narrow, if you know what I mean. Got a bit too hard for me own good. Which is why I thought I'd come over to church this morning. I didn't expect to see you here.'

'It's our local parish church.'

'Same here,' George said, with a smile which really did look genuine. 'Small world, eh?'

'Who was that, dear?' Aunt Hester asked as soon as George was out of ear-shot.

'Oh, just someone I met when I was round at Hannah's the other day. I think he knows her father. Just dropped in to ask how he was getting on.'

George had certainly made his presence felt during the service. His rendition of 'All Things Bright and Beautiful' had heads turning, and Marcus had struggled to keep from laughing as he bellowed *'Each little flower that oooopens, each little bird that siii-ings; He made their glowing colours, He made their tiny wiiiings . . .'* at a volume that even Mr Tenby couldn't match.

The only other unexpected outcome of the whole experience was the sighting of a live squirrel in the art block. The Head had made a particularly pompous announcement about how absolutely forbidden it was to bring any animal onto school premises.

Marcus smiled to himself. Then he felt a stab of anxiety. Joanna Leveridge was getting near the end of her piece.

They were up next. Compared to all the horrors of the previous weeks, standing up and playing a clarinet duet for two minutes should be child's play, he told himself; but he still felt nervous.

As the last notes of the piano died away, the audience broke into loud applause.

Mr Bishop waited till it had exhausted itself and then stood up, waving his baton. Marcus put his hand up to his shirt pocket, but, of course, the stone butterfly wasn't there to give him luck. Instead, in the luckiest break of his life, it had spread its wings and flown off into the sky.

The hall fell silent. This was it. Mr Bishop was giving them a meaningful look and raised his baton. Hannah leaned across and whispered in Marcus's ear: 'This is for your dad, OK?'

'And yours,' he whispered back.

They stood up together, and putting their instruments to their lips, began to play.

Acknowledgements

When I came to writing stories, rather late in the day, I sent my first book, *Unplayable*, to David Fickling. He liked it enough to commission two more – *Keras*, and then *Medusa's Butterfly*. I will always be indebted to him for this leap of faith.

Several people at both David Fickling Books and Random House Children's Publishers read the manuscript of *Medusa's Butterfly*, but I would like to mention three by name: Tilda Johnson wrote an extremely helpful and thorough report which has never been far from my desk; Hannah Featherstone, my first editor, helped me to jettison a complete red herring of a plot line, while Rachel Mann, to whom she handed over, sparked one last plot twist which sent me back to the revision process with renewed inspiration. All three have made a huge impact on the final version and I am extremely grateful to each of them.

Many others have played their part in the production

of the book, and I would like to thank Ruth Knowles who copy-edited and Pete Matthews who read the proofs. The designer was Alison Gadsby, and once again Richard Collingridge has produced a brilliantly atmospheric cover. My thanks to them all.

Thanks too, to my agent Bill Hamilton, and Charlie Brotherstone, also of A.M.Heath & Co, as well as my ever-supportive PA, Olivia Stanton.

I would also like to acknowledge the support of the Royal Literary Fund for timely funds, and in particular Eileen Gunn for helping me with my application.

Finally, I would like to say thank you to those closest to me: Susan read the first draft as I wrote it, her eagerness for the next instalment a terrific spur; Sian took a fellow-writer's interest in its progress, while Albertine, Michael and Naomi urged me on all the way to the finishing line. It is a huge sadness that I will not be able to give an author's copy to Penny, but the generous enthusiasm with which she read *Keras* in her last illness is something I will never forget.

SR

Little Tew
Oxfordshire